Dead For the Money

A Dead Detective Mystery

BY PEG HERRING

FROM GWENDOLYN BOOKS

Gwendolyn Press
Port Huron, MI 48060

Publisher's Note: This is a work of fiction. Names, characters, places, and incidents are a product of the author's imagination. Locales and public names are sometimes used for atmospheric purposes. Any resemblance to actual people, living or dead, or to businesses, companies, events, institutions, or locales is completely coincidental.

Dead for the Money/ Peg Herring – 2nd ed.
ISBN 978-0-9861475-4-8

Acknowledgements

The author would like to thank James Ecker, Retired Chief Engineer for the Mackinac Bridge Authority, for his help with the specifics of what it's like to climb around on the Mackinac Bridge. Though such activity is neither allowed nor recommended, Jim helped me imagine and describe what it would be like in the scenario presented in this book. If there are mistakes, they are mine, not his, because he has been everywhere on that impressive structure and knows it like most people know their own backyards.

CHAPTER ONE

"Who knew heaven was like a luxury liner?" the man across from Seamus speared the last bite of his steak. His head was shaved and shiny, and tattoos curled around his ears like ram's horns. He was called Joshua, but he didn't bring Jericho to mind. More like pure Jersey. "It's not what I imagined." Leaning back from his empty plate, he patted his stomach with a satisfied air. "I gotta tell you, it's pretty great."

"This is our introduction to the Afterlife." Seamus glanced at the speaker, a sweet-faced young woman in a diaphanous turquoise evening gown. Noting her work-roughened hands, he guessed it was the nicest thing she'd ever worn. "This ship, the feeling we're on a cruise," she waved vaguely at the elegant room around them. "It's designed to help us adjust to the fact that our lives are over."

"That's right," another woman put in. "They provide all the comforts while we prepare for the final step."

"Which they say is much better." The first woman looked around the table. "I believe that."

There was a moment of silence as the diners considered their own opinions. In the background, the band finished a smooth rendition of "The Impossible Dream."

As the notes of a new song began, a wide-eyed girl of about nineteen asked, "What about punishment?" Her food was hardly touched, and Seamus figured she hadn't yet adjusted to the idea of being dead.

"Oh, that will all be taken care of," said a woman a few chairs down whose facial wrinkles were intensified by a screaming red dye job on her hair. "My caseworker said not to worry about it."

Although he generally stayed out of such conversations, Seamus couldn't ignore the look of dread on the girl's face. "Think of all the good things you've heard about the Afterlife," he told her. "That's what's true."

Her spine relaxed a little and she smiled timidly. It was the same every night: new faces, but the same fears, anticipation, and wonder. The newly dead talking about being newly dead.

"This really is like a sea cruise," one man said.

"With everything you can imagine and more," Joshua agreed.

Seamus wondered how many of them understood that they'd soon forget the details of their former lives. In a day or two, the pretty girl in the red dress would know she liked musical comedies but be unable to name a specific occasion when she had seen one or who had accompanied her. Glancing around the table, he assessed the likelihood that someone here might object to losing their memories. No. Not a Portalist among them. Each of his dinner companions would accept the forgetting and make the crossing, content to leave the world, and even this ship, behind.

He was not like that. No matter how wonderful the next step might be, Seamus was unwilling to let go of Seamus. Like a small minority who chose to remain and remember, he stayed on the ship, waiting for the time when it felt right to give up who he was for whatever lay beyond.

Joshua's mind apparently ran along the same track. "I understand the workers on the ship are people who chose not to go on."

"Not yet," said a young man who'd begun refilling their water glasses. As ice plopped and water splashed, he explained, "Portalists can go on anytime, but we choose to stick around a while."

"If the next step is so wonderful, then why not take it?" asked the woman in turquoise.

The waiter, whose face was pleasantly freckled, thought about that for a few seconds. "I guess I want to enjoy this step," he said finally. "You gotta admit, this ain't bad. I work a few hours a day, and the rest of the time I get the same treatment you all are getting."

"It's really something," Joshua agreed. "Anything you want to eat or wear, lots of things to do. My wife and I used to take a Disney cruise every year, but it was never as good as this." His eyes clouded at the word *wife*, and Seamus imagined his thought: *My wife—now what was she like?*

"What if a person wanted to go back, back to Life? Could she do that?" asked the girl.

Everyone paused at the naive question. Most of them understood that their lives were over, but it was undoubtedly hard for the very young, who hadn't had much life at all, to accept that fact.

The waiter, who'd been on the ship longer than anyone present except Seamus, said gently, "It's not possible. No one goes back."

That wasn't true, but Seamus didn't contradict the speaker. He'd gone back many times. What *was* true was that returning to Life was not what the girl imagined, not what she'd want. It was a job, and only a few could handle it.

As the meal progressed, Seamus observed the other Portalists serving food, taking away empty plates, playing in the orchestra across the room. Those who stayed on the ship were given jobs: nothing too taxing, but work that made them feel useful. Waiting tables or handing out towels in the gym wasn't enough for Seamus. He tried not to feel contemptuous of either the guests who blithely journeyed forward or the Portalists who hung around to enjoy the ship's luxury. It was their choice, he reminded himself. *Maybe I'm the selfish one.*

He hadn't come to dinner tonight for the company, but because Mike, the guy Seamus thought of as the Manager Angel, had stopped by his stateroom earlier. The visit made Seamus' day, though he'd tried not to show it.

After knocking on the cabin door and being invited inside, Mike entered. "Are you up for some work?"

Seamus had been lying on the bed, fully clothed except for his hat, working a crossword puzzle with a pen. "You know I am." Setting the book down, he shifted his feet to the floor.

Mike held up a hand, signaling patience. "He's with Nancy right now, but she's pretty sure this guy will need you."

"Murdered?"

"He thinks so." Mike, who looked to Seamus like Leslie Howard, took a step into the room and closed the door behind him. "He's old, and I'd guess he was pretty shaky on his feet. He fell off a cliff while watching a yacht race. It could have been by accident, but he doesn't think so."

"So I'd go back and see what the police think?"

"Yes. If he decides to go ahead with it, you'll meet him after dinner and get the full story."

Seamus lay back on the pillows stacked against the headboard. "You're the boss, Mike." Mike grinned at his pretended reluctance, knowing his "employee" was thrilled when a new job came along. Seamus liked the idea of working for Mike, or better still, for Good.

Seamus had made his way to the dining room, located the man Mike wanted him to meet, and taken a seat one table away. Now, as conversation at his table continued, Seamus watched William Clark Dunbar. He was indeed old, though, like other guests on the ship, any infirmities he'd had in life were erased. Guests and Portalists alike were given an approximation of themselves on the Passage, not real in the sense they'd once been, but familiar and comfortable. Seamus himself had had a limp in the last few years of his life due to a shattered knee. One benefit of being dead was that everything worked. The disadvantages were obvious, at least to Seamus.

Dunbar was moderately tall and trim, with only a soft rounding at his waist to betray the passage of time. His haircut was G.I. issue, a buzzed style that might have been cut to fashion but was more likely old habit instead.

Judging from the freckled complexion, Seamus guessed that before his hair turned white, Dunbar had been a red-head.

He wore a tuxedo, as most of the men did, but he seemed at ease in it, as if used to formal attire, while other men in the room did not. Seamus had eschewed formal attire and stuck with his brown pin-stripe with the wide lapels. His fedora lay beside him on the table, and he touched it every so often, as if to assure himself it was still there. He always felt a little naked without it.

During the meal Dunbar was polite, making a comment from time to time and chuckling when someone made a joke, but it was obvious he had things on his mind. The staff on the ship encouraged mingling, but Seamus sensed Dunbar would have preferred to be alone, to ponder what had happened to him and come to terms with it.

Plenty of time for that later, buddy, Seamus told the man silently. *When you're alone in that stateroom, all you have to think about is why you died, how you died, and what will happen now.*

The noise level rose once the meal was over. Conversations hummed. The clink of dishes and cutlery sounded as the tables were cleared. The band switched to livelier tunes, and a few people moved to the dance floor. There was even laughter. Seamus saw Dunbar make his excuses and rise to go. One of the women tried to convince him to stay a while longer, but he resisted, affable but definite. Seamus made his own excuses to his tablemates. Not one of them asked him to stay.

On the way out of the room, Dunbar stopped to speak to Mike, which left Seamus standing near the table he'd just left. He surveyed the room idly as he waited, at the same time watching the exchange between Mike and Dunbar. The man seemed to be questioning Mike, who spoke reassuringly. His gaze slid once to Seamus, confirming what they had discussed earlier. As he waited, Seamus couldn't help but hear bits of conversation from the table he had vacated.

"—think he chooses to wear that suit?"

"—an Al Capone wannabe."

"He could have any clothes he wanted, just by going to the ship's store."

"It's kinda cool, I think." This was from the timid girl he'd reassured earlier.

Thanks, kiddo, he told her silently.

Dunbar finished speaking with Mike, and Seamus followed him out of the room. Outside, Seamus looked right and then left to see which way Dunbar had turned. Down only a short way, he leaned against the railing, staring into the void that surrounded the ship.

Seamus took a moment, as he usually did, to take in the view beyond the railing. What he saw was nothing, but the most beautiful nothing imaginable. The ship passed through something that was space-like, he supposed, but so much more than that. It was the most peaceful, amazing thing he'd ever encountered, and there was no way to describe it. Beyond the ship was something taken in through the senses rather than seen. Still yet moving, colored yet indistinct, real yet incomprehensible, Infinity was far beyond his understanding. It was not beyond appreciation, though, no matter how often he saw it.

Seamus moved to where William Dunbar stared into the void as if searching for something. If Dunbar didn't know who killed him, Life had left him with a bitter question: who? And if he knew who'd done it, the question might be even more difficult: why?

"Are you Dunbar?"

The man turned and surveyed Seamus with a slightly questioning air. "I am."

"My name is Seamus."

Dunbar nodded acknowledgment. "You're the detective?"

"Yeah."

The man rubbed the railing with a fingernail. "I'm trying to make up my mind about all this."

Seamus waited. It wasn't his way to press, though in his view, it was better to know. At least, for most.

"What did they tell you about me?" Dunbar stared into the distance.

"Not much. I guess they figure it's your story to tell."

"I see." There was another long pause. Seamus didn't mind. He sensed the job was his, that this man wanted to know. And in the meantime, there was the view.

When Dunbar began to speak, he kept his face averted. Seamus saw in the line of his jaw a tension that was undoubtedly visible in his pale blue eyes too. The man wasn't sure he wanted to know, but he had to.

"I am—I was—a very wealthy man," he began. "My family moved from Coatbridge in Scotland to Ontario when I was eight. As an adult, I moved to the States, to Chicago, and started a business. My product was simple, but its time came just when I started manufacturing it." He turned to Seamus with a slight smile. "As a consumer you wouldn't be aware of it, but every electrical gadget made needs one or two."

Seamus nodded. How Dunbar got to be rich didn't matter, though the fact he'd been rich probably did.

"Through that bit of luck and a lot of hard work, my wife and I enjoyed, from the time we entered our thirties, a lifestyle most would envy." He looked away. "It's true what they say, though. Money cannot buy happiness." His chin dropped, and he leaned more heavily on the railing. "When I was forty-one, my wife was killed in a car accident. And when I was sixty-four, my only son died of cancer. One of those inexplicable things: he was athletic, didn't smoke or drink. The doctors had no explanation— and no cure." He shook his head, apparently still unable to accept the reality of it. "He left behind a three-year-old son, who is now twenty-five."

Seamus did some quick math in his head. That made Dunbar eighty-six. *That's how I might have looked,* he thought, but added a moment later, *If I weren't a short Irish-American mongrel with a two-pack a day smoking habit.*

A couple of men passed behind them, discussing the

merits of the Bears versus the Vikings. One of them seemed to think raising the volume of his voice trumped his companion's statistics.

"This grandson was with you when you fell?" Seamus asked when the men went on.

Dunbar seemed reluctant to answer. "Yes."

"What was a guy of eighty-plus doing up on a cliff, anyway?"

The old man smiled. "I loved boats and bought a succession of them, starting with a trim little twenty-two footer and ending with something a bit more spacious. For years I sailed the Great Lakes whenever time permitted."

Seamus had a moment of doubt. He hated boats. If this job meant hosting with some yacht captain, he'd have to rethink it.

Unaware of his listener's inner conflict, Dunbar went on. "The highlight of my year was the Chicago to Mackinac Race, sponsored by the Chicago Yacht Club. Over three hundred boats take off from Chicago, near the Navy Pier, and head to Mackinac Island, in the straits between Lake Huron and Lake Michigan. For almost thirty years, I was in that race." He stood a little straighter. "There were times when I came close to winning it."

"That's good."

"My son was never interested in boating, but after he died, I became a presence in the life of my grandson, first simply as Gramps but later as his guardian." Dunbar smiled. "His name is William Clark Dunbar III, but I called him Buddy. As an adult, he became Bud to almost everyone. For a few years, he crewed with me in the race, but then he got busy with his life and lost interest. Eventually, my health began to fail, and I gave up racing and became a mere spectator." Regret was evident in his voice, but he shifted his feet and finished. "That was what we were doing on the bluff: watching for the racers on their way to Mackinac."

Seamus focused on a point the old man had omitted. "Where is Bud's mother?"

Dunbar gave a huff of disapproval. "One seldom knows where she is or which man she's with. Having a child cramped her style. When I demanded she either act like a mother or give me guardianship, she couldn't wait to sign the papers."

"I suppose there was money involved?"

Dunbar's shrug acknowledged Seamus' deductive power. "I don't think Callie ever saw Buddy as her child, only as a means to my money."

"What does the kid know about it?"

"He *knows* nothing, but I am sure he *suspects* a lot."

"They don't communicate?"

"No. Callie staying out of Bud's life was part of the deal."

"And he's okay with that?"

Dunbar stepped back, leaning his forearms against the rail. "I think he trusts my judgment, although I'm sure he is curious about his mother." He added as an afterthought, "I suppose a psychiatrist would say Bud suffered emotional scars from her abandonment."

"No sign of wanting marriage and a family?"

"Not so far."

"So Bud is what they call a player?"

Dunbar frowned "I wouldn't use that term. An eligible bachelor is always welcome, and plenty of women want to be seen on his arm. But up till now, no girl has lasted long there."

Seamus formed a mental image: Bud Dunbar, man-about-town. "Your grandson lived with you?"

"Until he completed his MBA. Now he manages Dunbar Enterprises in Chicago."

Running one hand along his jawline, Seamus asked, "Did you keep control of it?"

The old man's feet shifted, grating slightly on the metal deck. "I have final say, but we always made important decisions together."

So Buddy had *almost* all the power. "What happened that day up on the cliff?"

"As I said, I was a fan of yachting, even after I became too unsteady to stand on a deck. It became a tradition for Bud and me to climb up to the top of a bluff near my house and watch as the Chicago to Mackinac racers sailed north. The last few years I was unable to walk that far, so we took the golf cart. We'd spend hours up there, making predictions and critiquing the different crews as they passed."

"Okay. Tell me what you remember, starting from

when you left the house."

Dunbar closed his eyes briefly. "The day was a particularly beautiful one, although July has been very hot. Bud had everything in the golf cart when I came down: binoculars, water, and a couple of those chairs that come in canvas sacks."

"And where exactly is this bluff?"

"My property is—" He stopped himself. "—was near Frankfort, Michigan. I own two hundred acres with some beachfront, some open meadow, and a lot of woods. On the north end of the property, a bluff overlooks Lake Michigan. The area around it is wooded, but a parting in the trees at a spot fifty feet above the lake provides a magnificent view. That's where I—" His voice trembled but he coughed once and went on. "When I bought the place, I had a fence installed to prevent anyone falling over the edge."

"Smart move." Obviously, the fence had not done its job.

"As I got less steady on my feet, the fence became more of a necessity, something sturdy to hold onto. My handyman always made sure it was in good repair."

"Okay. Back to that day."

Dunbar's gaze lost focus, but with visible effort, he continued his narrative. "I remember peaceful silence on the ride up there. A golf cart doesn't make much noise, and Bud and I never felt like we had to converse if there was nothing to say. I was looking forward to the race. Small birds flew up and flitted away as we passed, startled by the movement. I felt small branches snap under the wheels. I could smell the pines, and a few cones had dropped into the sand along the track. I saw some prints left by animals, a couple of deer and a porcupine."

Seamus found himself enjoying Dunbar's description. Yes, that was Life: all the senses actually working, not some re-created facsimile that paled in comparison. It was smelly and noisy and inconvenient, but feeling, really feeling, was like nothing else.

"By the time we got to the viewing point, the sun was well up. To be honest, it was uncomfortably hot, downright tropical for Michigan, but Bud had brought an umbrella that fit into the frame of my chair for shade.

"We stopped. I was using a cane, and I waited while Bud unloaded our things from the cart. He hung two pairs of binoculars around his neck, put the water into his backpack, hefted the chairs, and we set off. It isn't far to the viewing point, probably thirty yards, but the trail is bumpy, and it took me a while to make it. I guessed from my grandson's expression that he was wondering if it had been a good idea to bring me up there." Dunbar smiled grimly. "Did you know that walking on an uneven surface is one of the most difficult things for the brain to handle?"

"No."

"They can't design a robot that can do it efficiently, because so many tiny adjustments must be made." He added with a hint of pride, "It took longer than it once did, but I made it on my own power."

That's what it's like to get old, Seamus thought. *Tiny victories over a rebellious body. Small achievements that help you believe it isn't over.* He recalled a friend of seventy who had insisted on demonstrating at every opportunity that he could still do push-ups. *See? I'm not dead yet.*

"Describe the area around this viewing point for me."

"As I said, it overlooks the lake, an open area the size of a mid-sized room. It drops steeply into some trees and slopes down to a tiny strip of beach." His lips pressed together briefly. "I don't remember much about the fall, just the helpless feeling that I couldn't stop it."

"We're not there yet. Go back to when you and Bud arrived."

Dunbar relaxed his shoulders with a roll and a deep breath. "Bud set up the chairs, but I wasn't ready to sit down yet. He handed me my binoculars. We didn't see anything coming, but you can't predict when the first boat will show up. So much depends on weather and conditions on the lake. After a while Bud said, 'Gramps, do you hear that?' I heard nothing."

"What did he hear?"

"He thought it sounded like an animal in trouble in the woods to our right."

"What kind of animal?"

"I don't know, but Bud heard it again, and a few moments later, a third time. He said something was hurt, and he was going to go and see what it was."

"You never heard the noise."

"No."

"So what did he do?"

"Well, he set his binoculars down on the chair seat and took off into the woods. I watched him disappear, then nothing. After a while I turned back to the lake, looking for the first boats."

Dunbar stopped, and Seamus knew they had come again to the fall. "Okay," he told the old man, "Slowly, tell me everything you recall."

He shrugged helplessly. "I was relaxed, focused on the water. Suddenly I was falling. I felt the resistance of the wooden fence rail against my stomach. My legs left the ground. I grabbed for the rail, but it was too late. I was over the fence before I could even call for help. My shoulder hit the ground on the other side." His jaw jutted, lips tight, but he continued. "My reflexes were too slow, my body too stiff, my mind too overcome. At forty, even at sixty, I might have saved myself, but—" Disgust tinged his voice. "It's like they say. Old age isn't for sissies." He turned once more to face Seamus. "One thing I am sure of, though. I did not *fall* over that fence. I was *pushed*."

CHAPTER TWO

Brodie Dunbar made her way up the trail, slowing once she was out of sight of the house. Scarlet would soon discover she wasn't in her room, but Scarlet would understand that she needed to be alone.

The trees smelled good, all piney and fresh, but Brodie willed herself not to notice. It had to be wrong to notice beauty in the world when Gramps was gone from it. A warm breeze touched her cheek as she finally stepped into the open space of the viewing point, but she tried to ignore that too. Nothing should matter now that Gramps was dead.

Before her, Lake Michigan sparkled in the July sunshine. The view could have been a postcard, except no camera could capture it completely. She was high above the lake, and the drop beyond the fence was dizzying, but heights didn't scare Brodie. In fact, she usually enjoyed the feeling of standing in lofty places. But this was where Gramps had fallen to his death. It was different now.

She willed herself to approach the rail fence that stood before her. Unable to look down at where Gramps must have landed, she kept her eyes on the rails themselves, searching for weakness. They looked as strong as ever. She knelt and took one in her hands, feeling the rough wood. Pulled on it hard. It gave slightly, as wood is supposed to, but it was whole, doing the job it was built for, keeping people from falling over the bluff edge.

So how had the fence failed Gramps? They said he must have had a dizzy spell, but if he got dizzy he could have held on, couldn't he? Why hadn't he? Was it her fault for not telling what she knew? She'd wanted to protect him, but she might instead have contributed to his death.

Brodie wished she could talk to Bud about what happened, since he'd been right there. But Bud was busy with police and family and business stuff. He had no interest in Brodie, who was nobody.

She tried to think of someone who would care, really care, if she never returned from this place. She peered over the edge at the drop she'd found exhilarating until now. Nothing below indicated the tragedy that had occurred. It seemed to her the earth and water should give some sign that a wonderful old man had died in this place. But it was a beautiful as ever, as peaceful as before. The lake moved below her as always, waves chasing each other to see which would travel farthest ashore. The sun had risen high enough to reach the spot, but barely, so the light was still filtered through the treetops behind her. It was the same place as always. Everything was the same, except that Brodie had no future, here or anyplace else she could imagine, without Gramps.

William C. Dunbar—Gramps—had been everything to Brodie, so much so that she was considering crawling over the fence herself and flying—or falling—to wherever he was. Everyone except Gramps thought she was ugly, stupid, and not quite right in the head. Maybe it was okay if she left the world. Maybe there was something better in the next one.

She looked again at the expanse of water on the other side of the fence. It sparkled invitingly. Every once in a while a wave slapped against the sand with a happy little sound. Without conscious decision she climbed onto the fence and over it, hanging onto the top rail and extending her arms so that she looked straight down. Had Gramps known he was going to die? Had he thought of her as he fell? The trees below seemed wicked now, though she'd always loved staring down at the contrast between their green branches and the soft sand beyond them. She hoped Gramps had lost consciousness, that he'd never known that his life would end that day, that hour, that second. It was all a kid could hope for when the one person who wasn't paid to like her was gone.

Seamus left the subject of Dunbar's death for a while, giving the man a chance to regain control of his emotions. "Tell me more about the property."

Dunbar pulled himself back once more from thoughts that obviously plagued him. The safer subject, his home, allowed him to relax somewhat. "I bought the land back in the '60s, when it was relatively cheap," he said. "The original buildings sat along a small lagoon, protected from the winds off the lake. That house burned long ago, and the site is almost completely overtaken by woods. I chose to build in a more open space down the beach. Lila would have loved it, had she lived." His shoulders twitched, and Seamus wondered if he was reminded that he too was now dead.

"When Buddy became my responsibility, I decided to

move to Michigan in order to give him the kind of childhood a kid deserves: room to wander and a small, supportive community.”

“Sounds nice,” Seamus lied. He couldn't imagine living away from a city center, where there was always something to do. “Anyone else live with you?”

“Everybody, it seems some days.” Dunbar looked a bit sheepish. “When you've got a house with twelve bedrooms, family tends to congregate.”

“Who's everybody?”

“My sister Arlis, for one.”

“What does she do?”

“Her hair, mostly.” Dunbar sniffed. “Arlis married one of my managers. When her husband died, she let her only child, Leland, handle her money, and he lost it all. Some hare-brained scheme that wasn't quite legal and not at all well-planned. When everything fell apart, Leland left the country to avoid legal ramifications. Arlis came to live with me.”

“So this Leland isn't around?”

“Haven't seen him in years, but he does call his mother regularly.” His lips tightened “None of it was his fault, Arlis says.”

Red flags went up in Seamus' mind. “Leland isn't an honest type.”

“He might only have been young and stupid. Apparently,

he has spent the last decade trying to atone. In fact, he became sadhu."

"What?"

"It's Hindu." Dunbar rolled his eyes. "I had to look it up. Rejecting everything life requires of most of us, sadhu have no home or possessions. They work when someone asks them to and eat when someone feeds them. According to his mother, Leland travels the world, helping out in disasters and out-of-the-way places." He raised both hands, palms up. "Believe me, I've heard more about it than I ever cared to. Arlis wants us to understand that Leland is a changed man."

"So he can inherit some of your money, maybe?"

Dunbar shrugged. "Arlis claims he's moved past wanting any earthly reward."

Seamus pictured a barefoot hermit with offensive body odor and a beard thick enough for robins to nest in. "Okay, so you support your sister. Who else lived with you?"

Dunbar's eyes softened. "There's Brodie."

"Another relative?"

The answer was oblique. "I didn't know she existed until she was three years old. She was—not being treated well. When I stepped in to help, her mother agreed to let me adopt her."

"More money changed hands, I assume?"

Dunbar grimaced. "What's money for if not to help those

who need it?"

Seamus could think of worse things a man might do with his money than rescue kids whose parents were screw-ups. "So what does Brodie do?"

"She's still a kid, just thirteen." His smile was rueful. "Her apparent purpose in life is frustrating anyone who tries to control her."

"A challenge, huh?"

"To put it mildly." He covered a smile with his fist. "She's the reason for another resident in my home, Scarlet."

"Another relative?'"

"No. Scarlet McMorran is Brodie's tutor. She's been with us for almost a year now, and she's done wonders." He paused, backing up slightly. "Brodie was almost feral when I adopted her. Over time she became civilized, but not completely socialized." Dunbar didn't try to hide his smile this time. "She has a reputation for innovative pranks that are aimed at people who deserve them, at least to Brodie's way of thinking."

A brat, Seamus concluded privately.

"Scarlet has had some success, I think because she truly cares for Brodie. At the same time, Scarlet is wise enough to pair caring with expectations of proper behavior."

"Okay. Your sister, the kid, and her warden. Who else?"

"My personal assistant, Arnold Wilk, is there most of the time, though he gets weekends off and often goes away with friends. Our cook-and-handyman couple, Shelley and Orville Briggs. Those are the permanent members of the household. Bud comes north when he can, but work keeps him in Chicago most of the time. My lawyer, Collin Marks, visits quite often and has a room assigned as his. Both Arnold and Collin were at the house that...um, last day. Collin rode up with Bud from Chicago for some R&R."

Seamus tried to picture a map of Michigan. "Isn't that kind of a long drive?"

"It is, but Bud likes it. M-22 from Manistee to Frankfort is scenic, with twists Bud claims are relaxing after negotiating the turns of the world economy all week."

"I guess. Anyone else?"

"We often have guests, as anyone who owns a home on a lake will tell you. But this weekend it was only the people I named."

"Do all of them figure in your will?"

"Well, yes. Arnold, the Briggses, and Collin get small bequests, Brodie inherits a substantial amount at eighteen, and Arlis gets support and a home until her death or remarriage. Bud controls it all."

"Is that everyone mentioned in the will?"

"There are charitable donations, of course. Oh, and the family home in Ontario goes to Leland." Dunbar sniffed. "Since he can't return to the States, it was the best I could do for him."

"You have land in Canada?"

Dunbar nodded. "My father, the last of the family except for Arlis and me, died a few months after my wife was killed. He was a simple man, rather dour and uninterested in modern conveniences. Having too much to deal with at the time, I simply paid someone to close up the house and never went back. When Arlis suggested it should be her son's inheritance, I agreed. Leland can sell the place and give the money to his charities or spend it. I don't care."

Someone called out behind them, and both men turned. The woman was speaking to someone farther down the deck. "Sorry," she said. Dunbar nodded graciously.

Seamus asked, "Is this place worth a lot?"

Dunbar grunted negatively. "A hundred rocky acres in northern Ontario. My father built several small cabins and called it a hunting lodge. I remember a collection of shacks." He shrugged. "It's peaceful there, I suppose, if one likes solitude."

"And the others? Did anyone seem impatient to get his or her inheritance?"

"No." The answer came too quickly. "I can't believe any of them would do anything—"

"Why don't you tell me why you think your grandson pushed you off that cliff?"

The question brought Dunbar up short. His spine stiffened, his mouth opened, apparently to object. Then he seemed to wilt. "I don't. But I'm afraid the police will."

"Why?"

"Bud and I had disagreed recently. We had a chance to sell the company, and he wanted to take it. Said he wanted to go in another direction. I was reluctant. I started that business. I made it a success. I...I wanted to keep it in the family."

Dunbar stopped, unable to put into words the desire of an old man to hold onto his young man's dream. "I might have been unreasonable," he admitted, more to himself than to Seamus. "A man's dream shouldn't be forced on his children."

"So you two disagreed about the business, he was the only one up there with you, and you distinctly recall being pushed." Seamus turned to Dunbar. "Are you sure you want to know what happened?"

A long sigh indicated Dunbar understood the implied warning. "I need to know. If Bud is in trouble, and if he didn't—if he's innocent, I hope you'll do what you can to see he is not unjustly accused."

"You know we don't have the power to make changes back there."

"I was told that. But my advisor—Nancy, is it?—indicated you can sometimes apply slight pressure in a direction."

"Very slight. A host can easily reject our efforts if what we ask is contrary to his own thoughts."

"Host?"

Seamus waved a hand as if wiping away a wrong impression. "We have no existence there anymore. We go back as an essence and depend on a living person for movement."

"I see. So you might...host with a policeman?"

"I often do. They move around, interview people, learn the facts."

"Then if this investigator began to suspect Buddy, you could communicate 'innocent' or something like that, and he'd look in another direction."

"I could try. *If* he'll listen. And *if* I'm certain your grandson is innocent."

Dunbar tapped a finger against his chin. "Could you host with Bud and read his thoughts? Then you'd know."

"I'll probably do that, but it isn't like mind reading. We only hear conscious thoughts, and only in spurts, the way people actually think."

"I understand. Fragments, thoughts that get interrupted, things like that."

"Right. And you'd be surprised. Guilty people are sometimes pretty good at not thinking about their crimes. If they feel justified or have no sense of guilt, the thought of doing murder might not even cross their mind for days at a time."

"Then it will be more difficult than I imagined." Dunbar sounded defeated.

"We have our tricks," Seamus said, taking a step away from the railing. "Try to relax and enjoy the Passage. I'll be back before you know it." He paused. "As long as you're sure this is what you want."

The man's jaw set, and he turned to face Seamus, holding out a hand. "It is," he said firmly. "And I appreciate your efforts, whatever the result."

The sun grew hot on Brodie's neck. Arlis was probably complaining even now about what the humidity did to her hair. Brodie looked down at the railing, noting signatures carved or inked into its surface over the years. "Buddy" appeared several times with a year added after each. Hers was there too, etched into the soft pine with Gramps' pocket knife: "Brodie, May, 2011." It seemed a long time ago now. She sat down on a patch of grass near one of the fence posts, leaning her back against it and staring at the trees.

It's okay, she told herself. *You can cry now, and no one will see.*

The tears didn't come, though her throat got so tight it felt like something was growing down there. No tears, but from somewhere, a phrase came: *A grief too deep for tears.* Was that what it was? Or did she not cry because she lacked normal human emotions?

Brodie tried to feel normal, but it never worked. Right now, a normal kid would be sobbing in grief at Gramps' passing, but she could not. And though she should be feeling nothing but sadness, she couldn't ignore the peacefulness of the place he'd loved. She tried to shut out the beauty of it, but it intruded on her thoughts.

The view was spectacular: the lake, spreading one hundred-eighty degrees over the fence rail. Although she'd turned her back to it, she could hear the water far below, always moving, always the same. In her mind, she heard Gramps pointing out landmarks.

"Up there, to the north, is Sleeping Bear." He insisted she get directions into her mind. "Michigan's western border runs like the side of person's hand, and we live a little above the knuckles." North of them was Traverse City, and to the south was Muskegon, her place of birth. Not that she ever wanted to see that town again.

"This area has lots of high and low spots because of glacial activity." Gramps would go on, naming islands, cities, and rivers until she lost track. To him they were vividly real, because for years he'd sailed these waters, both for pleasure and as a participant in the race to Mackinac. The course ran diagonally from the Navy Pier to Point Betsie, a few miles from where she now sat. It meandered a bit through the islands off the coast then made a beeline for Mackinac Island, one hundred fifty miles northeast, known world-wide for its beauty, Victorian charm, and prohibition of motorized vehicles. Brodie had been to the Island twice, and she loved its mix of history, ritz, and touristy junk.

No more of that now. Nobody cared what she loved. Someday, perhaps, she'd be able to go by herself, because

Gramps had arranged something called a trust fund for her. "You'll have the means to do as you like when you reach eighteen," he told her, adding, "You'll need to find out for yourself what that is." To help with that, Gramps had insisted on a good education, lots of experiences, and a lot of time spent with him, discussing whatever interested them at the time. Gramps advocated what he called informed decisions. "Opinions will always vary, because people are different," he'd say. "But if you make informed decisions, your view is as good as anyone else's."

Brodie doubted she could become as wise as Gramps or Scarlet, though they both insisted she was smart. Brodie didn't believe them, though it pleased her that they said it.

Her legs started to pick with numbness, and she shifted them to a new position. Around her, the birds in the woods had started making noise again, lulled into security by her stillness. The bluff was thick with tightly-spaced pine, cedar, and aspen with a white-barked birch here and there for contrast. She had thoroughly explored the property, wooded and otherwise, at the expense of her skin at the times when she didn't stop to put on long sleeves and pants.

"Brodie!" Arlis said at dinner one evening. "What happened to your arms?"

She didn't answer. She never answered Arlis; in fact, she rarely acknowledged the woman's existence. Scarlet stepped in, trying to protect Brodie from her own surliness. "She was looking for a bird's nest," she told the older woman. "We're studying birds, and I told her this was the time of year when the nests will have eggs in them.”

“She shouldn’t disturb the nests.” Arlis raised her voice, as if Brodie were deaf instead of unresponsive. “Brodie, you shouldn’t disturb the birds’ nests. They are procreating.”

Her expression betrayed her disgust. Did Aunt Stupid think she was she four years old?

“She was only going to look,” Scarlet said, keeping her voice light and non-argumentative. “She keeps a journal so we can talk about things she finds in nature.”

“Well, she looks like she had a fight with a grizzly bear.” Arlis’ nose twitched in distaste. “You should watch her more closely.”

Brodie had felt terrible then. Her activities—and her surly behavior—had resulted in a reprimand for Scarlet, who’d done nothing wrong. Brodie lowered her head almost to her plate, despite the fact it would probably bring another reprimand. Under the table, a foot nudged hers gently, and she glanced up. Arlis had turned to complain about something Shelley forgot, and Scarlet rolled her eyes comically. Brodie felt a little better. Arlis was an ass, but at least she didn’t scare Scarlet. Brodie was tempted to replace Arlis’ denture cream with some of Briggs’ caulking, but she’d promised Scarlet no more pranks. Who knew it would be such a hard promise to keep?

CHAPTER THREE

Seamus left Dunbar at the ship's rail, anxious to be on his way. The start of a case was always exciting: the mystery to be solved, the information to be learned, and—he admitted to himself—the chance to return to Life. He wasn't sure why it was so important to him, but going back to Earth was all he really wanted of Heaven.

As he passed the dining room, Mike stepped out of the doorway. "Did it go well with Dunbar?"

"Yeah. I'm ready to take off."

Mike looked as uncomfortable as an angel ever looks. "Uh, Gabe would like to see you before you go."

"Gabe?"

"He—I'll let him explain it." Mike led the way to Gabriel's office. It was beautiful: every surface polished, every noise muted. Even the smell of the place was hauntingly lovely, like the visitor's favorite memory of home.

In contrast to the inviting physical atmosphere, the current receptionist was one of those people who must be appreciated but not necessarily liked. Judging from his spotless desk, prim demeanor, and irritated frown at the interruption, it seemed efficiency was his sole talent. He emanated about as much warmth as a dental instrument. Setting his pen down with careful precision he said, "It's nice to see you, Michael." His mouth moved minimally, as if it were glued closed.

"Paul," Mike said, "This is Seamus. Gabe wants to see him."

Seamus was dismissed with the briefest of glances. "Gabriel is busy at the moment, but I'm sure he won't be long."

Mike turned to Seamus. "I'll leave you here, if you don't mind. When you finish with Gabe, I'll be in the dining hall."

Seamus realized he was sending a message. If he needed to talk about whatever Gabe proposed, Mike would be available.

"Thanks." Seamus took a seat at an angle from Paul. Facing the tasteful artwork on the wall, he could see the young man peripherally as he waited. Every movement was precise, every task completed in businesslike fashion, a regular assembly line approach to paperwork.

After a minute Paul surprised Seamus by asking, "Whom does he look like to you?"

"Who?"

"Gabriel."

"Oh." It was a common topic for those who'd been on board for any length of time. When they interacted with the angels, each person saw someone they trusted. Everyone's experience was different. "Leslie Howard, I guess."

"Really." The tone was ever-so-slightly disapproving.

"Who do you see?"

"Bob Fosse. They could be twins."

Seamus didn't know who that was but decided it didn't matter. *To each his own.*

After a few minutes, Gabe came to the door to invite Seamus into his office. "Sorry to keep you waiting. I know you're anxious to get started."

"Yeah, well, you never ask for much."

There it was again, that uncomfortable look. Gabe was going to ask for something, and it was not something Seamus would like.

Gabe closed the office door and even the muted noises ceased, as if they'd entered a sealed vault. Indicating Seamus should sit, Gabe took the high-backed leather chair behind the desk. "How long have you been with us now, Seamus?"

It was a subject that made him uncomfortable. "A while, I guess."

"Do you ever think of going on?"

"Sure. I'm just not ready yet."

"Of course. Totally your choice." Gabe pressed his fingertips together. "You enjoy working as a cross-back?"

"Yeah."

Gabe waited, but Seamus didn't think there was anything to add. He liked it. That was all.

"Did you ever think of taking someone along, a trainee?"

Of all the things he'd imagined Gabe might want to talk to him about, that one had not occurred to him. Seamus had worked alone his whole career. Well, except once. The crossing with a girl named Tori had worked out pretty well. Dunbar had shown no sign of wanting to cross-back with him, though. And Gabe had said *trainee.*

"I do all right by myself."

Gabe nodded. "You certainly do. No one has a better record of helping our guests than you do. It isn't that we think you need help, but you know candidates need guidance on their first cross-back."

"Oh." He'd almost forgotten Barnes, the guy who took him on his first return to life. He'd been patient, explaining everything, even stuff Seamus couldn't bring himself to ask. "You'll feel funny," Barnes had said before they left the ship. "Going back lets a guy see everything he left unfinished. It's kind of depressing, but you get over it."

Barnes had been right. Seamus learned to ignore the whispers of his own life and concentrate on the needs of his clients. Could he show some new kid the finer points of the cross-back?

"—candidate is somewhat troubling," Gabe was saying. "While the desire to help others is admirable, we must be certain our detectives see the difference between help and interference."

"You think this guy is gonna try to change things if he goes back?"

"Mildred is intelligent," Gabe said, watching Seamus' reaction to a female name. "We hope she'll pick up the idea of non-interference quickly. But she needs someone who can be firm if she happens to forget."

"Firm?"

"We paired her with Tellson first. When she began telling him her concept of crossing-back, he became nervous and asked to be excused from the job. I think she needs someone a little less…"

He paused, and Seamus supplied, "Tactful?"

Gabe smiled. "Tellson is a good man." He picked up a folder from his desk and set it on a different pile, as if temporarily setting Tellson aside. "I believe you can lay things out for Mildred and make sure she understands her role."

"Not a problem." Seamus had never been shy about telling the truth, and he was proud of it. If this woman wanted to be a cross-back detective, she'd have to learn the limits. Still, he hesitated. "I need to think about this."

"Fine," Gabe said quickly, and Seamus realized he hadn't expected to get this far. "You can let me know in the morning."

As he left the office, Seamus was deep in thought, but Paul stopped him. "Um, Seamus?" He grunted, his mind still on Gabe's proposal. "What's it like to go back?"

It was something many long-time Portalists wanted to know. Seamus avoided the question by speaking to very few people and never inviting confidences. Part of his reluctance was a desire to keep it to himself, a sort of secret pride in being strong enough to make the trip over and over, despite the pain and the hardships. Part of it was Seamus' natural tendency to be, if not anti-social, at least asocial. He didn't *dis*like other people; he just didn't *like* most of them much.

Another part of his reluctance to talk about crossing back was the inability to describe the experience. How did a guy explain existence without existence?

Paul waited, cool on the outside but eager to hear what it was like to return. "It's like love," Seamus finally said. "Frustrating, but mostly worth the effort."

Brodie spent most of the day on the bluff, thinking about Gramps and dying and what Gramps' dying meant to her. A few times she rose to stretch her legs. Other times she sat chewing on stalks of grass, watching the bugs do what bugs do.

Sometimes she turned, challenging herself with the view of the lake and the drop below her, leaning against the fence. She'd always loved the feeling of being up here, where it seemed the whole earth was below. Now her joy was diminished. Who could have predicted that such a beautiful place would turn deadly?

When the sun was directly overheard, an angry little growl from her stomach told her it was lunchtime. Leaving the house, she'd stopped in the kitchen to grab an orange and some crackers. "Where you going?" Shelley had called from the pantry. "Breakfast is almost ready."

"Not hungry."

Now she peeled the orange with her teeth, staring at the lake. She ate the segments slowly then munched on a cracker, ignoring the crumbs that fell into her lap.

When the first cracker was gone, she spoke aloud. "Cry."

After a long pause, she said it again. "Cry, damn you!"

Another pause, and then she said, "Sorry, Gramps. I meant 'darn'." She ate another cracker. "I miss you, Gramps. I really, really need you."

Mike was near the dining hall doorway, and Seamus guessed he'd been waiting for him to return from his meeting with Gabriel.

"You here to twist my arm?"

"You know better." Mike's gaze swept the room, always alert. "What do you think?"

Of all of them, Seamus liked Mike best, perhaps because, as the angel explained, he spent so much time around people that he'd become like them. Because everyone on board was his responsibility, Mike had little of the other angels' distance. He mingled with the guests all the time, unlike Gabe and Nancy, who sat in their offices and dealt with people one at a time. It was Mike who watched over them and tried to help them adjust to the biggest news of their lives: death. Mike was able to judge which guests struggled with questions of eternity, and he was always nearby, to talk, to listen, and to intercede when someone was unable to accept what had happened.

In the process, Mike had learned to enjoy eating food, especially anything fried. He played a mean game of pool and could even be caught taking a nap on deck from time to time.

Seamus watched Mike scan the crowd for signs of discontent. "I'm probably not a good choice to be somebody's guide," he said. "I do things my own way."

Mike shrugged. "Gabe knows that. But we think you're the guy who can handle Mildred."

"What is it about this woman?"

"She's very...sure of herself," Mike said. "We paired her with Drake, but the two of them disagreed from the very first."

"Drake and Tellson both turned her down?"

"Gabe thinks you're the right type. And he wouldn't ask if it wasn't important."

"What makes it important?"

Mike paused, and Seamus hoped their long association meant he'd be honest. Of course, he reminded himself, a long time for a dead guy probably wasn't that long to an angel. Still, he thought Mike respected him and knew he could handle the truth.

"The goal here is for everyone to find peace, you know that," Mike began. "Free will allows that peace to come when and how a person wants it."

Seamus glanced over Mike's shoulder at the dining room,

where the overhead lights had been turned down and pale colors glowed from recessed panels in the walls. A clarinetist stood and began a reedy solo. Most of these people, now dancing, chatting, and relaxing, would soon finish The Process, accepting gratefully what the Afterlife offered. Perhaps one in ten would hang back, nervous about what they found hard to understand. Some felt they weren't worthy of reward. Others liked the creature comforts and wanted to enjoy them for a while. Still others, like Dunbar, had unsettled questions that caused them to cling to their earthly connections. *And guys like me*, Seamus thought, *miss the feeling of being real.*

"What's this woman's reason for wanting to cross-back?"

"That's part of it. We're not sure. She has a good heart, but—" Mike stopped.

Unwilling to speak ill of the dead? Seamus almost chuckled at the thought. "She's not crazy, is she?"

"Nobody brings disease, mental or physical, when they cross over, Seamus, you know that."

He hadn't really thought about it much, but he'd never seen anyone who acted crazy.

"She has the right to do this. We've given her all the warnings, and she still wants to go. But she's a bit of a bull-dozer who'll need someone strong to keep her in line. And," Mike searched for the right words, "someone who can resist her. She's a charming bull-dozer."

What a mess, Seamus thought. All he wanted was to do

the job he was good at. Now they wanted him to babysit! Still, Mike and Gabe had been good to him, appreciative of his talents and his willingness to bear the discomforts of crossing back.

"I guess I'd better meet this Mildred," Seamus said with a sigh. "Then I'll make my decision."

Mike turned toward the room, searching the dance floor. "She's on the dance floor right now. I can put you at her table."

"The table next to it would be better."

"Whatever you like."

Mike led Seamus to a table where several chairs sat empty, vacated by dancers. Pulling up a chair from a nearby table, he introduced him to the two people sitting there. "This is Seamus. He wants to listen to the band for a while."

The two women smiled politely and returned their gaze to the dance floor. Seamus ignored their talk of clothing, watching the dancers and trying to guess which one was Mildred. He counted the chairs at her table: nine, three of them occupied. The number of guests at a table was always between four and nine. People function best in groups of that size, he'd heard.

As he waited, people came and went. Three didn't dance, an elderly man and two women. Other than that, the table's company included three women who seemed likely possibilities for Mildred. One was large enough to "hunt bear with a switch," as his father would have phrased it. One was young and cute in a twenty-something way. The third was a diminutive blond of about forty with sparkling blue eyes and a dazzling smile. One of those women who attract attention effortlessly, she was a popular dancing partner. Seamus found himself hoping she was Mildred.

She was. Looking around, Seamus saw Mike watching him. He nodded, brows quirked in a "see what you think" expression. Rubbing a hand along the back of his neck, Seamus wriggled his brows and turned back to the dance floor.

For once Seamus enjoyed a half hour in the company of his fellow passengers. He watched Mildred as she danced with different partners, moving gracefully, adapting easily to whatever tune was played. The dress she wore had classic lines and a filmy drape that seemed to caress her shoulders as she moved to the music. Her hair was swept back with two combs whose tiny jewels caught the light when she turned.

The evening's entertainment ended, and he waited as she took leave of her companions. One of the men told a story that involved much hand-waving and eyebrow movement. Mildred smiled up at him as if fascinated. However, at the doorway, she patted his arm, said something that seemed vaguely promising, and left him behind.

Watching her, Seamus had to admit he wouldn't mind having those blue eyes fasten on him, listening as he taught her what he knew about crossing back. Despite his reluctance to have any company at all, a woman of his own age, and a pretty one at that, wouldn't be too bad. If Mildred was interested in becoming a detective for the dead, he could help.

She made her way along the deck, almost to the exact spot where Dunbar had waited an hour earlier. There she stopped, leaning her weight against the rail and apparently losing herself in the scene before her. After a minute Seamus realized she was waiting for him, but he felt an unaccustomed shyness about approaching her. Not that he cared what she thought of him, but still.

"Pretty, isn't it?" he said, stopping some distance away to avoid startling her.

"I suppose one would say that words can't describe it," she replied. "But how could they? Words are our invention. This is quite something else."

They both stood for a few moments, looking at the view beyond the ship. The Passage to the next world was more perception than anything else. All the senses were engaged, but in a way they had never been in life: colors beyond what had been seen, sounds unlike any other, scents and feelings that were stimulating and calming at once, and even a taste in the air that was almost like a person's favorite but better. The total effect was, Seamus thought, whatever the opposite of sensory deprivation was. Sensory overload, but in the best possible way.

"You're the cross-back?" she asked, turning toward him.

"Yeah."

Her gaze flickered from his two-tone wing-tips shoes to his wide-lapelled brown-striped suit, ending at the fedora set low on his forehead. "Do they make you wear that outfit to meet new clients?”

“People wear what they want here.” It sounded defensive.

Mildred realized her mistake. “Of course.” She reached out and straightened his coat collar, tugging it into place then stepping back to judge her work. “You’d look nice in something a little lighter, though. It would brighten your complexion.”

He felt his nostrils flare. “I don’t need anybody to fix me, lady.”

She was immediately contrite. “I’m sorry. I didn’t mean to sound critical.” She smiled brightly. “Let’s start over. You are—”

“Seamus.” He waited for her to comment, but she didn’t.

“Mildred.” She made a little curtsey and smiled at him brightly. He noticed she was almost exactly his height. And that her eyes crinkled nicely at the corners.

“Good to meet you, Millie.”

“Mildred.” Her smile took the sting away, and she tilted her head slightly to one side. “I prefer Mildred. But I promise to stop correcting you when I’m your partner.”

He tried to suppress a sniff of opposition. “I *might* take you on a cross-back and show you the ropes. I am *not* in the market for a partner.”

Her lips tightened briefly, but she pressed on. “I promise you, I’m an excellent pupil. I know how to listen, how to follow orders, and how to keep quiet."

"Good, because that's important."

"I understand."

"Have they told you what it's like to go back?"

Her brow furrowed briefly. "I know it hurts."

"Like nothing you've ever experienced." He rolled his shoulders. "I can show you some things that will help, though."

There was that smile again. "That would be good of you."

"You know how we operate when we get there?"

"Yes. We find a host." Her voice turned recitative. "We move around with them, but they don't know we're there. They feel tired or think they're getting sick." She punched herself lightly in the stomach. "Tummy upset, like the flu."

"Two will make it harder on them."

"Really? I never heard that."

"I took someone with me a while back. We split up to make things easier on the hosts."

"I see. So we'll separate when we get there?"

"Probably." Recalling what Gabe had said about Mildred needing guidance, he added, "If I can trust you to do as you're told."

"How will I know what to do if we're in different hosts?"

"We talk while they're asleep. They kind of hear us, but

they think they're dreaming. We don't talk when they're awake."

"Unless it's really important."

"I guess if your host was on fire, you should tell me, but otherwise, keep quiet."

She pressed her lips together before saying, "You're the expert."

Seamus thought about what Mildred needed to know. "You can't make them do stuff."

"Yes, Angelo said that."

"Angelo?"

She licked her lips. "I was almost paired with a detective before. It didn't work out."

"Uh." That made three rejections. Seamus felt rising doubt, but he told himself maybe Mildred had rejected Angelo. Both sides had to agree on these things. "What didn't work out, exactly?"

"It was a mutual decision." Folding her hands, she rested them on the railing. "I haven't been told exactly how we get from here to there and back. Is that part difficult?"

"When we're ready to leave, the power will be there. The return requires living energy, so we need a healthy host. If you ever have to spend time with someone who's sick or hurt, make it quick."

"I see."

"We only get one try, so we don't want to come back too soon. You'll stay in contact with me so we can decide when we know enough." He raised a finger. "Just not when the hosts are awake."

"I'll do exactly as you say, Seamus. I'm not one to jabber, anyway."

"Good. Our voices sound like noise inside their heads. It disrupts their thoughts and makes them antsy. And if we interfere too much with their thoughts, they think they're going crazy."

"We can't let that happen." She gave him a conspiratorial smile. "Unless you say so."

Seamus scratched his jaw. "Right. What else have they told you?"

"That it's difficult to return once you've been here on the ship."

"True." His first time, he'd been shocked at the noise, the dirt, the heavy bodies that humans drag around with them, even the pain of physicality. Once a person was dead, those things seemed unbelievably troublesome. Yet Seamus found he missed them, so much so that in order to experience them again, he'd become, and remained, a cross-back. Though his efforts on behalf of the dead didn't change things on earth, they helped his clients get over whatever doubts held them back. Once things were explained, most forgot earthly concerns and moved to the next level with eager anticipation.

That brought him to Dunbar's fear he'd been murdered,

perhaps by his beloved grandson.

Mildred seemed to read his mind. "They told me you have a case. I'd be very grateful if you'd let me come along and observe how you handle it."

"It might be a good one for a first timer," he said, weighing the options. He could make Gabe and Mike happy by acceding to their request, and the case seemed likely to be open and shut. Either the grandson did it, or Dunbar had fallen due to age and infirmity.

"Is it a murder?" she asked.

"Possibly."

"What exactly would I be doing?"

"Exactly what I tell you." Seamus summarized what Dunbar had told him.

"And you're willing to let me come along?"

"I'll let you know in the morning."

She reached out as if to touch his arm then apparently thought better of it. "I'd like to help you solve this case, Seamus."

"We don't have to solve it. Dunbar wants to know if his grandson killed him, that's all." Seamus glanced out into the distance, adding, "My guess is he did."

She looked surprised. "Should detectives form an opinion before even beginning?"

"Millie, fifty million dollars is a lot of incentive."

"Mildred," she corrected. "But it does sound intriguing." She leaned close, allowing Seamus a hint of a haunting perfume. "Please let me come along." With that she left him, her retreating figure swaying in a most feminine manner until she disappeared from sight.

The sound of a motor alerted Brodie to the approach of intruders. She jumped to her feet, scraped the sand around her with her cap to smooth out her footprints, and headed into the trees. She didn't leave but crouched in the foliage, hidden from view. Brodie cultivated the skill of observation without detection, which was how she knew that most of her family wished they'd never heard of her. *Brodie the spy*, she thought of herself, although Arlis phrased it differently. "I wish you wouldn't act so sneaky, Brodie," she'd said more than once with a disapproving sniff. Sneak or spy, Brodie knew that Arlis drank more than she admitted, that Arnold told more than he should about his employer's family to friends on the phone, and that Briggs kept a stash of nudie magazines in a crate at the back of the garage. It made her feel a little less abnormal to know others had secrets too.

The vehicle she heard was Gramps' golf cart, but two people she'd never seen before rode in it. One was a youngish man in the uniform of the local sheriff's department. The other was a woman in a green pantsuit, a no-nonsense type, judging from her flat shoes, short hair, and focused expression.

They parked the cart a short way from where Brodie lay in

the dense brush. She followed quietly as they walked the crooked path to the viewing spot. Once there, they both took in the view for a few seconds. It would have been hard not to pause and appreciate it. Then they looked over the edge, around the fencing, and into the trees on either side. Neither spoke for a long time, but finally, the woman said, "Vertigo."

The deputy's response came a beat too slowly. "Possible."

She picked up on it. "You think something else?"

He smirked, and Brodie decided she didn't like him. "Lots of money to be had if the old guy died."

"Yeah. But the grandson pretty much had control of it. He could have anything he wanted."

"Except *total* control." The deputy tapped his chin lightly with a closed fist, letting that sink in. "Rumor is they'd disagreed about things lately."

"Yeah?"

"I'm just sayin'."

"Office Reiner, if you've got something more than suspicion, I'd like to hear about it." The woman's tone was mild. One of Brodie's former tutors had often spoken to her in that tone, which the girl interpreted as, "I have to deal with you, but I don't like you."

"Don't you think we should investigate a little more, Detective Schell? Mr. Dunbar was a respected member of this community—"

"Who had a dizzy spell and fell off this bluff. He had no business being up here, old as he was. If the grandson did anything wrong, it was leaving him alone for even a few minutes."

"That's the other thing. This animal crying in the woods. Don't that sound fishy to you?"

"Not really. If I heard it, I'd probably go see what it was too." She made an impatient move. "There are a dozen things I should be doing, and I don't see anything here to convince me Dunbar's death wasn't an accident. You can't prove young Dunbar pushed his grandfather over the edge."

"But you can't prove he didn't."

"Reiner, the grand jury, the district attorney, and the voters of this state don't ask me to spend my time proving that a murder did *not* happen. They're only interested if I can prove that it did." With that, Detective Schell took a final glance at the lake and turned to go. She disappeared from Brodie's sight almost immediately, but Reiner hung back.

"There's got to be a way to prove he did it," Reiner said to Lake Michigan before he too left the scene.

When they were gone, Brodie climbed out of hiding and started for the house. Their exchange had ruined even the tiny bit of peace being in Gramps' favorite spot had brought her.

CHAPTER FOUR

Seamus found Mildred the next morning as she left the breakfast buffet. She wore pink. Everything. "I'd like to leave as soon as possible."

Her face lit like a candle. "Oh, I'm so grateful, Seamus. Thank you." She moved forward, almost certainly intending a hug.

He held up a hand. "You should meet our client. Let's see if Dunbar's around somewhere."

They found him reading in a deck chair, his feet propped on a low table. When he saw Mildred, he rose politely.

"Mr. Dunbar, this is Mildred. She's going with me while I investigate your case."

Dunbar frowned slightly, and Mildred stepped toward him, extending a hand. "I'm a detective in training. Seamus is going to let me observe, so I can learn what he knows about crossing back."

Seamus almost sneered at the implication she could learn in one trip what he knew, but he stuck his hands in his pockets and examined the deck instead.

Dunbar took Mildred's hand and she moved closer, so he looked down at her upturned face. "I wonder, Mr. Dunbar—"

"Please, call me Will."

Now Seamus quashed an urge to sniff in objection. Dunbar hadn't invited him to that familiarity.

Mildred smiled coquettishly. "Will, then. Could you tell

your story again, for my benefit? Seamus has given me the basics, but it would be so much clearer coming from you."

I wasn't clear? Seamus almost said it aloud. Still, it couldn't hurt to go over the facts of the case again.

Dunbar obediently told the whole story once more. As he talked, Mildred stopped him occasionally, touching his arm lightly and asking a question. Seamus had to admit they were all good ones.

"So your sister lives with you. Does she have a good relationship with the child, Brodie?"

"Well, no. Arlis tried, of course, but Brodie is...difficult. She was treated badly by her mother, and unfortunately, she took a dislike to my sister from the first. For my sake, they came to a sort of compromise. Arlis generally leaves Brodie alone, and Brodie generally pretends Arlis doesn't exist."

Disrespectful, Seamus thought, but he didn't let disapproval show on his face. He sensed Dunbar thought the kid made the sun rise and set each day.

Later, Mildred had another question. "You say your grandson went into the woods to find a creature in pain, but you didn't hear it. Did he say what it sounded like?"

"I don't remember him mentioning a particular animal. He might have, but—"

"That's quite all right. I just wondered."

As Dunbar described the members of the household, she stopped him once more. "This Scarlet. Does she benefit in any way from your death?"

Dunbar seemed shocked. "Certainly not enough to be involved in it. She was a waitress I met last year when Bud and I were on Mackinac Island for a conference. She's Irish, and she mentioned she'd trained to be a teacher but hadn't yet found a position."

"An Irish schoolteacher waiting tables at a tourist spot in Michigan?"

"Young people come from all over the world each summer to work in the hotels up there. The money's good and they get to visit the States."

"I see." Mildred didn't seem convinced, and Dunbar flushed slightly.

"Because she was intelligent and lively, I took a liking to Scarlet. When I returned home and learned Brodie had driven yet another tutor away, I contacted her to ask if she'd take the job." He raised a hand. "After I'd checked her out thoroughly, of course. We extended her visa, and things worked out very well from there."

The questions went on a while longer. Mildred was, Seamus had to admit, a shrewd interviewer, getting Dunbar to expand on things he hadn't thought to ask. She learned that Arnold Wilk, Dunbar's personal assistant, was "a bit of a worm but very efficient." Shelley the cook had been a surrogate mother to both Bud and Brodie. And it had been Bud who first suggested Scarlet might become Brodie's tutor.

Finally, Mildred seemed satisfied. "I appreciate your candor, Will," she said, patting the man's arm. "We'll do our very best to find out the truth for you."

Seamus thought her use of "we" was a little presumptuous.

They left Dunbar to his novel, walking the deck as they discussed what they'd learned. Mildred took Seamus' arm, as if they were on promenade. Her pink heels clicked softly on the deck surface. "I think that went very well."

"Yeah?"

"I'm sure you noticed the same things I did."

"Okay, what did you notice?"

"Well, there are two ways to explain why Will didn't hear an animal crying in the woods."

"Yeah, like there wasn't any animal."

"That's one. But there is another possibility. Will is—well, he was—quite deaf."

"Deaf!"

"Yes. Of course, here, everything works fine. But you must have noticed that he turns one ear toward whoever is speaking. It's habit, left over from years of straining to hear with what was undoubtedly his good ear. It was the left ear he turned toward us, so his right, where the sound supposedly came from, was possibly so bad he wouldn't have heard a thing."

Seamus was impressed. The woman was intelligent, as Gabe had said. Not just book-smart, college intelligent, but observational and deduction-type intelligent. "That's pretty good."

Mildred looked pleased. "The other thing I got from his

story is more important. I think we can narrow the list of suspects already."

"Didn't you recently lecture me about keeping an open mind?"

"Oh, I will," Mildred said airily. "I always do. But I think we'll find that a woman is our focus."

"The sister, Arlis?"

"Arlis seems unlikely to go tromping through the woods, no matter how much money was at stake. But Scarlet seems much too good to be true."

"The tutor? What does she gain from Dunbar's death?"

"She's after the grandson, you silly man. He's wealthy, and she's been under his nose for the past year, working on getting him hooked."

Brodie had intended to return to the viewing point the next morning, preferring its solitude to the presence of people who disapproved of her, but when Scarlet asked her to remain in the house she obeyed, lying on her bed and watching tiny white clouds drift by her window like passing ships.

Gramps had been half of Brodie's life, and that half was gone. The other half she divided among Scarlet, Shelley the cook, and her husband Briggs, the handyman. Everyone else she imagined as outside an invisible circle. There were times when she had to speak to those outside people, but she had as little to do with them as possible. They made her feel like a misfit. They spoke louder than normal when they talked to her, and something in their eyes conveyed discomfort at her presence.

Just because she'd set one tree on fire.

It had been an accident. She'd been a kid then, and she'd taken it into her head to build a fire in her tree house and roast marshmallows. The stupid thing wouldn't go, and she used up all but one of her matches on it. Finally, she had a brilliant idea: gasoline would make it burn. But how to get some up into the tree? She'd hit on an idea she thought was clever. Using a narrow tube, she sipped some gas from the can Briggs kept in the barn into her mouth then climbed carefully back up to the tree house. Lighting her last match, she spit the gas on the kindling she'd amassed. That was pretty much all she could recall for a while. When it was all over, she had no eyebrows, a receding hairline, and a reputation as a budding arsonist to add to her other crimes. When she thought about it, she could still taste the gas in her mouth. *Stupid.*

Scarlet knocked softly on her bedroom door. "Brodie? Can you come downstairs? There are things we have to discuss."

Dragging herself off the bed, Brodie made herself presentable, knowing Scarlet would send her right back upstairs if she didn't wear shoes and comb her hair. No doubt funeral arrangements were being made. They'd bury Gramps, then what? Would they send her away? Put her in some snobby girls' school so they didn't have to look at her? She was pretty sure nobody wanted the ugly crazy girl around. Nobody ever had, except Gramps. Briggs and Shelley were good to her. So was Scarlet. But it was their job.

When she'd come to the Dunbar house, Brodie ate only with her hands. Her caregivers would put her to bed in her lovely room only to find her asleep on the couch in the family room the next morning. Over time, she'd adapted to society's simple demands. She ate with a fork, combed her hair once a day, and learned to sleep in a bed. Although not as wild as she had been, at twelve years of age Brodie still refused to go to school, associated only with a few people she was used to, and would not eat meals in company. A long line of nannies, caregivers, and tutors had been endured with little grace. Each was tested, most beyond their ability to withstand it. Brodie considered it a kind of duty.

Then, a little less than a year ago, Scarlet had arrived. Brodie learned, through her usual spying, that the new tutor came on Bud's recommendation. Since Bud didn't like her, she figured the woman would be horrible, but Gramps had urged, "Give her a chance. Most people are okay if you treat them well." Brodie didn't buy it. Best to find out right away what a person was like when she was angry. Anger told you a lot.

On her first day, Brodie had waited for the new girl to try to befriend her, as all those before her had done. But Scarlet hadn't come looking for her. Instead she sat down in the back yard in an Adirondack chair shaded by a large maple tree. It was a spot Brodie herself favored. Idly she paged through an oversized book with a medieval castle on the cover. Brodie watched from her favorite hiding place, a spirea bush that drooped branches onto the ground, making a space for a slightly undersized girl to hide and spy on her elders.

The new woman was not much fun to watch. She looked at every page for what seemed like forever. Sometimes she stopped and rested her eyes, and when she did, the book would tilt forward on her lap, giving a tantalizing glimpse of more castles. It was apparently all about them, and Brodie wondered if someone had told this Scarlet person that such books were her favorites. She had several, but this one was new to her, with pages of bright greens and stark grays against blues that seemed to draw her to them.

Finally, the Scarlet person rose, set the book down on the chair, and disappeared into the house. Brodie decided with some satisfaction that she had out-waited Gramps' most recent hireling. She crept out from her leafy lair, looking around to be sure the woman wasn't lurking somewhere near the French doors.

Satisfied she was alone, Brodie took up the book and sat down on the chair. The cover depicted Blarney Castle, one of her favorites. Like her, it wasn't fancy or prettied up. It was what it was. Carefully, she opened the book's pages, and within a few minutes was transported across the ocean, visiting Edinburgh Castle, Floors Castle, Conwy Castle, and others she'd never heard of. She wondered what it must be like to see those places for real, not as pictures in books or on TV.

"I've been to Blarney, and some of the others as well," said a voice behind her. Brodie knew in an instant she'd been had. The Scarlet person had left the book on purpose. Someone had blabbed, probably Arnold the Mouth. She tried to be angry, but she was fascinated that this woman had been where she wanted so much to go. In fact, she heard a lilt in Scarlet's voice that revealed more.

"Are you Irish?" Brodie used her voice so little that she had to clear her throat before asking.

Scarlet made a little curtsey. "Have you heard of the Ring of Kerry?"

"No."

She came a step closer, and Brodie caught the scent of apples. "May I see the book? I can show you Ballycarbery, the castle nearest my home town."

What must it be like to live near a castle, to see it as you passed by every day? Brodie handed the book over, and while the woman paged through to find the picture, she made a decision. She loved Gramps. She liked Shelley and Briggs. For reasons she didn't fully understand, Brodie decided Scarlet might be a fourth person on the earth she could enjoy spending time with.

From then on Scarlet had been her guide, helping Brodie see that behaving herself wasn't so bad. There were no lectures about expectations, no fake "Let's be friends" talks. Scarlet was firm but not demanding, authoritative but willing to listen to Brodie's side of things and compromise.

In the last year Brodie's reading skills, which were good but had been limited to what she chose to read, widened and deepened. Scarlet let her dress as she chose, never criticizing her odd clothing choices the way Arlis did. Scarlet served as a gentle example of what was proper and gave advice, but only when asked. She also showed Brodie ways to manage her wild mop of hair, having her own unruly auburn curls to conquer.

With Scarlet's encouragement, Brodie began to mix with the people who came to the house. Scarlet suggested she might spend a few polite minutes with Gramps' dinner guests before returning to her own pursuits. Once she found that none of them pointed at her or went into hysterics, Brodie agreed to remain through dinner from time to time. She and Scarlet practiced together which fork to choose and how to eat and answer questions at the same time. Scarlet made it a sort of game, and Brodie did okay. She decided she didn't mind people too much, at least for short periods of time.

The first time she stayed for dinner, Gramps embarrassed her by asking all sorts of questions about what she'd been reading. She'd been uncomfortable, balancing questions about *Great Expectations* with concerns about ending up with a lapful of succotash. Scarlet explained later that he was proud of her and wanted his guests to know she read things other kids her age had never heard of. "He wants everyone to see how intelligent you are."

Brodie never thought of herself as smart. She had learned a lot of stuff from the array of companions Gramps had hired over the years, but it wasn't hard. Stuff stuck in her head, but that didn't make a person smart. Brodie had learned early on what she was.

"Watch this," Jeannie said to the current boyfriend. "Hey, Brodie! Hey, little girl. What's Brodie?" She held up a cookie, just out of the child's reach, and repeated, "What's Brodie?"

"Tupid."

Jeannie chuckled, elbowing the guy, who smiled disinterestedly. "What's Brodie?"

"Tupid."

"—and what else?"

"Ug-wy."

"Ug-leee," Jeannie corrected." Ugly. And what else?"

The child hesitated, trying to recall the word that would get her something to eat. "Weed."

Jeannie shook her head. "Not weed. Weirrrrd."

"Weerrd."

"Right." She gave the child the cookie and watched her bite into it. "Stupid. Ugly. Weird. That's Brodie."

Even if she knew some stuff, Brodie was still ugly. Maybe better now with Scarlet's help, but nothing anyone would want to look at for long. And surly. Arlis reminded her of that often enough. And crazy. Not normal, not like normal people. Weird.

She knew her oddness had bothered Gramps. He hadn't said it out loud, and it wasn't something Brodie talked about, even to Scarlet. She could tell Scarlet lots of stuff, but not what went on inside her head. She couldn't tell anyone, though she always thought if she ever had to, Gramps would have understood.

But Gramps was gone. And she was afraid to tell anyone else how weird she felt, how unlike everybody else.

CHAPTER FIVE

As Seamus considered the case and his responsibilities to both Dunbar and Gabe, he began to have doubts. Mildred was intuitive and intelligent, but he'd already noted her strong will and tendency to speak first and think later. Her charming apologies might smooth the way in face to face conversations, but a cross-back couldn't apologize or explain to her host that she was sorry to have spoken out of turn.

"Keep in mind what I said," he warned as he went over the specifics of the trip. "We aren't there to change anything."

"And you're the boss. I get it." Mildred's tone was politely impatient. "I won't do anything you don't explicitly tell me to do."

"Good. Then you won't get into trouble." Seamus took a step toward her. Realizing the moment had come, Mildred stepped back. "I can't go like this!" she protested. "I have to change."

At first he didn't comprehend. When he did, his brow furrowed in disapproval. "They won't—"

She put a hand on his arm. "Five minutes," she pleaded. "I will run—literally run—to the ship store and get something suitable. I promise. I won't be long. I can't go feeling unprepared."

Seamus didn't agree or disagree. She was gone before he had a chance to.

As she hurried off, he looked around blankly. Finding an empty lounge chair, he threw himself into it, already regretting the decision to take Mildred along. His gut told him she was trouble, but when she was standing right in front of him, he found it hard to say that to her. "It's those eyes," he muttered aloud. "And a woman's eyes are the worst reason ever for agreeing to anything."

Mildred went first to the store, where a pleasant woman with a French accent helped her choose an outfit for the trip, complete with earrings, shoes, and a scarf for her hair. She marveled, as she had the first few times she'd visited, at the endless array of choices. Anything a person could ask for seemed to be a touch away, and the woman behind the counter took the right tone, helpful but not pushy. Mildred went to her stateroom and changed, turning before the mirror to be sure the outfit looked good from all angles. She laughed at herself for caring about something no one but Seamus would see, but it was important to *feel* like she looked good. How could a person accomplish anything otherwise?

As she came onto the deck, Mildred passed the ship's salon. She paused, unsure, then turned and went inside. Seamus could not begrudge her the time to make herself look her best.

Much time later she emerged from the salon, hair styled and peach-scented, and all twenty nails colored to match her outfit. She was ready to go.

As she navigated the hallway, however, she thought of Nancy, counselor for the recently dead. Nancy had first explained the possibility of crossing back, and she deserved word of Mildred's imminent departure. Seamus would understand.

When she knocked on the door, Nancy called out, "Come in." Mildred entered the tastefully appointed office, approaching the angel with arms outstretched. Nancy bore a strong resemblance to Mildred's mother, though without the half-glasses Mom had worn the last decade or so of her life.

"I've come to tell you how grateful I am for your help," she said, giving Nancy an enthusiastic hug before sitting in a chair opposite the desk.

"You found a detective to take you back?"

"Yes. He's an odd duck but very sweet. Seamus."

"Oh, yes, I know of him."

"He's given me all the background, and we're ready to go." She wriggled a little in her chair. "It's just so exciting, to be going back to Life to share with others the assurances I have."

Nancy's brows rose. "Seamus did tell you it's not your place to share anything with the Living, didn't he?"

"Oh, of course. I didn't mean I'll *talk* to anyone. I meant that I hope my presence will give the *feeling* of comfort, like a spirit of peace."

Nancy was direct. "I'm told your presence makes them feel sick."

Her smile faltered. "I intend to be very light, so they won't even know I'm there."

"That's the idea." Nancy folded perfect hands on the perfectly clean desktop. "Listen to Seamus. He knows what to do."

"Oh, I will," Mildred said. "I can tell he's very good at what he does, although men like that are a little bossy sometimes, don't you think?" She held up a hand when Nancy seemed about to object. "But I'll listen very carefully to his advice."

"I hope so," Nancy answered. Her tone was even, but something in her eyes conveyed doubt that Mildred's words, however much she meant them at that moment, were true.

Seamus had no idea how long he waited in the chair before dozing off, no idea how long he slept, but he woke with the sense he was losing time. Mildred was nowhere to be seen. Should he go without her? He glared at the empty deck, disgusted with himself. Why shouldn't he leave her behind? Let her go on to Detective #5 and see if *that* worked out!

Three guys had been smart enough to pass Mildred by, so why had he taken her on? With a disgruntled, tooth-sucking sound, he admitted the reason. Because Gabe was wrong about him. *I am a sucker for a beautiful woman,* Seamus thought. *A sap.*

"There you are!" Mildred's tone implied he'd been hiding on her when he was no more than three steps from where they parted. She wore white pants and a long, flowery top that draped almost to her knees on one side. She'd done something different with her hair too and the shoes she wore matched the brown tones in the top. "I'm sorry to be a little long, but a person has to feel right, don't you think, when starting something new?"

Seamus could think of nothing to say, having worn the same suit for—well, eternity seemed like a good word for it.

"Let's go."

"One more thing." She held up a finger, looking at him sideways in a flirty manner. In a moment, she was gone again, disappearing into a shop whose door stood open down the way. She was only gone a few seconds, and she returned proudly holding a chrysanthemum. "Just what that suit needs," she told Seamus, tucking the flower into his buttonhole. Standing back, she nodded. "Perfect. Now we can go."

He touched the flower's soft petals, almost unbelieving. A flower? Sighing, he chose not to comment lest they delay any longer.

Seamus took Mildred's hands in his, and immediately, the pain hit. Despite long experience, the agony surprised him every time. It was like being stretched in every conceivable direction, maybe worse than that, if there was something worse. Only one thing helped. He said aloud, "Moan!" He heard his own voice, in his head and all around him, giving sound to his suffering in low, anguished tones.

Beside him, Mildred wailed like an Irish banshee. Around them both, something, or maybe nothing, swirled furiously. When the pain became so bad Seamus thought he couldn't stand any more, he counted breathlessly: "One, two, THREE!"

He opened his eyes. Mildred, who seemed to be leaning on him though there was no longer any of her to lean or of him to lean on, asked, "Where are we?"

"The last place William Dunbar saw in his life."

"So this is where we pick up—" She stopped. Before them

a young girl hung suspended on the wrong side of the cautionary fence. Her toes extended over the edge of the cliff, her arms reached backward, gripping the top rail. Most of her stretched over thin air.

"Seamus!"

"Hush!" He was thinking furiously. They had to enter a host within seconds of their arrival or return to the ship. But if they jumped to this girl, she might let go of her precarious hold, reacting to fear and physics. Within seconds of arrival, he had to make a critical decision.

The girl made it for him. As lightly as a mountain goat, she pulled herself back from the edge, vaulted the fence, and landed directly in front of them. Once she landed, facing them, her eyes opened wide in disbelief. She saw them, or at least saw something her brain didn't know how to interpret.

"Jump!" He told Mildred, and they propelled themselves toward the girl. She stumbled forward a step, caught herself, and muttered something like, "Shit!" Immediately, she replaced the word. "I mean, shoot! What was that?"

"She saw us," Mildred said. The girl shook her head. "She's Brodie, isn't she? What if she tells someone?"

"Hush!"

Instead of obeying, as she'd promised to do, Mildred spoke in distinct tones. "Brodie, don't worry. Everything is going to be all right."

If Seamus had had teeth, they'd have clenched. He should have gone with his instincts. Within ten seconds, Mildred had demonstrated she was everything she'd insisted she was not:

talkative, meddlesome, and completely unwilling to follow orders.

Brodie had escaped again to the viewing point after funeral plans were explained. Funeral—the word itself was awful. There would be people, emotion, ceremony, all the things she hated. But it would be for Gramps, so she would tolerate it.

She hung from the fence rail, staring down at the trees and water below, until she was dizzy. *I'd better be careful, or I'll fall,* she thought with a grim smile. Was that what she was hoping, that the fence would give or her hands would tire, and she'd plunge to her death like Gramps did? She imagined the feeling of falling through the air. Would it be freeing to not hold on to anything ever again? Death might not be so bad if she and Gramps were reunited. If a person knew what it was like to be dead, she could decide if that's what she wanted. It was not knowing that made the decision so tough.

Not that life offered a lot of prospects. She had nobody left. With Gramps gone, someone else, probably Bud, would take over as her guardian. Where would she end up? Scarlet was important to her, but Bud might decide she was old enough to be on her own. He might send Scarlet packing and save the estate's money.

This morning he'd been pretty nice, but it was obvious he had no idea what to say to her. Arnold the Mouth had tried to help, but he was as clueless as Bud. He kept asking Brodie if she was all right, which had to be the dumbest question ever. She listened for a while, learned the funeral would be tomorrow, and escaped before Arlis started in again on her visit to the mortuary. Arlis had insisted on choosing the casket, the flowers, the music, and the readings from scripture. Bud seemed relieved to let her deal with those things, but Brodie knew Arlis had done it for herself, just like she did everything.

"I made all the arrangements," She'd tell the guests. "After all, he was my brother."

And your meal ticket, Brodie would have added if Brodie ever spoke in Arlis' presence, which she didn't if she could avoid it.

She'd watched Bud, trying to figure him out. He was everyone's meal ticket now, even hers. As trustee, Bud had control of Brodie's life for the next five years. She didn't know him well, but she knew there was almost no chance he liked her.

For one thing, she'd been a real pain as a kid, playing dumb, sometimes horrible, pranks on people. Bud had been the recipient of a few of them—not that many, she tried to tell herself. He'd lived with Gramps when she first came, but their age difference kept them from interacting much. Bud had been into cars and girls at the high school, not half-wild three-year-olds with the table manners of an orangutan. He had ignored Brodie whenever possible. Then he went off to college, becoming one of the people who visited from time to time and had to be avoided.

When she asked about Bud's parents, Gramps had been truthful but not forthcoming. "My son didn't marry well," was all he said. "When he died, I thought it best that Bud live with me."

"You rescued him, like you rescued me?"

He smiled. "Something like that." Brodie pictured Gramps, swooping down like an avenging angel on Bud's mother and taking the child home with him.

So Bud had been unwanted, like Brodie. But unlike her, Bud was useful and normal. Gramps' charity cases had come out fifty-fifty: one worthwhile, one not so much.

A funny moaning sound came from behind her, but she could not turn from her present position to see what it was. It had to be wind in the pines, but it was kind of creepy. At the same time, her arms began to ache from the strain of holding onto the fence rail. Admitting she was not going to do the right thing and off herself, she jumped back over the fence. As her feet hit the ground on the safe side of the fence, Brodie saw something in front of her. It was nebulous—no, *they* were nebulous: two misty shapes that looked vaguely human.

Then they were gone. A wave of nausea hit her like a punch in the gut. She staggered under the weight of it, put one hand to her head, the other to her stomach. A few seconds later, a second phantom punch sent her staggering to one side. Her stomach turned queasy, like the time she'd eaten a whole loaf of uncooked bread dough. Her head filled with the sound of swarming bees. She didn't understand Mildred's assurance that everything was going to be all right. In fact, for Brodie, everything felt even worse than it had before.

Entry had been difficult, and Seamus paused to regroup. His worst fears had manifested in one place and time. Their first attempt had been repelled by the girl's essence, a mix of hormones, misfiring axons, and some sort of cellular rebellion. Like a prize fighter on the ropes, Seamus had had to shake his (metaphorical) head and reconnoiter. Their prospective host was off-balance from the first attempt. "Again!" he ordered Mildred, and they'd tried a second time. Although it felt like they'd be shot backward again, the girl's body gave way at the last second, and they were inside.

Seamus had been relieved until Mildred started yapping. "Shut up!" He'd never in his life spoken so loudly inside a waking host's head. Still, he'd had to get his point across to this woman who hadn't been on the job thirty seconds and was already breaking the rules.

To his relief, Mildred did as ordered, although she too might have been too exhausted to speak. The girl they both inhabited seemed totally disoriented for a while, but gradually her heartbeat returned to normal and she stopped massaging her forehead. She would be fine. It irked Seamus that Mildred had made him lose his temper. *Not like me at all,* he thought, but at least they were in. Mildred was silent, cowed, he hoped, by his disapproval.

There was a span of a few seconds where only the lap of waves could be heard. Seamus shuddered when the girl formed the first thought he could comprehend. *Crazy,* she said to herself. *I really am crazy.*

Her name was Brodie, and she was the child Dunbar had spoken of, the one he'd rescued from some horrible situation. Seamus saw right away she wouldn't be a useful host.

The girl was odd. He had been inside a lot of heads, but he had never felt more resistance. It was what cross-backs called the Curse of the Teenage Girl. Young women just into puberty were notoriously bad hosts. In fact, they were lucky to have gotten into this girl's head at all. Other cross-backs told stories of bouncing off young females and having to flounder back to their original host. Things got upset, knick-knacks went flying into walls, and there was a general feeling of atmospheric distress in the vicinity that gave rise to stories of poltergeists.

If Brodie was relatively permeable right now, he sensed it was due to sadness. Grief hung on the girl like weighted netting. Everything she saw was filtered through sadness, dread, and fear. The cause of the grief he could guess at. The fear he didn't understand, but her thoughts on the matter were closed, as if she pushed them away with continual, active effort. It had to be a gargantuan task, not to think at all about something that loomed so large in her mind.

The girl's only clear thought was that she was crazy. After a moment Brodie pushed that thought away too and stumbled down the path, her mind stubbornly empty.

"Seamus—"

"Millie, for the last time, shut *up*!"

There was a poignant silence.

"It's Mildred."

CHAPTER SIX

Brodie felt sick, weighed down and nauseated, but she should have expected it. She'd been obsessing about Gramps' death and her future, or lack of one. She hadn't eaten much of anything over the last twenty-four hours. Gramps always said worry didn't change anything. She tried to stop thinking about death and uncertainty, which led to worrying, but it wasn't easy.

She'd stop thinking about anything at all. She would concentrate on her feet, watching them, steering them, hating them. It worked fairly well. Her mind stayed empty all the way down the steep incline, across the open meadow, past the barn, and up to the house. It didn't help much, though. Her head felt too heavy for her neck, and her gut felt jumpy and kind of squishy.

With nothing to do until the funeral the next afternoon (which she would *not* think about, would *not*!), Brodie wandered the house listlessly. Shelley was busy preparing for the guests who would come to the house after the service. Seeing no sign of Briggs outside, she guessed he was cleaning everyone's cars so they'd be ready for the funeral procession. Bud was in Gramps' office, talking to someone on the phone, Arnold hovered outside the room, obviously hoping to become useful to the new Mr. Dunbar. *The king is dead; long live the king.*

Arnold the Mouth was not Brodie's favorite person. Gramps had always smiled when she said that, explaining that Arnold was competent and willing to live in a small town west of everywhere. *Likeable* was not one of the terms in the job description. Scarlet spoke no ill of anyone in the household, but she did smile once when Brodie, required to use the word *officious* in a sentence, used it to describe her grandfather's assistant.

As Gramps had done fewer business-related tasks, Arnold's role had shifted to more general duties. Arlis often used his expertise for church or social events. Seeing herself as the grand dame of Frankfort, Arlis hosted teas, Twelfth Night suppers, and garden tours for the supposed benefit of the locals. Since it was all for charity, Gramps had played his part when the day of each event came, allowing Arnold and Arlis the spotlight as his home and property were made available to the public.

Arnold was a fake and a sneak, one of those people who thought if he smiled when he said something awful, people wouldn't realize what a sneak he was. Brodie had heard him on the phone sometimes (yes, she'd been spying) and knew he told stories about her, dramatizing her minor mistakes to make her seem worse than she was. She tried not to let it bother her, but she had outgrown a lot of that stuff.

Watching Arnold now as he waited for Bud to notice him and give him something to do, she wondered what he'd told Bud about her lately. She had glued his shoes to the floor last year, but only with hot glue. It wasn't like she'd used the tough stuff.

Scarlet had gone into town to find Brodie a pair of real shoes, insisting that flip-flops were not appropriate for a funeral. When Brodie mentioned she had a pair of Reeboks, Scarlet had given her The Look. "You have to buy something nice," she said firmly. "It's for your grandfather."

Brodie liked that Gramps had never explained to Scarlet—or to anyone who did not already know—that she was not really his granddaughter. Still, she hated shopping. "You go."

"But what if the shoes I buy don't fit?"

"I'm only going to wear them for an hour."

Shaking her head, Scarlet had gone, leaving Brodie with nothing to do. She passed through the living room aimlessly, wondering how to keep from thinking about Gramps. The sound of crunching gravel caught her attention. The front wall was mostly windows, but Shelley had closed the blinds to keep the house cool. Pulling them aside, Brodie saw the county sheriff's car pull into the drive. That gave her a head start to a spot where she could overhear what the deputy had to say to Bud.

Seamus saw the car through Brodie's eyes, and his interest picked up. He had to work his way to someone in authority, and here was an early opportunity. Law officers knew things he wanted to know: autopsy details, salient facts, and what witnesses said about the incident. He wanted to jump to the deputy who now approached the house and hoped Brodie would get close enough to allow it.

Brodie was on the move. Seamus didn't understand her purpose until she slid under the staircase and crouched down in a shadowed recess. A hiding spot. She wanted the same thing he did, information.

The girl's position was well-suited to eavesdropping, since the open stairway faced the office where Bud Dunbar sat sorting through old photographs. The deputy was shown there by a fifty-ish woman who moved as if her feet hurt. As he passed not four feet from them, Seamus easily made the jump to him. He had a moment's misgiving, hoping Mildred understood she shouldn't chat with her host.

The deputy was a better fit all around. Seamus preferred hosting with men—not, he told himself, because he had anything against women. He simply felt more comfortable with the male linear thought process. Men spent less time wavering between alternatives. They chose a path and made it work.

William Dunbar's fears had been correct. This officer believed Bud Dunbar was a murderer. Seamus sensed nervousness, however. Those above him in rank were convinced the old man's death had been an accident. He'd come to the Dunbar home on a fishing expedition.

"Mr. Dunbar—"

The man who occupied the desk smiled slightly. "I was Bud when we were in school, Frank."

The man's feet shifted. "Well, this is business, so I thought I'd keep things businesslike."

"All right." Bud laced his fingers atop the open album. "What can I do for you, Officer Reiner?"

"Um, it came to my attention,—I mean, I heard some things—"

Bud's chin lifted a little. "What things?"

Seamus felt Reiner's defensiveness and caught a name, *Arnold.* "It wasn't like anybody was tryin' to do you dirt or anything. Word is you and your grandfather had some problems."

"I spoke with the detective about that. It was nothing serious."

"You wanted to sell the company, and he didn't."

"Something like that." Dunbar's gaze challenged Reiner to make more of it.

"I wondered—" Reiner shifted uncomfortably. It wasn't as easy as he'd imagined, Seamus sensed, looking a man in the eye and accusing him of murdering a helpless relative. "Why did you want to sell?"

"I thought the business had gotten to be too much for Gramps and he'd do better without the worry of it."

"Are things going downhill?"

Bud sighed softly but answered politely enough. "As you know, our company makes electrical parts. We've reached a time when those parts will soon become obsolete. I proposed that we get out of the business while we could still sell at a profit."

"Makes sense."

"There's a prospective buyer who has plans to retool the whole business and shift production to more modern manufacturing."

"You couldn't do that yourselves?"

"We could. But I had no interest, and Gramps—He was too old to start over."

Seamus sensed Reiner's doubt. "You didn't want to

manage the company anymore?"

"No." It was a refusal to go into more detail.

Reiner's thoughts centered mostly on disbelief that anyone would voluntarily giving up a job with such prestige, not to mention the financial rewards. "How, um, how serious did the arguments get?"

Passing a hand through his hair, Bud met Reiner's gaze. "Not serious at all, Frank. I brought it up a couple of times, Gramps said he didn't want to sell, and I dropped it."

"And now that you have control?"

Dunbar's eyes went a shade darker. "I'll do what I think is best for everyone involved, as I did when Gramps was alive." He rose from the chair. "Now unless there is something specific you need, I have a lot to take care of before the funeral."

From her hiding spot under the stairs, Brodie heard it all. Reiner didn't close the door, which made it easy. Other times, she'd had to creep up and put her ear to the door, and at those times she heard only bits and pieces. Now she heard everything and even saw the anger on Bud's face when Reiner went too far with his insinuations.

She didn't like Reiner, but then she didn't like cops. She'd had dealings with a few over the years, and they had no sense of humor at all.

It had been a sheriff's deputy, although not this one, who caught her on the night Arlis had thrown a Halloween fundraiser for UNICEF. It was in the B.S. days, Before Scarlet.

Brodie had no objections to the fundraiser, but Arlis had been a pain, lecturing her on how eleven-year-old girls were ladies and should behave accordingly when guests were present. She had arranged dumb activities, like a hay ride and some really lame games. In Brodie's mind, a Halloween party should include scary stuff, so she borrowed Arlis' cloak, which had to be from 1965, and made up her face to look all bloody and beaten. When it was time for the guests to arrive, she'd made her way up the long drive and chosen a spot that was dark. When a car turned into the driveway, she staggered out in front of it, gasping and moaning. She only got to do it a few times before the cops arrived and spoiled everything.

Pushing aside her dislike of deputies, Brodie thought about what this one suspected. Bud wanted to sell the company. Buyers didn't wait around forever, even she knew that. So if he'd wanted it badly enough, might Bud have done something terrible?

She hoped not. Gramps had loved Bud better than anyone else in the world. He'd trusted him completely, and she had never seen evidence those feelings weren't mutual. So could Bud, a guy who had always been around, a guy she was sort of related to, be a murderer? It was a lot to think about. Brodie decided an informed decision required more information.

Seamus left with Reiner, gathering a sense of local geography as they drove. The house—it probably deserved a more impressive word like *mansion*—sat back from the beach about fifty feet. Bluffs rose on either side, although the southern one was softer and lower than the one he'd come down earlier as Brodie's unwitting guest. Around the house were several outbuildings: a large garage, some sheds, a barn, and a boathouse, all in the same Edwardian style as the house. Behind them, a stretch of flat land spread in both directions before turning to deep woods.

Reiner rolled the windows of his patrol car down for a few minutes, letting the heat dissipate in order to give the AC a chance. The smell of clover gave way to pine when they entered the cooler, darker section. They traveled for some time before the driveway rose sharply and ended, meeting the county road that paralleled the lake. Reiner turned right, and they drove along the shoreline.

They traveled southward, passing several impressive homes, a golf course, and a yacht club. Finally they descended a winding, tree-lined street to the town of Frankfort, which lay between Lake Michigan and a much smaller lake, which he learned from a sign was called Betsie. The town was not large, and the marina dominated. It seemed there were boats everywhere. Sunlight sparkled off the clear water and off the metallic bits of every sort of watercraft. Expensive yachts dwarfed tiny one-person sailboats, and clunky rowboats shared space with sleek cruisers with massive double motors.

Seamus didn't approve of any of them.

Reiner drove through Frankfort slowly, watching for signs of trouble. He cruised a few side streets, checked motel parking lots for a car they'd been asked to watch for that morning, and drove by some of the places the kids liked to hang, making his presence known and watching for infractions of the law, major or minor. Finding none, he took Highway 115, which inclined its way out of town. Seamus learned from his host's thoughts that the sheriff's department was headquartered in the nearby town of Beulah.

When they arrived there, it was almost four o'clock. The sheriff's department was quiet, the few people around busy with their work. Reiner stuck his head into the sheriff's office, which smelled of coffee left too long on the warmer. "Done for the day, boss. Pretty quiet out there."

The sheriff looked up from the report he was reading. Leaning against the wall behind him was the cane he used since his knee replacement two months ago, which didn't seem to be coming along well. Seamus heard Reiner's thought: *Lose fifty pounds. That might take the pressure off.*

"You went out to the Dunbar place?"

Reiner's jaw tightened. "Yeah. Checked to see if they were doing okay."

"And?"

He shrugged. "Seems like it. Funeral's tomorrow."

The sheriff regarded his deputy's eager face. "Would you be able to go? Getting out to the cemetery isn't easy with that." He waved resentfully at the cane.

"Sure, I can go."

"They're pretty important people in this county."

They're rich, Reiner thought. *That isn't the same as important.* He rubbed his nose with a knuckle. "You don't think we should look at this some more? See if it was really an accident?"

The sheriff's expression indicated it wasn't the first time the subject had come up. "Listen—"

"That doctor said a strong push could have unsteadied the old guy."

"He also said Dunbar was in rough shape and probably lost his balance."

"It's convenient for Bud, having his grandfather die after they argued about the future of the business. Arnold says—"

"Arnold Wilk is an old woman, gossiping where he shouldn't and trying to look like he's sorry to have to say it."

Reiner didn't argue that point.

"Sergeant Schell thinks Bud came off as truthful. Completely distraught, she said."

"He could always do that." Reiner sniffed disdainfully. "Wrap women right around his finger."

His shift over, Reiner switched to a Ford pickup and drove to a modular outside of town. The house was over-laden, at least in Seamus' view, with items in a forest motif. On every surface and wall, bears, wolves, and moose cavorted. Candles, pine-scented, of course, burned in several rooms. If this was cabin chic, he'd pass.

Mrs. Reiner looked like a life-long dieter: too thin, unable to relax, and impatient with everything. As her family ate the meal she had prepared, she drank a glass of tea to which she'd added cayenne pepper and some drops from a small brown bottle. Seamus heard reference to a "cleanse" but did not want to know more than that.

Reiner spent the evening watching extreme boxing on TV

and wrestling with his two boys, who looked like miniatures of him. Later he made love to his wife, which Seamus always found uncomfortably voyeuristic. Unable to opt out of the process, he tried instead to concentrate on the case and what he knew thus far.

His time with Reiner had been informative, but he was finished with the deputy. Having learned what the authorities knew and having seen what Reiner suspected, which seemed to him mostly wishful thinking, he wanted to return to the Dunbar home, where there might be real answers to the questions Will Dunbar wanted answered.

Seamus was brought back to the moment by a cessation of bedroom activity. In minutes, maybe seconds, Reiner was asleep. Seamus called to Mildred.

"I'm here." With no interference from their hosts' conscious thoughts, Mildred's voice was distinct.

"I would never have guessed how different it is," she began. "How come we didn't know our bodies were so darned heavy?"

"Nothing to compare it to."

"And why does everything seem a little gray, like I'm wearing sunglasses?"

"The kid is sad. They don't know it, but their mood affects how they perceive things."

"Isn't it all really interesting? It's fascinating. I never imagined how it would be."

Seamus suppressed a sigh. "What have you found out?"

"Okay, Mr. All-Business. Just the facts."

That would be nice, he thought. He doubted she'd stick to it for long.

"I met Arlis at dinner, and I can't say I like her very much. She's bossy and intrusive."

Seamus thought that sounded a lot like someone else he'd met recently, but he didn't say it aloud. "Does that make her a possible murderer?"

"Probably not," Mildred admitted. "But she and Brodie don't get along. Maybe she quarreled with her brother about it. Maybe he was about to kick her out of his home."

"He'd have told us."

"I suppose. There might be something he didn't know about, though, something she thought she'd get if he were dead."

"Like what?"

"I don't know yet." Mildred seemed unwilling to let go of Arlis as a suspect. "She's so sure she's right about everything. At dinner, everyone had to listen while she prattled on about her son, who's helping at some disaster. To hear her tell it, he's the national hero of wherever he is, Tibet, I think."

"What do the others say?"

"They keep trying to change the subject, but everything out of her mouth starts with 'Leland says' or 'My son thinks.' He sounds like one of those fanatical types, you know, like smokers who quit then try to make everyone else quit too. This guy's going to fix the world to make up for the mistakes of his youth, and his mother is convinced that puts him in the same category as Mother Teresa."

"Okay. So Arlis is a pain. That isn't a crime. We haven't got a reason for her to kill her brother, so we need to look at the rest of them. What else did you pick up?"

"Well, Brodie isn't sure Bud didn't push Will over the edge. I think it's part of what is bothering her. I thought maybe I could—"

"Do nothing." Seamus spoke louder than he intended, and Reiner stirred in his sleep. "We aren't here to counsel anybody. We're here to learn what we can about Dunbar's death."

"But she's so pitiful, the poor little thing. She thinks she's ugly, did you get that?"

"Mostly what I got was interference."

"Yes. She tries not to think. And there's that whole teen-aged angst thing, 'I hate myself.' I think hers is worse than usual because she doesn't feel like she belongs anywhere. Her grandfather was everything to her, and he's gone. If she thought someone cared—"

"Someone will. But it can't be you, get it?"

"I know. I don't exist, not really. Isn't it odd how everything smells funny?"

"I never noticed."

"You've got to be kidding! Nothing smells like it's supposed to."

"I suppose different brains process odors differently."

"But isn't that amazing?"

"Yeah. Listen, who are you going to jump to next? I'd say the tutor, because she knows the others on an adult level."

"I can't leave Brodie. She needs me."

"Millie—"

"It's Mildred, and I have to stay with the child. Even if I can't really talk to her, I can do that thing you told me about, the one-word suggestion. I'll tell her she's okay."

"She won't believe you. She doesn't want to."

"I have to try."

Seamus was disgusted, with Gabe, with Mike, with Mildred, but mostly with himself. Instinct had told him this woman was too subjective to be a good investigator. Now she was proving it. Again.

Maybe they should return to the ship. The police would almost certainly call Dunbar's death accidental. Reiner wanted to believe Bud had killed Dunbar, but the deputy envied Bud, the guy who had everything, including the starting pitcher's job Reiner had coveted back in high school. He might make noises about murder, but his superiors thought otherwise.

Was that enough for Dunbar? Was it sufficient to know Bud would not be prosecuted, or did he want to learn what really happened? Seamus decided he should stay at least until he could get to Bud Dunbar and see what he was feeling. He'd have to work on it alone if Mildred insisted on sticking with Brodie, but he preferred working alone anyway. In fact, he wished he were alone on this job.

"Okay, stay with Brodie but do *not* interfere with her thoughts. I told you before, it makes them think they're going crazy. This kid doesn't have far to go, so leave her alone."

"I understand," Mildred said pleasantly, and Seamus winced. It was the same sort of tone his wife used to use when she intended to ignore his advice entirely and do precisely as she pleased.

CHAPTER SEVEN

Brodie awoke feeling strange. It wasn't the bolt of nausea she'd experienced yesterday, but she felt slow and sort of groggy. Then she realized why: today was Gramps' funeral.

It was every bit as awful as she had imagined. She dressed in the new outfit Scarlet bought her, a pair of soft black jeans (Scarlet knew better than to buy a skirt) with a gray top that wasn't too disgusting. The shoes from Classens were okay too, though they felt constricting and heavy, unlike flip-flops. "You don't want to slap-slap all over the church," Scarlet pointed out. "We're going for dignity here."

Dignity sounded like something Gramps would have wanted, so Brodie pulled her hair back with a black plastic headband, taming its wildness somewhat. The band felt tight, and in an hour it would press into her temples like a vise, but she had to try to look good. She turned to the bedroom mirror to see the total effect. Her reflection showed a skinny girl with bony elbows, a mouth that was too wide, and hair like one of Macbeth's witches. "Ugly," she said aloud, but from somewhere inside, a voice answered, "Pretty."

"Yeah, right," she told her mirror image. "Pretty ugly."

But when she came down the stairs, Scarlet smiled approval, and even Bud seemed pleased with her appearance. Maybe he was relieved she wasn't too big an embarrassment.

The service went on forever. Arlis had prepared a little speech, of course. Then she asked some of Will's friends to speak, and a lot of them were so old they didn't know when to stop. The minister seemed to feel he should have his time even if the others overran theirs, so it was almost two hours before they were done. Brodie tried to be patient, to remind herself it was all for Gramps, but she knew if he'd been there, he'd have dismissed it as pure silliness. She suppressed a sigh. Everyone said the funeral was the worst part. Maybe she'd feel better afterward.

Seamus jumped from Deputy Reiner to Scarlet as she passed him in the doorway of the lovely old Presbyterian church. Scarlet tensed in reaction, but her grip on Brodie's hand didn't falter. Seamus heard her thought clearly. *Poor kid. She's doing pretty well for someone who hates crowds.*

Scarlet McMorran felt an appreciation of the good that life offers, and Seamus welcomed her spirited outlook after experiencing the confused Brodie and the negative Reiner. Scarlet was an optimist, and while Seamus couldn't exactly call himself that, he appreciated a host with a bright outlook.

The tutor was affected by Dunbar's death, but most of her sadness came from sympathy for Brodie. Scarlet saw life and death as natural, and Dunbar had been old and increasingly feeble. *He's better off*, her thoughts said, *but Brodie isn't.*

Questions flitted through Scarlet's mind concerning what her own future might be, but Seamus sensed an assurance that seemed odd, given the situation. Scarlet glanced at Bud, who was talking to the minister near the door. *He could fire me*, she thought, *but he'd best not try it.*

As the attendees headed to their cars for the trip to the cemetery, Seamus looked for an opportunity to jump to Bud. To his frustration, Scarlet and Brodie remained apart from everyone else, apparently due to a promise Scarlet had made earlier. They rode to the graveyard together in Scarlet's sporty little Chevy.

"Do you think he'll let you keep the car?" Brodie asked when they were shut inside, waiting for the procession to line up. She seemed much more at ease when she and Scarlet were alone, almost like a normal young person. Not that Seamus knew many young people.

"I think Mr. Dunbar left it to me." Scarlet started the engine and the AC went to work, providing a blast of cool air.

"Cool. I wouldn't want you to lose your wheels." She watched the funeral home attendants putting little flags on the cars. "Scarlet, do you like Bud?"

Seamus sensed confusion in Scarlet's mind: embarrassment mixed with something else. He didn't quite grasp it, but it made him uncomfortable. It was like a door had opened as he walked by a hotel room, revealing a passionate tableau he wasn't intended to see.

"I don't know him very well."

"Me neither. He's always pretty much ignored me."

"Bud was good to your grandfather." Scarlet checked the rear view mirror for pedestrians then pulled away from the curb to join the stately parade.

As they followed the lead car Brodie asked, "So you don't think Bud killed Gramps?"

"Brodie! How can you say that?"

"I heard the cops talking about it. One of them thinks Bud

pushed Gramps so he could do what he wants to with the company."

"Bud would never hurt your grandfather." Scarlet downshifted as the procession began its slow passage through town. "He couldn't kill anyone."

Brodie thought about that. "I saw him get mad once. He was pretty scary then."

"Really? What made him so angry?"

Brodie lifted her headband slightly to ease the pressure. "When he was in high school, Bud was all about girls. He had this girlfriend, Candy."

"Candy?"

Brodie rolled her eyes. "I know. Couldn't you gag? Anyway, him and Candy—"

"Candy and he."

"Right. Candy and *he* were gonna go somewhere one night. I heard him say it was a castle."

Scarlet smiled. "A magic word."

"Yeah. I was a kid then, maybe eight. Anyway, I wanted to go and see the castle too, so I got into the back seat of his car and scrunched down. I covered myself with an old blanket he kept back there, and he didn't see me. He picked this Candy up, and we drove for a long time. I could hear them talking, but it was really dumb stuff like what band is the best and which teacher should be fired.

"It was hot back there, and I finally fell asleep. When I woke up, we were going through a town. I said something like,

'Can we stop at that McDonalds before we go to the castle?'" Brodie chewed on her lower lip. "Bud went ballistic."

"I can imagine." Scarlet was having a hard time keeping a serious expression as she pictured Bud finding his adopted sibling stowed away on his big date.

"It was some concert they held at this place called the Castle, but they couldn't go, 'cause they couldn't leave me by myself. They had to turn around and drive all the way home."

"And Bud was angry."

"Yeah. Really."

"But he didn't push you off a cliff."

"I think he wanted to."

"But he didn't."

"No. But he kinda was mad at me ever since."

Scarlet braked for the turn into the cemetery. "Can you see why he was angry? It was probably going to be a really special evening for him, and you ruined it."

Brodie smiled grimly. "That's what I do. Ruin things."

Seamus heard fragmented thoughts in Scarlet's mind: consideration of where she should park, along the road or on the grass. Brodie's natural tendency to think the worst of herself, which worried her. The question of whether the grass was still damp from the morning's rain. And an odd little bump of jealousy for Bud's long-ago girlfriend named Candy.

Through some horrible quirk of fate, Brodie ended up seated

next to Arlis at the graveside ceremony. One minute she was waiting for Scarlet, and the next, an attendant from the mortuary was ushering her to a chair beside the grave. There were only three: one for her, one for Arlis, and one for Bud. Everyone else stood around the gaping hole, trying not to look at the casket positioned over it.

Collin Marks stood across from her, and he smoothed his trim mustache with a familiar gesture. Collin had been around most of her life, though Brodie knew little about him. He was the perfect lawyer, Gramps said, lacking strong opinions and wanting only to serve his clients' interests.

Next to Collin stood Arnold, trying to appear sad but looking more bored than anything else. Arnold had weaseled a spot in Gramps' car, probably at Arlis' invitation. Bud had looked at Brodie as if to ask if she wanted to ride with them, but she'd stuck with Scarlet. Arnold saw her looking at him now and gave her what was supposed to be a brave smile. In deference to the occasion Brodie didn't put out her tongue at him, but she didn't acknowledge their solidarity, either.

When all was ready, the mortician signaled a worker who pressed a switch that activated an almost silent device that lowered the casket. Arlis grabbed Brodie's hand, digging her nails into the skin until it hurt. Arlis' other hand went to her mouth, and she pressed it against her lips dramatically. *Like a soap opera actress*, Brodie thought.

Then her own distress rose inside her like a bubble in her chest. That was Gramps in the box. He was dead. He wasn't coming back, ever. The pain of Arlis' deep-red nails biting into her hand was almost welcome, almost enough to keep her from feeling the finality of the scene before her.

Now she felt like crying, but now was the one time she would not. People would see. They would know what she was feeling. And Brodie didn't want people to know what she felt. It was always better if they didn't.

Scarlet stood back, feeling her place was not with the family. Still, Seamus knew she'd liked old Mr. Dunbar. Her eyes lingered on the younger Dunbar, but with a force of will she lowered them, concentrating on the minister's voice. *So Millie had one thing right*, Seamus thought. *The little tutor has designs on the new boss.*

But maybe not. Scarlet worked hard *not* to think about Bud Dunbar and the thoughts Seamus discerned were firm denials of any feelings for him. The more he put bits and pieces together, the clearer it became. Scarlet didn't have plans for Bud's future. She and he had a past, which she was determined to bury, in a symbolic grave as deep as the real one waiting to be covered over.

Why? he wondered, but Scarlet concentrated on the scriptures being read. Seamus caught only a snippet of judgment on Bud Dunbar's character: *Snake.*

As soon as she could, Brodie escaped the guests who came for the funeral dinner. She forced herself to circulate once, putting up with fatuous condolences and even a few pats, though most people were leery of her and kept their hands to themselves. She tried to act in a way Gramps would appreciate and even managed to smile at Mr. Zimmerman, whom she disliked intensely. "Z" was an old business acquaintance of

Gramps' who sometimes visited for a weekend. Once, when Gramps wasn't around and Brodie was too little to stop him, he'd grabbed her and given her a "whisker rub," scratching his stubbly face across her soft one in what he thought was a huge joke. She had repaid him by topping off the gas tank of his car with water from the garden hose.

Having paid respect to Gramps by tolerating his friends as long as she could, Brodie slipped upstairs, changed into shorts, a T-shirt, and her beloved flip-flops. As she came downstairs, Arnold was passing. "You were really good today, Brodie. Your grandfather would have been proud of you."

What Gramps would really have been proud of was the fact she bit back the acidic reply that came to mind. Instead she said, "Thanks, Arnold." Then she left by the back door, avoiding Shelley's eagle eye, and headed for the spot where she would really say goodbye.

Everything was a little damp from the rain, but Brodie liked that. She liked the smell of the earth and the extra-green color of the washed leaves. As she made her way to the viewing point, some of what the minister had said played back in her mind. Death was part of life. Those who left—died—were gone, but those left behind still had what the dead had given them: love, joy, and understanding. Gramps didn't want those he loved to grieve forever. It was okay to enjoy the sunshine, okay to laugh.

Gramps had given her a life much different from the one she'd have had otherwise. If not for him, she might never even have known that life had a good side. Though she tried to forget, scenes of horror played in her dreams, even in waking hours if she dropped her guard. There was a woman who seemed to hate her and a succession of men who either ignored her or swatted her out of their way. She recalled hunger, a tattered blanket she wrapped up in at night, and a lumpy couch that smelled bad and made her sneeze. It all seemed unreal now, as if it had happened to someone else, but at times the mists parted and Jeannie's voice would come to her, telling her she'd ruined everything.

Stupid! Ugly! Weird!

According to Scarlet, the brain cannot recreate feelings of the past, which was a good thing. "Who could carry on if the emotions of each hurt remained as clear afterward as when they happened?" she'd asked, and Brodie had to agree it would be impossible.

Gramps had rescued Brodie. It was hard to forget Jeannie and her constant abuse, but affection, security, and time had helped. Brodie wondered if this new tragedy would break her, erase all the progress she'd made in the last ten years. She hoped Scarlet was right, that her brain would learn to forget, and she wouldn't have to live with this crushing grief forever.

A memory came of the first time she'd ever seen Gramps. He had knocked at the door of their apartment. She never knew how he'd found them, how he knew of her existence and the life she endured. But when he saw Brodie wrapped in her filthy quilt, he had acted swiftly. Before Jeannie could react, William had swept the child up in his arms, announcing he was taking her home with him.

Brodie didn't remember exactly what was said. Jeannie— she'd never been taught to call her Mother—screamed obscenities, which was nothing new. What was new was the strong arms that enfolded her, the soothing voice that told her it was going to be all right. She reacted in the only way she knew to this strange man's attention—she bit him.

Instead of swearing, Gramps soothed her, petting her matted hair and speaking softly. She didn't remember the words, only a feeling she'd never experienced before, the feeling that someone actually cared what happened to her.

It scared her to death. And it had continued to be scary for years, though she'd gotten used to most of it. She believed Gramps loved her, despite her oddness. She'd even come to understand that there were people in the world who were all right, who could be trusted. But it hadn't been easy.

From determined spying efforts, Brodie learned later that for the first few months Gramps fought a multi-faceted war. Jeannie, sensing he'd do anything to keep the child she didn't want, threw all her resources—not much intelligence but lots of craft—into getting every cent she could from the wealthy William C. Dunbar. Shelley and Briggs often discussed Jeannie, their voices disapproving as they rehashed what a mother had done—and not done—to her own child. Gramps dealt with Brodie's mom brusquely but fairly, and in the end, Jeannie relinquished custody of her daughter for a sum of money she had, in Shelley's opinion, never imagined he'd agree to.

There had been problems at home too. Arlis wanted proof Brodie was related to the Dunbars. She objected strongly to Will's taking in a "damaged child" without DNA testing. It was true Brodie didn't look like the Dunbars, who were attractive people with light hair and normal-shaped eyes. Brodie had dark, round eyes and wiry black hair. It must have been hard for him to argue that she belonged. He refused to discuss Arlis' objections, however, insisting he felt a bond and didn't need DNA to prove it. Shelley approved of his stance, and Briggs approved of whatever Shelley approved.

Now that Gramps was gone and she had to face life without him, Brodie admitted she was the biggest problem William Dunbar ever faced. Like a wild thing, she had at first refused any sort of affection, instruction, or civilization. Until she was almost ten, it took two people to make her presentable: one to hold her, one to de-snarl the mass of curls. If Gramps was at home, he'd be the holder, and Brodie would allow the current caregiver to perform the torturous process. A succession of women came and went, and some made it through a year before her tantrums, language, and stubbornness drove them off.

She had eventually succumbed to most of society's demands. She slept in a bed. She learned to use a knife, fork, and spoon, though she still preferred hand-held foods. This brought on some bargaining. Brodie found cooking interesting and could usually be quieted if allowed to sit on a stool in the kitchen and watch Shelley prepare meals. Shelley gave her small tasks to do, like cleaning carrots or stirring cookie dough. When Scarlet came, she suggested Brodie be allowed to participate fully in meal planning and preparation if she ate the resulting meal with the family. As a result, Brodie became a semi-regular presence at dinner. Gramps always declared her contributions outstanding. The others seemed to enjoy her cooking, even Arnold, who had cause to doubt her good intentions.

Overall, the verdict on Brodie was mixed. Gramps loved

her in spite of her oddness. Shelley enjoyed her company and her willing hands. Briggs liked to talk, and since Brodie was mostly silent, let her tag along while he talked about anything that came to mind, from his tour in the Nam to aphids that eat the vegetables if a guy isn't watchful.

On the other side, there was Arlis. Though she claimed to have grown fond of Brodie, it was a pitying sort of affection Brodie had no use for. Early on, she pegged Arlis as a fraud whose every action was for her own benefit. Gramps loved Brodie, so Arlis claimed to.

Brodie the Spy had more than once heard Shelley tell the story of her first few weeks at the house. "When she saw Mr. Dunbar couldn't be talked out of adopting Brodie, Arlis declared she'd transform that child into an acceptable member of the family," Shelley would say. "But her idea of helping was the wicked stepmother type, all smiles and coos when others were around and all snotty and disgusted when nobody was. That little girl knew Arlis didn't like her, and boy, did she react."

Brodie had been so awful that Arlis gave up after only a week. She allowed hired caregivers full sway and warned each new one it was impossible to deal with that "recalcitrant child."

Then Scarlet came. "No bigger than a minute," Gramps said of her. He'd feared she might be too petite to handle Brodie, who, though not large, was capable of vigorous resistance. She'd proven it with former employees.

"I won't need to subdue her, sir," Scarlet had insisted. "Brodie will want to do as I say."

Gramps always chuckled when he got to that part of the story. "That I had to see," he'd say.

A rustling startled Brodie from her reverie, and she jumped to her feet. Too late. A man emerged from the woods, holding a small device that might have been an MP3. He seemed as surprised at their meeting as she was. As she considered retreat, he stopped, raising his hands in apology and assurance.

"Sorry. I didn't mean to intrude." When Brodie made no reply, he added, "I'm watching birds."

She nodded, wondering whether she should tell him he was on private property. Gramps wouldn't have, so she decided not to.

He held up the device. "I record their songs with this. They're all different, you know."

Of course she knew. She had an excellent teacher, and they spent a lot of time on natural science, a subject that interested them both.

The man peered at her as if she were a species of finch he'd never encountered before. "Are you, um, are you a local girl?"

Brodie tried her voice, trying to make it neutral but firm. "Yes."

"Do you know Mr. Dunbar, then?"

"He died." Too late, she realized he might have meant Bud, being about his age. "William did."

"I'm sorry to hear it," the man said. He was dressed in jeans and a T-shirt, so it was hard to tell, but he seemed an unlikely type for bird watching. She thought of such people as nerdy, anti-social, and all scientific, but then she'd never met a birdwatcher before.

"If you don't mind my asking, how did Mr. Dunbar die?"

Brodie could not help but glance over her shoulder at the water below. "Accident."

The man's gaze went to the fence too, and he took a step toward it. "Terrible!"

She said nothing, and he hesitated, apparently unsure of what to do. "I'm sorry." He was still looking at the fence, and he indicated the signature carved into it. "Is that you?"

"Yeah."

"Well, I'm sorry for your loss, Brodie." The man turned back the way he had come. "Sorry to have disturbed you." With a wave, he melted into the trees. Brodie watched until he disappeared, glad he was gone. She'd had enough of being polite to strangers for one day.

CHAPTER EIGHT

Scarlet started picking up the dishes and trash as Bud said goodbye to the last of the guests at the front door. Closing it with a snap and a sigh of relief, he leaned his back against it and said to no one in particular, "Funerals. Who needs 'em?"

Arlis, who'd sat in state most of the afternoon and now watched placidly as Scarlet and Shelley cleaned up the mess, gave him a look of mild rebuke. "They are necessary for the grieving process, like putting away your white shoes at the end of summer."

Scarlet almost smiled at the puzzled look the comment brought to Bud's face. He turned to her, but she looked down, apparently concentrating on neatly the stacking dishes left on various surfaces.

Seamus had sensed all afternoon that Scarlet avoided speaking to Bud. Worse, she avoided thinking about Bud, which meant he got no take at all from her on his likeliest suspect. *If Dunbar's death was murder,* he reminded himself. Scarlet had opinions on the others in the household. Arlis she considered spoiled and more than moderately irritating. Arnold she treated with cold politeness, and Seamus suspected she had warded off more than one pass. Shelley, the cook/housekeeper, was a force to be reckoned with, but Scarlet seemed to respect her and didn't mind pitching in when possible to make her work a little lighter.

"It's a shame Leland couldn't be here," Arlis said with a sigh. "I called him, of course, but he's still in Nepal. Something to do with orphans. He sends his love to all."

"Hmm." Bud again tried to catch Scarlet's eye. She wiped

a coffee stain up with a napkin, taking longer with the task than was strictly necessary.

"Did you see the outfit Carol Olds was wearing?" Arlis asked. No one answered, but a one-sided conversation never stopped Arlis. "It was ghastly. She's much too old for florals."

"Scarlet, have you seen Brodie?" Bud asked.

"And that perm! She looks like she belongs under the Big Top."

"I think she went for a walk."

"Why a person doesn't know enough to grow old gracefully, I will never know." This from a woman who'd tottered through the afternoon on heels much too high for eighty-year-old ankles.

"Did you see which direction?"

"I think..." Scarlet indicated the road up to the bluff with her eyes.

Arlis gave Bud a coy smile. "Buddy, you'll tell me if I start dressing like a silly old woman, won't you?"

"Of course, Aunt Arlis. Now, I have some things to do." With an apologetic smile at Scarlet, he left the room. Whether he was sorry for leaving her with the clean-up or for leaving her with Arlis, Seamus didn't know. A few seconds later, the back door clicked softly closed. Scarlet seemed determined not to notice Bud's departure at all.

After listening to the birds and the breeze for a while, Brodie climbed the fence again and tested its strength. Holding on with one hand, she peered down at the treetops directly below.

Again the thought struck her that she might be able to find Gramps if she followed him. If she thought it was true—

"Brodie?" The call made her jump. Bud was coming, apparently on foot this time, for she'd heard no sound. Deputy Reiner's hinted accusation returned to her mind, giving her a funny feeling. She'd told the stranger Gramps' death was an accident. Did she believe that? Or was the criminal returning to the scene of his crime?

"Here." She scrambled over to the proper side of the fence just before Bud appeared.

"Scarlet said you might be up here. I—" He paused, and she had another eerie thought. Had Bud been watching, hoping she'd jump so he had one less problem to deal with? He didn't seem disappointed to see her alive. "I thought maybe you could use some company," he finished.

You own the place now, she thought. *I don't suppose I have any say.* She shrugged, the universal teenage signal of rebellious resignation.

Bud stayed where he was, well back from the fence. "I don't much care for funerals, but I thought it was a nice one."

If anyone else had said that, Brodie would have whooped in derision. What was nice about saying goodbye to a loved one and setting his body into a dark, damp hole? Somehow, though, she sensed Bud meant it. Looking at it a different way, she supposed the service had been worthwhile. A tribute to Gramps, the last thing those who loved the old man could offer him.

"Yeah."

Brodie looked at Bud—really looked at him—for the first

time in years. Gramps had been his Gramps for real, and Bud had the look of him: the twinkly eyes, the complexion that would redden but not tan, the thin lips that smiled easily and often. Bud didn't smell like Gramps, who never gave up his Aqua Velva, even when he could afford something better. He did not have Gramps' white hair, of course, nor his wrinkles. Those would come later.

Bud had been up here when Gramps fell. If he hadn't done it, did he feel guilty about bringing him? The yacht race was the high point of the year for him, and Gramps would have come by himself if he'd had to. Was Bud sad that Gramps was dead? It seemed so, but Brodie's experience taught her that what a person seemed to be in public was different when they didn't think anyone who mattered was looking.

Bud was rich, in control of a large company he could get rid of now. If he and Gramps had argued about whether to sell the business, she sided with Gramps, not because she knew anything, but because he was Gramps and therefore always right.

Bud pointed vaguely back the way he'd come. "Did you eat anything at all?"

Brodie glanced at the Judas fence that hadn't done its job. "Not hungry."

"You want to talk about, uh, anything?"

It was the chance she'd been wanting, to hear his version of what had happened, but now she felt shy. Bud was everything she wasn't: mature, handsome, self-confident, sane. He was also Gramps' real grandchild. Gathering her courage, Brodie asked, "Do you?"

Bud ran a hand through his hair, worn longer than his grandfathers' but the same shade she'd seen in pictures from Gramps' youth. "I told the police a half dozen times. But I don't mind talking if you want to hear it."

In answer, she slid her back down the fencepost, taking a seat on the ground. Bud stood, looking out over the lake, eyes focused on nothing. "We got up here, no problem. I set a chair out for him and handed him his binoculars. Then I heard a noise over there." Bud pointed into the trees on his right. "Like an animal in pain."

Brodie waited expectantly, but it was a while before he went on.

"When I got back, he was gone." The last word sounded choked, and she looked down for a few seconds to give him a chance to pull himself together.

She knew what had happened after that. Bud had run into the house like a madman. "He fell!" he screamed at Arlis, Arnold, and Shelley, who came at his call. Scarlet had been in town. Brodie had been in her room with her ear buds in. Shelley told the story in the kitchen later, as she prepared a dinner few of them would eat. In the way people have of repeating a story until they accept that it's true, she told it more than once, wiping away tears and at times stopping to blow her nose on a tissue.

Bud had been frantic, Shelley said. "Arnold called the police. Briggs and Bud took the golf cart down the shoreline to the—the spot where he landed. He was dead, like Bud figured." She stopped to gulp back tears. "The sheriff's men got here pretty fast. Then a lady came, a detective with the State Police. They took Mr. Dunbar away to do one of them authopies or whatever."

Brodie shivered at the thought, having seen Ducky do lots of them on *NCIS*. "It's an autopsy."

No one had come upstairs to tell her what was happening. Either they thought she was too young or she didn't matter. She'd heard doors and cars but had no idea Gramps was lying dead among the pines down the beach.

"Authopsy. That's what I said." Shelley washed her hands yet again, having disposed of another tissue, and went back to rolling Swedish meatballs. "Anyway, Mr. Dunbar was gone, and Bud was in a state, I tell you. 'Course we were all in a state, but he felt like it was his fault, 'cause he left him alone."

"Did you find the animal?" Brodie asked Bud now. It was more words at once than she'd said to him in the last five years.

It took him a minute to re-focus, to drag himself away, she guessed, from the mental image of what he'd seen when he leaned over the railing. "Uh, no. The cries stopped, and I never found what made them."

She nodded, scanning the trees around them as if the critter might show itself now. She'd seen lots of them in her travels through the woods: raccoons, possum, skunks, deer, and even a coyote once. She thought about asking Bud what the cry sounded like, but she didn't think he wanted to talk about it anymore.

There was a silence, and Brodie knew there was more he'd come to say. Scooping, Bud picked up a pine cone and began shredding it onto the ground. "I—um—I wanted to tell you there won't be any, um, changes in your life here," he finally said. "Unless you want them, I mean."

"Can Scarlet stay?"

He probably hadn't thought about it at all. Why would he? He had a zillion other things to think about. Brodie guessed she was far down his list of important items to be dealt with, and Scarlet's job was even farther down. With only a second's consideration, however, he nodded. "Sure. As long as you need her."

Need her? Brodie conceded she did need Scarlet. She had no friends, no family except the guy who stood before her, uncomfortable in her presence. If he was willing to pay Scarlet to be her friend, Brodie would take it.

Bud seemed relieved to have finished the onerous duty of talking to her. "Let's go back to the house." He moved toward Brodie, and for a horrible moment she thought he was going to hug her or take her hand. Either she was wrong about that or he came to his senses, for he simply gestured for her to precede him down the pathway. She did, without looking back.

"I wondered—" Bud said when they were away from the bluff and headed down the hill, "I wonder if you might like to go out on the sailboat tomorrow."

Brodie's heart leapt. Sailing was her passion, one denied her in the last few years as Gramps became unsteady on his feet. Because he couldn't go, she'd pretended it didn't matter, but the truth was, she missed it tremendously. There was nothing as free as the feeling she got on a sailboat. Everything the poets said was true about wind in your face and the keel slicing the water.

Then the distrustful side of her brain kicked in. She'd heard Gramps say once that Bud lost his enthusiasm for boats when he discovered women. Although he'd come home more often than usual this past year, he'd never before offered to take her sailing. What if Bud planned to shove her overboard so he could have all the money?

Stop it, dork! You're being dumb.

Bud apparently sensed her doubt. "Look, Brodie. We don't know each other very well, but we're practically all we've got." A glint of humor shone in his eyes as he added, "Except for Arlis and Saint Leland of the Long Beard and the Homemade Sandals, of course."

Brodie almost smiled. He seemed to be admitting Arlis was a pain, which was satisfying.

"I'm not the sailor Gramps was, for sure. But I know how to handle the Catalina, and I thought you might like something to take your mind off...all this." He paused before adding casually, "If you want, you can ask Scarlet to come along."

Brodie considered all aspects of the proposal. She'd get to go sailing. Scarlet could serve as insurance that Bud wasn't going to drown her. And maybe Scarlet would talk to Bud, so she wouldn't have to. It could work.

That night, when Scarlet and Brodie were asleep, Mildred told Seamus about Brodie's day. Her account included more detail and more teenage angst than Seamus would have liked: Brodie's fears, insecurities, and thoughts that the world might go better if she were gone from it. She finished with, "The child is really quite sweet, once you get past all the nerves and self-doubt.”

Sweet, my eye, Seamus thought. He’d picked up Scarlet’s concerns with her charge’s behavior. Apparently, things she had done in the past to people she didn’t like were legend in the household. Scarlet hoped the girl wouldn’t regress now that Dunbar’s influence was removed.

While Scarlet and Shelley cleaned up after the reception, Shelley had wandered down memory lane, as people often do on the occasion of a funeral. Many of her stories had been about Brodie.

“We didn’t know what Mr. D was thinkin’ when he brought that child into this house. You shoulda seen her! All she had on was a pair of filthy underpants and an adult-sized T-shirt from some rock concert. Had skulls all over it! Here it was, dead of winter. She’s got no shoes or coat, jus’ wrapped up in a old blanket that smelled like pee.” Shelley paused to wipe a wisp of graying hair back into place. “Mr. D was still mad, and he’d brought her all the way up from Muskegon like that. He says to me, ‘Give this child a bath while I go to town and get her some clothes.’ Well, I did it,” Shelley said with a grim smile, “but it wasn’t easy. I think the poor little thing thought I was gonna drown her.” Shelley shook her head at the memory. “When he come home with her new stuff, I said to him, ‘I can’t handle that one, Mr. D. Bud was easy to have around, but that little girl? She needs a lotta help.’”

“So he hired someone?”

Shelley lowered her voice. “At first, Arlis said *she* would handle things. That didn’t last long, I can tell you! About the second time she got called a whore, Arlis gave up. Mr. D hired—uh—I think the first one's name was Cecilia. After that, they came so fast we didn't bother to learn their names. We just called 'em all Miss."

"Were they horrible to her?"

"Oh, no, Honey! Mr. Dunbar tried real hard to find the right kind of woman, and some of them was nice." Shelley's smile beamed on Scarlet. "But you're the one she needed."

Scarlet was modest. "Brodie's growing up, that's all. It's a natural process."

"Maybe so. But she's been happier this past year." Shelley wiped the sink dry and spread the wet towel on a rack. "She's turned into a pretty good kid, and you're helping her get better at being around people." Her expression turned serious as she echoed Scarlet's fear. "Let's hope Mr. Dunbar bein' gone don't set her back too far."

They left it at that, neither knowing how much Brodie's behavior would be affected by the loss of her grandfather. Scarlet was concerned, but Seamus sensed determination to help the girl through her trouble. *If I'm allowed to stay*, she thought.

Seamus told Mildred what he'd learned about Scarlet and Bud Dunbar's past relationship. "I'm not sure what they meant to each other, but she's determined to forget it now," he concluded.

"That's it! Scarlet hates Bud, so she pushed the old man over the cliff hoping he will get the blame for it."

"That doesn't make any sense, Millie."

"Of course it does! If Bud went to prison for murder, Brodie would be the principal heir. Since she's under age, chances are the court would appoint Scarlet as trustee."

"I think Arlis would have something to say about that. And Arlis is at least as likely as Scarlet to have murdered the guy."

Mildred was dismissive. "She'd have poisoned his tea or something. I think we have to look closely at Scarlet."

"If she wanted to frame Bud for murder, she did a lousy job of it. The police are calling Dunbar's death an accident, and that may be what it was, despite his recollection."

"*Might*, Seamus. *May* is used to give permission, *might* indicates possibility. And you said that deputy thinks Dunbar was pushed."

Seamus ignored the grammar lesson. "That guy has his own agenda. He's so jealous of young Dunbar he can hardly stand to look at him."

"So?"

"So he's looking for something suspicious."

"That doesn't mean he's wrong."

Frustration got the best of him. "I guess he's like a lot of people who are never wrong—in their own minds, anyway."

There was a miffed silence, which Seamus savored briefly before going on. "I want you to try to get to the cook in the morning. She seems to have been around a long time and *might* have insights on the family that will help us."

There was a pause, and he guessed Mildred was trying to decide how to argue her point that Brodie needed her. "What are you going to do?"

"I'm going to try to make my way to Bud."

"That shouldn't be hard. He's taking Brodie sailing."

"On a boat?"

Mildred snickered. "I assume it will be on a boat." At the growling noise he made, she asked, "What is it?"

"I don't do boats."

"Don't be silly. It won't kill you to—" She stopped and began again. "Seamus, what possible threat could a boat pose to a dead man?"

He didn't answer because he couldn't explain it. That was the problem with keeping your memories: they came back to bite you at the worst times.

After a few seconds, Mildred said, "All right. I want to stay with Brodie anyway, so I'll go on the sailboat. You stick around the house and learn what you can from the staff. We'll talk again tomorrow night."

Unwilling as he was to let Mildred have her way, Seamus was relieved to be able to skip the sailing expedition. Sometimes a partner *might* be useful after all.

CHAPTER NINE

Brodie looked out her bedroom window to make sure the weatherman hadn't been mistaken. He was right: another gorgeous day, a cool morning heating to the mid-eighties by afternoon, and just enough wind. She could already feel the pull of it in her imagination.

By 6:30 Brodie had finished breakfast and was waiting impatiently for Bud to appear. She knew they wouldn't start much before 9:00, when the air had warmed. Scarlet came down at 7:00 and helped herself to a portion of the omelet Shelley had made and a cup of tea. She acted funny when Brodie asked her to accompany her and Bud, but in the end she agreed, murmuring something about distracting Brodie from her unhappiness. It sounded like she was arguing with herself.

While Shelley packed a cooler for them to take along, Arlis wandered in and, learning of the outing, began a list of catastrophes they were to avoid. "Now don't be silly out there, Brodie. And make sure you put on lots of sun-block."

Shelley intervened to make the order less offensive. "You'll come back smelling like a coconut, but at least your nose won't be all red and peeling."

Arlis continued as if Shelley hadn't spoken. "Wear your life vest. Don't set it nearby. Wear it."

Thanks, Aunt Stupid! Brodie kept her lips tightly closed. What real sailor didn't observe proper safety precautions? Though she swam like an otter, Gramps had taught her to be smart on the water.

"And don't go swimming until an hour after you eat lunch." When Arlis said this, Scarlet glanced at Brodie and raised an eyebrow. They'd talked about such myths at length, because Scarlet didn't want Brodie to be an ignoramus. She'd cautioned it was useless to contradict those who spouted such nonsense. "If they want to believe going around without a hat brings on a cold, let them," Scarlet said. "People believe what they like, but I agree with your grandfather. Informed opinions are best."

As Brodie made a list of things they would need, Arlis told them how Leland, "an excellent sailor," had almost met with catastrophe when a storm came up on the lake unexpectedly. "Will had to go out in the rowboat and help him get the boat back to shore," she said. "It wasn't his fault. On the Lakes, a storm can arise quickly. He couldn't have known."

That was how it always was with Leland stories. He was blameless, innocent, but oh, so smart.

When Bud finally came downstairs, he found Brodie waiting with ill-disguised impatience while Scarlet read a novel. They wore bathing suits. Scarlet had put khaki shorts and a soft cotton shirt over her one-piece and pulled her hair up, ready for a day in the wind and sun.

"I think you told me you've sailed before, Miss McMorran."

"I have."

His smile was tight. "I guess there aren't many places in Ireland where one isn't near the sea."

"That's true."

Brodie thought the conversation had some sort of edge to it, but she didn't see why. Scarlet seemed tense; Bud defensive. Things would be better on the boat, she figured.

Or not. Scarlet remained reserved, even prim. As soon as they were aboard, she took out her novel and started reading, as if banishing her companions from her mind. Brodie and Bud cast off, motored out into the lake, then set about getting ready, falling into a surprisingly easy rhythm. She kept the tiller steady as he raised the mainsail, expertly clamping the lines into their cleats and tightening them. Watching Bud, it occurred to Brodie that they worked well together because Gramps had taught them both. They did things the way he had done them.

The sail caught the wind and they were off, pulled across the water by unseen but powerful forces. It was thrilling for Brodie to be out on the boat again. It had been in storage for a couple of summers, shut away so as not to remind Gramps of his advancing age. Everything came back to her, though: how to belay the lines, how to steer toward a point, and when to tack.

Bud seemed to be enjoying himself too. "Gramps told me you were good," he said, "but I thought he was bragging."

Her face warmed at the first compliment Bud had ever given her, and she asked an impulsive question. "Why don't you like sailing?"

He frowned slightly. "Who said I didn't?"

"Gramps."

Bud chuckled. "I love sailing. What I don't like is racing,

which is pretty cut-throat." She must have looked surprised, because he added quickly, "Gramps was never unsportsmanlike, but some of them are. If they don't win, it has to be someone's fault." He paused. "Kind of like corporate America."

She thought about that for a while. "You don't like business either?"

He chuckled again. "I really, really don't." His expression turned serious. "I don't want to be the guy who drives some other guy out of business so I can pick up more customers. I'm the guy who likes this." He pointed at the clear water around them. "Sailing around in circles if I want to, with no particular place to go."

"But you said Gramps wasn't a cut-throat."

"He wasn't." A note in his voice made her think there was more he could have said. "When he started, his product was the only one of its kind. People needed it, and he sold it to them. Now it's all sales projections and market share and loss minimization." Bud sighed. "I thought we both would have been better out of it."

Brodie looked at Bud with new interest. She'd always assumed he wanted to be what he was, a businessman. But here he was, explaining his feelings to her as if what she thought mattered. "If you sell the company, what will you do?"

He eyed her warily then grinned, leaning toward her and lowering his voice. "You want to know what I'd like to do?"

"Sure."

Glancing at Scarlet, who paid them no mind at all, he said,

"I'd like to own a little inn somewhere around here, one with a really nice restaurant."

It was about the last thing Brodie expected. "A restaurant?"

"I'm a pretty good cook."

"But you've got more money than Donald Trump."

Bud put up a hand. "Not quite. And even Donald Trump doesn't want what he's got. He's always trying something else, isn't he? I guess it's what makes people people."

She thought about that. "I like to cook too."

"There. We could be partners." She looked up, suspecting he was making fun of her, but his expression was serious. "Look. Neither of us ever has to earn our living. That's the gift Gramps left us. I say we do what we like to do and forget about adding to our assets."

Brodie felt almost giddy. Bud didn't hate her, didn't hold a grudge for those long-ago pranks. He spoke as if they were going forward together.

Encouraged by his attitude, she made a timid request. "Do you think I could use some of my money to help kids like me?"

He shrugged casually. "It's your money. Gramps did some things along that line. I can show you the details and you can consider expanding on it. He had a soft spot for kids, that's for sure."

Brodie brushed some sand from the seat beside her. "I always think about the ones who don't have a Gramps to come and take them away."

Bud turned to her. "It was bad, huh?"

She shrugged. "I guess." She considered telling him about Jeannie, but she didn't. No sense risking their new friendly feeling by turning into a whiner.

Bud was watching the lake, automatically checking the wind and adjusting the steering. His thoughts seemed to parallel Brodie's. "My mother never mistreated me, but I figured out early on she had better things to do than take care of a kid. She left me with Gramps for longer and longer periods, and I think finally he told her she should either be a mother or give me to him for good." He tried for levity. "Guess we know what her choice was."

Brodie thought about the things her mother had chosen over her: hypodermic needles, odd-smelling cigarettes, and men whose laughter was insincere, even to the ears of a toddler.

Bud adjusted a line, pulling it snug. "I think we have the opportunity to do some good with Gramps' money. If you have no objections, I plan to sell the company and look for a place around here where I can try my hand at restauranteuring. Is that even a word?" She shrugged, watching the arrow at the top of the mast and adjusting the tiller.

"You have time to decide what you want to do with your life. But if I stick around here, you won't have to—" He paused, unsure how to phrase it. "Um, I mean, Arlis will be good to you, but she's a little—" He gave up trying to put his thought into inoffensive words.

"You don't want to leave me at the mercy of Aunt Awful."

Bud grimaced. "Well, I wouldn't have put it like that."

"I wouldn't mind if you stayed." Brodie glanced at Scarlet, who still did not appear to be listening, though her face was flushed. The wind, maybe.

"You could go to culinary school," Bud suggested. "There's one in Traverse City, at the college. Then someday we really could work together."

"Yeah." Brodie could hardly believe it. Bud, the Perfect Grandchild, the person she'd always envied, was proposing a future where the two of them lived in the same house and possibly even worked together. "Thanks."

Looking slightly uncomfortable, Bud spoke what might have been a prepared statement. "Brodie, Gramps thought you were pretty amazing, and he was never wrong about people." She didn't know what to say, but he lightened the moment, "Now, find us a picnic spot, First Mate. I'm starving."

They put in for lunch at an island that was barely there: a single lump of land with a few scraggly trees and a rounded sandy spot on one side big enough for three people to spread out in the sun. There was no dock, so Bud dropped the anchor, hefted the cooler onto one shoulder, and slid over the side into waist-deep water. Scarlet and Brodie followed, gasping a little at the change in temperature. Once in, Brodie enjoyed the coolness and swam around the boat a couple of times while Scarlet and Bud waded ashore and set up the meal.

Scarlet acted funny with Bud, like she was trying too hard to be nice. With Gramps she'd been warm but respectful. With Shelley and Briggs, she was friendly, listening with apparent interest to their accounts of mundane things. When she had to deal with Arnold or Arlis, she said little but was carefully polite. That was how she sounded now when she spoke to Bud.

Hanging onto the ladder at the back of the boat, Brodie peered around it to observe them. Scarlet was setting out lunch on a towel she'd spread on the sand. Bud tried to help, but she pretty much ignored him. Brodie wondered again why she didn't like Bud, or at least didn't trust him.

Scarlet's reserve caused Brodie to rethink the morning, and she began to berate herself for the ease with which she'd fallen under Bud's spell. There had to be something wrong with his easy charm that a kid couldn't see but Scarlet could. *And you, dumbass, fell right in with his plan.* "Sure, Bud, we can work together to benefit mankind and make delicious veal scampi!" He was probably laughing to himself this minute about how easy it was to get the kid to go along.

Brodie resolved to be different on the way back. *Cool, like Scarlet, not stupid like Brodie.*

A voice almost at her ear—maybe *in* her ear—said, "Smart!"

"Huh?" She spoke aloud in surprise, turning to see who might be nearby.

"Smart!" the voice repeated. Brodie shivered. Time to get out of the lake and warm up. Hunger was causing delusions. "Smart!" the voice repeated.

"Flippin' nuts!" Brodie countered. With a strong kick, she pushed herself through the clear water, heading for shore. She didn't know where the voice came from, but maybe the company of others would block it out.

As Scarlet passed Shelley at breakfast, Seamus jumped from the tutor to the cook. Shelley was quite a change, rather like passing from a formal living room to the area where a family really lives. Shelley had opinions about everything, and they were almost too easy to read.

As Bud, Brodie, and Scarlet left on their planned excursion, Shelley waved approvingly from the kitchen door. "Nice," she muttered to herself. "That's nice."

Seamus learned a lot as Shelley cleaned the kitchen and reminisced about her years with the Dunbar family. She'd been employed by William Dunbar in 1985, at first only when the family came to northern Michigan on vacation. Back then, Shelley and her husband had made a business of opening and closing summer homes, readying them for winter by draining the pipes and closing and insulating drafty spots. In spring, they reversed the process, turning on water and electricity, opening windows to air the place, and vacuuming up the hundreds of dead flies that magically appear in unused rooms.

When Dunbar moved permanently from Chicago to Frankfort, he'd come as a widower, without his beloved Lila but with his young grandson instead. Shelley and Briggs became full-time employees, and Bud had become Shelley's pet. She'd loved to watch him roam the property, returning with boy treasures for her: pretty rocks, almost-whole shells, and live creatures he always carefully replaced them where he'd found them once she'd had a chance to admire them. Shelley had been sad to see Bud go away to school and sorry he'd stayed away so much since. *Always busy, the young ones!* "That's what funerals are for," she said aloud. "Bring them all home. Bring them together."

Briggs came into the kitchen precisely at eleven forty-five. He took a seat in a chair under the clock and turned his body sideways, watching his wife prepare their lunch. "Everybody gone?"

"Yup. Arlis went to run some errands, Arnold took the day off, and Mr. Marks is on his way back to Chicago." Shelley had fried several pieces of bacon until they were crisp and set them on paper toweling to drain. Cutting a tomato thinly, she covered two pieces of bread with the slices. Next came lettuce, then the bacon. On two more pieces of bread she slathered mayo, then put them atop their mates, pressing the whole until the lettuce and bacon crunched. Finally, she cut the sandwiches diagonally with a sharp knife.

"I sent them three off on the boat." Briggs took a bite of the sandwich and spoke around it. "That Scarlet sure don't like Bud."

Shelley gave him a look. "I think it might be the opposite. I think she'd like to like him, but he did something that made her mad."

Briggs grinned. "Maybe it's what he didn't do!"

"Oh, stop. Everything's about sex to you."

"No, it ain't. There's baseball."

She punched him playfully on the arm. "You want tea or milk with that?"

He pinched her rear. "I'll have the sheepherder's special. A glass of milk and a piece of—"

"Stop, or I'll send you to the shed to eat your sandwich." She laughed, though, and sat down across from her husband to eat her own lunch. "We'll see how things are when they come back. Maybe that girl will warm up a little with a day in the sun."

Seamus thought of his time with Scarlet. Something had turned her against Bud, caused her to think of him as a "snake." Was it something Bud had done, or was Briggs correct, and he'd somehow failed to be the man she had imagined him to be?

The wind picked up as the three boaters finished lunch and packed the cooler with the remains of their meal. The sun had become hot, so the breeze on Brodie's skin felt good, even where her wet swimsuit clung to her body. Once they'd waded back to the boat and hoisted themselves aboard, Scarlet dug some sun-block out of her bag. When Brodie was protected to Scarlet's satisfaction, she looked uncertainly at Bud. After a brief hesitation, she offered the sun-block to him. When he took it, she didn't offer to cover his back, as she had with Brodie. Following her example, Brodie didn't offer either. Bud pulled on his shirt, covering the spots he couldn't reach.

After stowing the cooler and pulling in the anchor, Bud set sail for home, raising the jib as well as the main to better catch the wind. For a few seconds the sail whipped noisily, but soon it quieted and they raced over the water. Caught up in the joy of it, Brodie forgot her vow to remain silent. She called out, "Let her go, Bud!"

With a grin of agreement, Bud let the little boat have her

way with the freshening breeze. Soon Brodie was filled with the sheer joy of speed. The wind pulled at her hair, and she played with it, turning her head so the strands slapped against her face then facing the wind so the hair flew out behind her like a flag.

Sitting near the back of the boat, Scarlet tried to keep reading, but the wind fluttered the pages of her book, almost lifting it out of her hands. Her bookmark flew up, and she grabbed at it too late as it twirled in the air behind them and settled on the waves. When Brodie laughed at her squeal of objection, Bud turned to see what the commotion was about. At that moment the mainsail corrected in response to the jib's shift. The boom swung toward Bud, who was turned away. Despite a yell from Brodie at the last second, he took the full impact of the metal pole on the side of his head and dropped like a stone. The tiller banged against the transom. The boat tilted sharply then righted itself, swinging into the wind.

"Oh my god! Oh my god!" Blood spurted from Bud's scalp, and he lay dazed on the deck.

"Brodie!" Scarlet called above the flapping of the loose sail. "Take the tiller and hold it steady." Scarlet moved to Bud's side. He was conscious but unaware, mumbling incoherently. She used the ends of her shirt to wipe the blood away. "I think he's okay," she said, "but he'll need stitches."

At the tiller, Brodie tore her gaze away from Bud and looked ahead. They were a couple of miles from shore, headed toward the center of the lake. Could she turn the boat and guide it home by herself? She wasn't sure.

Scarlet moved to the storage compartment and took out

one of the half-frozen ice-packs Shelley had put in with the drinks. Tearing the back section of her shirt into strips, she bound them tightly over the wound. Next she put the cold-pack inside the shirtsleeves and laid the bundle over the improvised bandage. Finally, she wrapped Bud's whole head in a beach towel.

He was still groggy when she finished, but he was starting to be Bud again. "I've got to—"

"Sit still," she told him. "You don't have to do anything except rest until we get you to a doctor."

"But—"

"Just rest, machree. Rest." She patted his cheek in a manner very different from the Scarlet of moments before.

Bud obeyed, closing his eyes. Scarlet came to where Brodie stood at the tiller, shaking with fear and unable to decide what to do as the shore receded. "Sit with him," Scarlet ordered. "Try to keep him still."

Brodie sat down on the deck beside Bud, who was pale but awake. He opened his eyes and smiled faintly at her. "Sorry to ruin your trip."

"It was an accident."

"It was stupid. I always screw things up."

Brodie was surprised. Bud doubted himself? She was the one who always did stupid things.

The voice in her head spoke. "Okay," it said. "Okay." Brodie didn't know if the voice meant she was okay, Bud was okay, or the situation was going to be okay. She did notice, however, that Bud looked at Scarlet as he repeated, "Stupid."

Scarlet was impressive, taking charge of the Catalina as if she'd sailed it for years. First she dropped the sail, leaving it furled on the hatch as she moved to the outboard motor and started it up. With an expert hand she turned the boat in a wide circle and headed for shore, angling toward their dock.

"Call Briggs and have him meet us," she told Brodie. "We have to get Bud to hospital."

Bud made a weak objection, but Brodie ignored him, digging her phone out of her pocket and calling the house. She got Shelley, which was lucky. She wouldn't have wanted to deal with Arlis' reaction to an emergency.

They arrived at the dock to find Briggs waiting beside Gramps' SUV. He'd folded the seats down, and they made Bud lie in the back, his head still wrapped in the towel. He insisted he felt fine, but none of his listeners let that change their minds.

"Really, you guys, I don't need a doctor."

"No," Brodie quipped, surprising herself. "You need a caftan to go with that turban."

Scarlet and Briggs drove off with Bud, promising to let the others know as soon as there was a diagnosis. Brodie followed Shelley into the house, head down.

"Now look here," Shelley said in a voice a little too loud to be normal. "This flip-flap got me all behind on my work. Do you think you could help me get supper going, honey? When Bud gets back, and all the others, they'll be ready for something to eat."

Brodie knew Shelley was trying to get her mind off things, and she knew it would be good for her to have something to do. Soon she was wrist deep in potato peelings. As the metallic ring of the peeler accompanied her movements, she tried to push away images of Bud lying bloody on the deck. Had it been her fault? What if Bud died too? She'd be left with no one. Well, there was Arlis, but Brodie suspected if Arlis had the power, she'd bring Saint Leland home and send Brodie to a place like the one Jane Eyre was sent to, where everyone was mean to the orphan. Only the clothes would be different.

"He's gonna be all right." Shelley had her phone at one ear. "Briggs says the doctors are stitching him up right now."

Brodie felt the tightness that had been growing in her chest relax somewhat. Bud would be around a while longer.

It was a while before she noticed the voice again. Along with the rhythmic sound of the metal peeler rattling in its handle, she heard, "Happy." It repeated every few seconds. "Happy." "Happy." Strangely, she didn't mind it, at least not much. People who heard voices were crazy, but still, if the voice in your head said you were pretty and smart and okay and happy, maybe it was good to be nuts.

CHAPTER TEN

Seamus was frustrated. When lunch was finished, he'd jumped from Shelley to Briggs, whose pace was leisurely and whose thoughts were, to say the least, mundane. Briggs' concerns centered on his garden and rabbits. He was for the former and against the latter. Among thoughts of rabbit remedies, Seamus gleaned a few details about the Dunbars' background, but not much of importance.

He'd been two days on this case and had yet to get a chance to host with Bud. The cook and the handyman thought Bud was perfect, but Seamus wanted to hear what Bud himself was thinking. If he wasn't guilty, he might have seen or heard something that would answer the questions of the case: was it murder, and if not Bud, then who?

A guy who might have a concussion didn't need Seamus' presence weighing him down, however. When Briggs carted Bud off to the hospital, Seamus returned to Shelley.

There was a period of quiet as they waited for word. Everyone in the house seemed to tiptoe, to hold their breath. Finally Briggs called. "The doctor don't think he's hurt bad, but to be safe, they're gonna keep him overnight." He paused dramatically. "I'll be home in a while, but the little lady is gonna stay."

"Yeah?" Shelley let a hint of humor creep into her tone.

Briggs chuckled. "I hate to admit it, Old Woman, but I think you was right all along. She definitely likes him."

Shelley chuckled low in her throat. "See? It ain't about sex, neither. She's a good girl."

"You was a good girl, once upon a time."

"Hush and get back here. Somebody's got to clean the blood up off that boat."

Dinner was painful, though the pork roast smelled wonderful and the Yorkshire pudding that accompanied it was perfect. Arlis shared her opinions with Brodie and Arnold, who had returned from his day off to find he'd missed the excitement. Bud had suggested he take a week after the funeral, but Brodie suspected Arnold didn't want Bud to find out he could survive without a personal assistant. Even though she didn't like Arnold much, she appreciated his current attempts to derail Arlis' monologue.

"Boating is dangerous. I should have told him not to go. That lake is treacherous. Not as bad as Superior, of course, but bad enough. I hated it every time my brother went out."

"Great sauce on the pork, Shelley," Arnold said. "What do I taste in there?"

Shelley knew what was expected of her. "It's thyme." She pronounced the *h*.

"What distracted him, Brodie? He should have seen that boomer coming. Were you acting up again?"

"And a little bit of allspice," Shelley said. "I think allspice just wakes things up."

"I suppose she was playing with the ropes or something and loosened one. Is that what happened, Brodie? It was an accident, dear, but you have to tell the truth."

"Whatever you did, it tastes great." Arnold looked around helplessly as Shelley left the room, out of his depth without another adult to help divert Arlis.

"I'm sure he'll sell that awful thing now that he's seen how dangerous it is. At least something good will come of this."

No one answered, and she tried another subject, helping herself to more corn and a second slice of gravy-covered pork. "Arnold, have you filed whatever is needed for the will?"

"Um, everything is ready to go. Bud and I went over it with Collin before he left, and I'm to file in the morning." He looked momentarily confused. "I mean, I was supposed to. I don't know if I should wait now or not."

"I don't see why we should wait. The sooner it's done, the sooner things will be settled." She gave what Brodie recognized as her "brave" smile. "It doesn't mean a thing to me, of course. But others might be waiting for some sort of settlement, and it would be unkind to make them wait any longer than necessary."

Arnold wasn't quite as wimpy as he appeared, and he said in a neutral tone, "I'll run it by Bud when he comes home. There'll be plenty of time to file the papers in the afternoon."

A sniff was all the response Arlis gave, but she managed to put a lot of personality into it. "Leland is supposed to get the lodge in Canada. I'd like to think he won't have to wait long for his inheritance."

For once, Arnold seemed relieved to have the conversation turn to Leland, or at least away from his duties.

"Is the place something he could fix up?"

"I doubt it." Arlis shuddered delicately. "It's never been modernized, no electricity or running water. I'm hoping he can sell it and make enough money to get a place in Toronto or Sarnia. Then I could go and see him when he isn't away on some mission."

For a second Brodie almost felt sorry for Arlis. The woman had nothing: no power, no money, no independence, and her only child had been absent from her life for more than a decade. She'd lost everything when Leland screwed up her finances.

"Brodie, please don't slouch," Arlis said. "You look so much better when you sit up straight."

Obediently, she pulled herself back until her spine touched the chair back, in no mood to fight with Arlis. She wanted to escape, but that would cause yet another fuss. Arlis always insisted she ask for permission to leave the table, which was apparently proper behavior for children back in the Victorian Age. She wanted to tell Arlis to kiss her—*Sorry, Gramps.*

To shut Arlis up, Brodie had taken to catching the eye of either Gramps or Scarlet when she finished eating. Either would nod permission, relieving her of the irritation of asking while satisfying Arlis' demand. Neither was there tonight. In fact, Gramps would never—

"Brodie, can you help me in the kitchen?" Shelley had seen her dilemma and solved it. Arlis couldn't object to her helping Shelley, but Brodie didn't have to suffer one of her not-so-great aunt's long lectures on propriety.

As she stood to go, the doorbell rang. Brodie turned, left the dining room, and crossed the open living area to see who was there. Through the sidelight she saw a striking woman with spiky hair, large brown eyes, and a perfectly oval face. Tall, she added emphasis to the fact with a pair of strappy little heels so high as to be ridiculous and a clingy, hot pink dress with a flirty ruffle that ran from one shoulder to the hemline.

When Brodie opened the door, the woman put her hands up in mock shock, sending shoulder-length earrings spinning. "You must be Brodie. You are gorgeous."

From habit—and from surprise, Brodie said nothing. The woman leaned into the doorway, smiling with big, white teeth. "Is Billy here?"

"Billy?"

She frowned briefly. "Bud."

"Uh, no."

"Oh." The visitor seemed to downshift a gear. "Can you tell me when he'll be back?"

Shelley had come up behind Brodie, and there was a noticeable chill in her voice when she asked, "What do you want?"

The woman's smile stayed in place, but it froze to equal Shelley's coldness. "I'm here to see Billy. I heard William died, and I figured he might need me." She turned to Brodie and said by way of explanation, "I'm Callie, Billy's mom."

Seamus was surprised by the reaction of the usually

unflappable Shelley. *The nerve!* was her first thought, followed by, *Not coming in this house, Missy!*

Next he heard Arlis gasp behind him—or rather, behind Shelley. "What are *you* doing here?"

"I came to see my son."

"Well, you can't."

"Listen, Aunt Arlis—"

"I am not your aunt. I was your husband's aunt, despite his horrible taste in wives."

The woman's lips pulled inward and her eyes narrowed. "When will Billy be back?"

Arlis and Shelley glanced at each other and tacitly joined forces. "We don't know," Arlis replied.

The woman fluffed her hair as she considered her options. A jasmine-y aroma wafted toward her opponents. Finally she said through tight lips, "I'll come back tomorrow."

Neither woman answered, but Seamus heard Shelley's thought: *Don't bother.*

Brodie closed the door, put her ear-buds in, and buried her head in the pillow. When people started yelling, her stomach always tied itself in a big old knot. It wasn't only the yelling. The appearance of Bud's mother, a woman she'd always imagined as Cruella DeVille, shocked her. What kind of woman gave away her child, especially a perfect son like Bud?

Her own mother had given her to Gramps, but that was different. When she was six years old Gramps told her, very gently, that her mother had died. He explained she'd been sick, which was why she hadn't taken good care of Brodie. "Mothers aren't usually like that," he'd said. "If Jeannie hadn't been sick, she'd have loved you and taken care of you."

"Like you do?"

"Yes."

Brodie looked up at him. "Then you must be my Gramps *and* my mom."

"Yes," he said softly. "That's exactly what I am."

"You could have knocked me over with a feather," Mildred told Seamus late that night as their hosts slept in their respective beds. "Apparently no one in the family had any idea the woman was even in the country, much less expected her to show up here."

"She's a piece of work, all right," Seamus responded.

"She's after money, or I don't know anything. She obviously read of the old man's death and showed up to get what she could for herself. And did you see that dress? Teeny-bopper style!"

"Yup."

"Well, she reckoned without Arlis! That woman is like a rhinoceros, large and slow-moving but a formidable opponent when enraged."

Seamus agreed the comparison was apt.

"Brodie left," Mildred said regretfully. "I wanted to hear the rest, but she apparently can't abide confrontation. She practically ran to her room, which is all black and white, by the way. Very unhealthy, I think. Anyway, she buried her face in the pillows, so I didn't hear any more."

"There wasn't much more," Seamus told her. "They sent her packing."

"Good for them!"

"Oh, she'll be back."

"How do you know?"

"First, there's too much money at stake for her to give up now. And second, because I jumped to Callenda Dunbar when Shelley stepped up to slam the door in her face."

Mildred gasped. "Do you think that was wise, Seamus?"

"Wise?"

"You can tell by looking at the woman she's sleazy."

"So?"

"I don't know if it's right for you to host with someone like that."

He almost laughed aloud. "What do you think investigating is about, Millie? We can't stick only to nice people."

"You don't think she killed Mr. Dunbar, do you?"

"Well, no. She seems to see his death as a stroke of luck. Apparently she's hurting for money right now, and she thinks Bud will be generous now he's got lots of it."

"What is it with these women? Don't they know how to do anything but stand around with their hands out? Arlis lives off her brother, now Callenda wants to live off her son."

"She prefers to be called Callie."

Mildred made a sound of disgust." She must be my age, at least. Did you *see* the dress?"

"She's fifty, but she claims forty when she can get away with it."

He had to admit, Callie could get away with it if the lighting was right. Not only were her hair, skin, and muscles under the care of experts, but she concentrated on acting young, copying the speech patterns and vocabulary of thirty-somethings. She constantly monitored herself, dumping phrases she thought sounded like something only an old person would say.

He quickly tired, however, of Callie using every reflective surface available to check her lips, eyes, and hair. He didn't mention it to Mildred, but he was repulsed by the woman's habit of drawing attention to her breasts by touching them, apparently unconsciously. A lady didn't need to hear about that. Many men would enjoy it, he supposed, whether inside Callie or out.

What he sensed in Bud's mother was total self-absorption. Callie wanted everyone looking at her, men in lust, women in jealously. She had expensive tastes, and her attractiveness allowed her to indulge them. A beautiful woman can get away with a lot, and she had, for half a century.

Seamus sensed a shift in Callie's outlook in recent months. Age was catching up to her, and though she could slow it, she couldn't stop it. It was harder and harder to keep up the illusion of youth. Her eyes pouched if she stayed up too late, and her upper arms had begun to jiggle underneath.

The money Will had given her long ago, the money she'd demanded in return for giving up custody of her son, was long gone. Since then Callie had lived with, slept with, and sometimes married a succession of men, most of them wealthy enough to indulge her as long as she amused them. Her relationships ended either when she got bored or when the men got wise to being used as ATM machines.

Lately, it had become harder to attract the rich ones. Callie found herself being pursued by younger men who clearly thought *she* was wealthy enough to support *them*. She'd managed to keep up appearances, but the realization had begun to set in that she was regarded as a cougar. The men she wanted to attract were charming, flirtatious, and noncommittal. Seamus guessed that was due to the desperation Callie radiated like plutonium.

"So what did she do when they turned her away at the house?" Mildred asked.

Seamus gave a slightly sanitized version. "She was pretty mad."

"Bitch," Callie had said to the door before stalking back to her rental car. Returning to Frankfort, driving much too fast for the narrow roads and seething all the way, she pulled into the parking lot of a run-down, twelve-unit motel, the only place that might have a room available in mid-July. "If Bud had been home, he'd have given me my old room," she muttered to the steering wheel. "Instead, I get insults from Acid Arlis and a room at the Bates Motel."

With conscious effort, Callie relaxed her stride as she entered the motel lobby. A lifetime of practice allowed her to hide her anger, allowed her hips to sway slightly and her mouth to relax into a smile. Seamus picked up her thought. *You never know who might be watching.*

In the closet-sized room, she threw her weekender on the bed, fished her phone from her purse, and made a call. "You told me he'd be there," she said as soon as it was answered.

"There was an accident on the boat this afternoon. He's in the hospital."

Seamus felt Callie's gasp and for an instant thought it was maternal concern. That was contradicted by the thought he picked up next: *I need to pay something on that hotel bill in London by Friday!* Her question to the person on the phone was more subtle. "Is he all right?"

"They think so. The boom swung and hit his head. There was a lot of blood and a nasty gash. The doctors kept him overnight, but more because he's a millionaire with good insurance than because he's in any danger, I think."

Callie was looking at herself in the mirror, and she brushed at her neck, wondering if plastic surgery could erase the lines that had begun to show across it.

"All right. Give me a call as soon as he gets home, hear? And see if you can't distract Arlis tomorrow morning so I can talk to Bud without her yammering in his ear."

"How should I do that?"

"That's your problem."

He sighed. "I guess I could offer to help with

acknowledgments of funeral gifts and donations.”

“There, see? I knew you could do it.”

“It’ll cost you extra.”

“Everything you do costs me extra, you little jerk.” Callie glanced at her face in the mirror and made a conscious effort to stop frowning. “Once I talk to Bud, you’ll get your money.”

“You really think he’s going to let you walk back into his life?”

“What’s Bud got for family? Arlis? That kid you keep saying is nuts? Tell me I won’t look good compared to them. Better yet, do your job.” She ended the call with an abrupt tap of a cerise-tipped finger.

Seamus was intrigued—and disgusted—by the nerve of Callie Dunbar. She was in a spot. She owed lots of people lots of money. The news of William Dunbar’s death couldn’t have come at a better time for her. Although the elder Dunbar would have refused her request for more money out of hand, Callie thought her son would not. “Thirty thousand will do it,” she said aloud. “Once I talk to Buddy, everything will be all right.”

CHAPTER ELEVEN

Brodie came downstairs the next morning and stopped to listen when she heard Shelley talking in the kitchen.

"That woman!" Shelley said to Briggs, who had missed the whole episode. "Just waltzin' up to Mr. Dunbar's door like she forgot she promised to stay out of that boy's life forever."

"Where ya think she's been?" Briggs asked. He'd probably heard the story a dozen times by now and asked the same question every time.

"Someplace expensive," Shelley replied in disgust. "She spent all the money old Mr. Dunbar gave her and now she's going to gouge young Mr. Dunbar for more."

Brodie often wondered what it would be like to have a mom, one who wasn't sick like Jeannie had been. Other kids spoke casually of their parents, unable to imagine not having them around. TV children had at least one parent, and the moms were always hip and understanding. It was hard to know what to want, though, since memories of Jeannie still gave her nightmares.

What was Bud's mom like? Would she tell Bud she missed him, ask him to be her son again? Maybe that was what last night had been about. Callie wanted to be a mom after all this time.

Footsteps behind her alerted Brodie to someone's approach, and she turned and began straightening, or appearing to straighten, the pictures on the hallway wall. Arnold mumbled a morning greeting as he turned in at the dining room doorway, holding his ever-present phone to his ear. "Yes. It was a scare, but they tell us he's all right." There was a pause as he listened to the other person. "Okay, so you'll drive back up after that?" A chuckle. "Yeah. It's a bad idea to count on judges sticking to a schedule. Don't worry. I can handle things until you get here."

Brodie rolled her eyes. Arnold made it sound like he was so important. What was he going to handle—breakfast? She guessed he was talking to Collin, wanting to be the first to report Bud's accident. Anything to get a little attention, even from the family lawyer.

Arlis' groan sounded on the stairs, and Brodie hurried into the dining room. Judging the old woman's nearness by grunts that accompanied each step, she piled scrambled eggs on a piece of toast, squirted ketchup over the eggs, and slapped a second piece on top. Grabbing a quart of milk from an ice-filled bowl on the sideboard, she was almost through the kitchen doorway when Arlis appeared on the opposite side. "Brodie!" Her name on Arlis' tongue was seldom anything but a prelude to criticism. The swinging door's *whump* was the only answer Brodie gave.

She didn't stop in the kitchen but made her way out the side door and down toward the lake. A flagstone pathway led to the boathouse and the dock, and she noted the sand that sifted its way over the flat rocks during the night. Briggs made it his mission in life to keep those stones sand-free, but it was an unending battle.

Between the dock and the boathouse was a glider, and she sat down to eat her breakfast. With her egg sandwich in one hand, she drank from the milk jug by slinging it over one shoulder like Johnny Depp did as Jack Sparrow in the movies. It wasn't rum, and the plastic jug tended to collapse and push the milk out faster than she expected, but it was doable.

She didn't like rum, having tried it—and every other liquor in her grandfather's study—one day when no one was around. How adults could drink that stuff was beyond her. She'd asked Scarlet later, which got her into trouble, because Scarlet knew the question hadn't come out of thin air. It had led to a talk about adult things and kid things, which, Brodie had to admit, made sense. According to Scarlet, when you were a kid, you could get away with things adults could not.

"If Arnold put salt in your aunt's sugar bowl, as you did last summer, what do you think would happen to him?"

"She isn't my aunt, but if Arnold did that, he'd probably get fired."

"But because you're a kid, you didn't get sent away, did you? Kids can do things adults can't, so it's only fair that adults do some things kids can't."

She was reluctant to admit the difference. "I had to apologize, though."

"As you should."

Brodie had not liked apologizing to Arlis, so in her head she'd added phrases that made it easier. "Arlis, (you ass) I'm sorry that (you are an ass) I put salt in the sugar (but your ass is so big you don't need sugar anyway).

Remembering that now, she apologized to Gramps, who had explained patiently when her choice of words mimicked Jeannie's rather than his own that swearing is the sign of a weak vocabulary. *I didn't mean 'ass', Gramps. I meant 'jackass'.*

After the salt-for-sugar prank, Arlis had taken a dislike to Scarlet, claiming she was too young to be in charge of Brodie. Fearing someone might believe Arlis, Brodie had altered her behavior. There had been no more pranks, though she'd recently confessed to one or two for reasons of her own. She hoped her improved deportment demonstrated that Scarlet really was good at her job.

Arlis remained unconvinced. Whenever she came upon the two of them doing something that was fun *and* educational, her mouth bent funny, like she tasted something bad. She'd say things to Scarlet like, "Well, you're young dear, but—" or to Gramps, "She's no more than a child herself." She kept at it, and it made Brodie nervous. Arlis was nothing if not determined.

"She's only twenty, Will," she said one evening when she thought Brodie was absorbed in a TV show. "The child needs someone mature, someone she can respect."

I do respect Scarlet! Brodie had wanted to shout, but she knew it would do no good. When she turned, though, Gramps had been looking at her. With a smile he'd let her know he wouldn't be persuaded to can Scarlet, no matter what Arlis said.

But Arlis would probably go to work on Bud now with that same old song. Brodie promised herself she'd be nice—well, nicer—to the old biddy, so she'd lay off trying to get Scarlet fired.

Just after at eight o'clock, Callie got the news that Bud had been released from the hospital. "I offered to help Arlis with thank-you cards at ten," her spy reported. "That should give you until lunchtime."

"You're a prince, Arnold." Callie closed the phone and moved to the closet. She stopped at the mirrored door to check her stomach, which apparently stuck out more than she wanted it to, because she slapped it disgustedly and dug a body-briefer out of her suitcase. Tossing it on the bed, she slid the mirror aside and began choosing the outfit she would wear to visit her son.

Seamus always tried to be businesslike when hosting with females. It was inevitable he would see personal things, so he concentrated on keeping his thoughts clinical. When Callie picked out what she considered a conservative outfit, however, he wasn't in the least objective. It looked to him like something Gypsy Rose Lee might have chosen for a publicity photo.

When Briggs brought Scarlet and Bud home just before nine, he was still wearing his swim trunks from the day before. Briggs had taken him a fresh shirt, since the one he'd been wearing was bloodied beyond saving. Brodie stood back as the rest of them fussed. Embarrassed by the attention, Bud kept assuring everyone he was fine. Brodie noticed no one mentioned the visitor from the night before.

Scarlet insisted the chair the hospital had provided in Bud's room had been perfectly comfortable for sleeping, and she was rested and ready to return to her responsibilities.

"We'll work inside this morning," Scarlet told Brodie, "and go outside later, as we planned." Turning to Bud she explained, "We're catching spiders, to see how much variety there is in a small area."

"Sounds great," he said sarcastically. "If there's anything I hate, it's spiders."

"Be sure to wear bug dope, Brodie," Arlis ordered. "And a hat. You don't want to get sunstroke."

Behind Arlis' back, Bud actually winked at Scarlet. Brodie saw it and noted Scarlet's blush. It made her think, since she'd looked up *macree* on the internet and learned that it meant something like "beloved" in Irish. Why had Scarlet called Bud that when he was half-conscious in her arms?

Although Arlis fussed and clucked at him, Bud insisted he didn't want to lie down. "I've been doing that for hours," he protested. "I'd like to sit in the sun for a while." Ignoring Arlis' arguments, Shelley escorted him to the glider Brodie had vacated, and they left him alone. Arlis ordered Shelley to bring him a hat. Apparently sunstroke was rampant these days.

Brodie and Scarlet went upstairs to do lessons. Scarlet felt it would be beneficial to get back to a routine, and Brodie had to admit that doing equations and studying the Crimean War restored a sense of normalcy. She liked knowing stuff and always pictured herself as the characters in history they read about. Scarlet seemed to find at least one woman in every era who knew what she wanted and went after it. Crimea undoubtedly meant Florence Nightingale, but after seeing Bud's head wound, Brodie was pretty sure nursing was not her destiny.

She was still thinking about yesterday's disaster an hour later when she was supposed to be listing the causes of the war. Spying on Scarlet through her lashes, she wondered if she and Bud had talked at all during his night in the hospital. Had Bud been pleased to see Scarlet there each time he opened his eyes?

"You were pretty good with the boat yesterday."

Scarlet smiled, though her eyes remained on the essay she was correcting. "Lots of experience. Although," she added, "most of my seafaring was done on aging fishing boats."

"Do you like Bud?"

Scarlet still did not look up, but her voice sounded funny. "I suppose he's all right."

"You were scared when he got hurt."

"Well, of course, silly. We didn't know how badly he'd cracked his skull."

"But—" Brodie didn't know how to express what she was thinking. "It looked like you really cared. Not like 'Oh, this poor stranger' but more like—I don't know."

Scarlet looked up now, and Brodie saw in her eyes a struggle between truth and falsehood. She'd never lied to her, and Brodie felt a lump growing in her chest. This was going to be the first time. Everyone lied. People said how pretty you were and how sweet, but their eyes said differently. People said they would buy things or take care of you, but instead they went into the bedroom and shut the door. No one could be trusted except Gramps, and he'd died, leaving her behind. If Scarlet lied, who was left?

"There was a time when Bud might have meant something to me," Scarlet said, and Brodie felt the lump start to ease. "It was before I met you, and it didn't turn out well. When he was hurt, I suppose that feeling came back in the crisis, but I'm over it now."

"You and Bud?"

"Yes."

"Where?"

"On Mackinac Island. He was there with your grandfather, though I didn't realize at the time they were related. I worked in a restaurant there, and Mr. Dunbar came in early each morning for several days. Bud came later, with a group of men his age. I never put them together in my mind."

"So you and Bud knew each other for one weekend on the Island?"

"Well." Scarlet's smile was like La Giaconda's. "He stayed on after the conference ended."

"Because of you?" Brodie's imagination soared as she pictured moonlit walks along the road that circled the Island, the scent of lilacs, the sound of ferry horns, a trip to Arch Rock or a carriage ride through the tiny, crowded town.

"I thought he stayed to be with me," Scarlet said, her eyes averted. "But I was wrong."

"You saw him with someone else?"

She smiled grimly at Brodie's quick deduction. "I didn't, but a friend did. We'd planned to meet, you see, then Bud called and said he couldn't make it. I thought nothing of it until my roommate reported he'd left the hotel with a woman."

"Did you ask him about it?"

"I never got the chance. The next day, he checked out and caught the earliest ferry back to Mackinaw City."

Brodie thought about that for a while. There was no disaster she was aware of that summer that required Bud's immediate return to Chicago. "So when you took this job, you didn't know Bud was related to Gramps?"

"No. Mr. Dunbar and I had talked a little. He was interested in where I came from, and he told me about his boyhood in Scotland. But we were never formally introduced."

"So you didn't know about Dunbar Electronics?"

"Bud said business was the last thing he wanted to talk about." Scarlet pushed her hair back from her face. "Anyway, the night he called to cancel our date, he was seen with a woman." Scarlet's mouth twisted. "My roommate couldn't wait to tell me how attractive she was and how she snuggled up tight to him."

"Wow."

Scarlet shifted, as if throwing off an emotion. "Bud never promised me anything. We had a few conversations over tea and some walks on the shoreline. He was funny and sweet and interesting. I guess I put too much stock in the fact that he asked me out that night."

Brodie tried to picture Bud teasing, Bud laughing, Bud being romantic. All that came to mind was Bud sitting on the glider outside, listening politely to Arlis' instructions that he not stand up too quickly lest he faint.

"You didn't try to find him after he left?"

"You have seen too many movies!" Scarlet's smile was rueful. "The Island is the perfect place for romances that end when the summer does."

"Were you surprised when the job offer came?"

Scarlet shrugged. "When Arnold called with a job offer in Michigan, I told myself it was a coincidence. I knew Bud lived in Chicago, and there are thousands of Dunbars in the world. Arnold said he worked for an elderly millionaire, but he didn't mention that he and I had met." She gave a little chuckle. "I think he was busy trying to impress me with his own importance, because he made it sound like he'd located me all by himself through assiduous, diligent effort." She glanced out the window to where Bud sat. "When I arrived and saw pictures of the two of them, I got the connection."

"And then it was too late because you were captured by my charming personality." Brodie heard the sarcasm in her own voice.

"Actually, I *was* captured by you, almost at once."

"Pity?"

Scarlet leaned toward her. "Brodie, do you really think that?"

It was Brodie's turn to look away. "I don't know."

"Then here's the truth. I saw a bright, beautiful girl who trusted no one except her beloved grandfather. I hoped I might help her see the rest of the world isn't so bad."

Brodie could think of nothing to say. *Beautiful?*

Movement outside the window caught her eye, and Brodie looked out to see a woman teetering down the flagstone pathway on heels that were not only ridiculously high but dangerous on the uneven surface. A closer look, and she said to Scarlet, "Bud's mother is back."

Scarlet looked for herself. "Oh, my." She looked around as if wondering who to tell, but there was no one. Bud was on his own. Callie was his mother, and he had to deal with her.

Seamus had seldom been more ready to leave a host than he was by the time Callie Dunbar arrived at the Dunbar home. Self-absorbed and shallow, Callie's innate cunning combined with a lack of any sense of self-respect made her a formidable force. He wondered if Bud was in any condition to deal with his determined mother.

At ten after ten, Callie pulled carefully into the driveway, stopping far enough back that she hoped Arlis wouldn't hear the car and come out to investigate. Her thoughts on the way over had been about how to get inside the house, but her plotting was made unnecessary by the fact that Bud was down on the beach, sitting on a swing overlooking the lake.

Seamus heard her thought. *Perfect!* Heels clicking on the stones, she made her way toward her son. Hearing her approach, Bud turned. A bandage covered the shaved patch on his scalp.

"Billy?" Callie began, then switched. "Bud?"

"Mother." The tone was as flat as Seamus had ever heard.

"I heard about the accident, honey. You might have died out there on the lake when that boom swung around. Are you going to be all right?"

Bud paused, and Seamus wondered what he was thinking. He finally said, "I should have been paying attention, and I wasn't, that's all."

Callie had stopped on the pathway. Seamus felt her nervousness, but it was more about what approach to take than about her son's condition.

"I came home because I heard about your grandfather. Honey, I'm so sorry."

Again Bud paused. "Thank you."

She shifted her feet, grating sand against the stone. "You don't seem very glad to see your mother, Bud."

He smiled grimly. "I'm wondering how much you want this time."

At Bud's direct statement, Callie took the offensive. Sitting down beside Bud, she put a hand on his arm. "Buddy, you're angry because I took your gift and left. I get that, but please believe me, I needed that money. I didn't think you'd understand why, but it was important, and you helped me more than you can imagine." She widened her eyes and lowered her chin. "You don't know what it's like to be alone and broke."

"You've had plenty of company in the last year. I have a list somewhere, if you'd like to see it."

Callie bit her lip. Bud was better prepared than she'd expected. She adopted an attitude of shocked outrage. "You've been snooping into my private life?"

Bud snorted what might have been a laugh. "Not much that you do is private. I know more than I want to know about Callie Dunbar/Michelson/Brannon/Sanders' activities."

"It's Dunbar. Your father was the only man I ever really loved. When he died—" Callie turned her face away, but her shoulder brushed Bud's lightly.

Bud pulled away, his expression unsympathetic. "Within a month of your last visit, I found your picture in half a dozen newspapers from Dubai. I didn't even need to translate them into English to get the idea." His tone turned accusing. "Did I pay for that party you threw for the sheik?"

She smiled in remembrance. "It was a hell of a party, Babe."

He glared at her coldly. "It's a game for you, isn't it, charming wealthy men and living high and wild on their money until it's gone."

"Babe, a certain lifestyle is expected in the circles I travel in."

"Well, you'll have to find a way to pay for that lifestyle other than me."

"But I'm your mother, Buddy."

His lips pulled into a tight line. "Then where have you been for the last twenty years? When you asked me for $50,000 last summer I was shocked at the amount, but I thought my mother needed me and I had to help. Then you disappeared without even a thank you. I couldn't believe it, so I started researching where you've been since you left me with

Gramps."

Callie's eyes widened, and she blinked several times as if clearing away tears. "I was devastated when your dad died, Buddy. Cancer is a terrible disease, and I needed time to forget. Everything reminded me of him, even you." She leaned toward Bud, who sat as if he were part of the wooden bench.

"Is that why you sold me to Gramps for two hundred thousand dollars?"

Again she was truthful. "It sounded like a lot of money at the time."

"And you couldn't wait to get out from under the responsibility of having a kid."

She reached out to touch his hand, but Bud didn't respond. "I was young, Buddy. I felt like I'd missed out on life."

Bud turned a little too quickly and grimaced as a stab of pain reminded him of his head wound. Another wound seemed to hurt more. "You missed out on my life too."

"I know, and I'm sorry. I want to make it up to you. I really do."

His face turned red, the color rising slowly from the open collar of his shirt. "Don't you remember saying those same words a year ago on Mackinac Island? I believed you then. I did what you asked. Now I know better."

"Babe, I admit it was a story. I owed a lot of money. I didn't think it was wrong to ask my only son for a little help."

"I gave you everything I had saved."

"William would have given you lots more if you asked, but

he wouldn't have given me a dime." She smiled, a little too smugly. "Now you've got more money than you'll ever need."

His voice was almost a growl. "And my mother has arrived to help me spend it."

Callie leaned toward him, her voice silky. "Think how embarrassing it would be for you if the world heard that Mrs. William Dunbar II, widowed mother of William C. Dunbar, millionaire, was about to lose everything while her son lives a life of luxury."

"Anyone who knows you would understand."

Her voice quavered. "I didn't think you'd be like this, Bud. I'm all you've got now."

"I need time to think about things." He sounded defeated.

Callie caressed his face lightly. "All right, hon. I just want you to know I'm here for you."

Seamus had remained with Callie, fearing Bud wasn't strong enough to accept a host. He felt her insincerity as she pleaded her case, her triumph when Bud didn't totally reject her. Bud was no match for his mother in cunning.

"I won't leave you all alone." As Callie rose to leave, wiping away tears Seamus knew were fake, he had to make a decision. Bud seemed all right physically. His mind was clear, even though it was obvious he was in turmoil over Callie's presence. Making his choice, Seamus jumped. It was too bad that a guy with a head injury who'd just had an unpleasant surprise had to absorb the physical jolt of becoming a host, but Seamus decided it had to be done.

As Callie retreated, Bud sat on the bench, looking at the

lake that offered timeless beauty but no answers. Seamus discerned sadness at his grandfather's death, guilt that he was unwilling to continue the company Gramps had founded, dejection at the state of his personal life, distress at the nausea he thought was caused by Callie's visit, and disgust that his mother would stoop to blackmail. *I'm a failure,* Seamus heard in Bud's mind.

Bud was ashamed of Callie. All his life, he'd believed—or tried to believe—that his mother had good reasons for giving him up. Gramps had said she was "unable to care for a child." He'd fantasized that his mother had some debilitating disease or crippling mental disorder. After her appearance on Mackinac Island and her subsequent disappearance with his money, he'd hired an investigator. Pictures the man provided showed Callie partying, and never with the same man twice. Mention was often made of her lavish spending, always on some unique, often outrageous, form of entertainment. In Bahrain, she'd thrown a reception for the national netball team. In Shanghai, it was a New Year's celebration that included many of the local glitterati. Bud found no mention of anything worthwhile. Callie was no philanthropist, just a partier whose time was running out.

"Bud?" He turned, and Seamus saw Brodie standing hesitantly behind the bench.

"Hey, kid."

"Was that your—was that Callie I saw down here?"

"Yeah."

"She's—" Brodie didn't seem to know how to finish what she'd started. "She's pretty."

"Yeah." He turned to Brodie. "I heard your mom was pretty too. Do you miss her?"

It took a long time for Brodie to answer. "I think I miss the idea of having a mom."

He nodded. "I remember that. You feel different, like everyone else has something you don't."

She apparently didn't know what to say next. There was a long silence. Finally she said, "If you're feeling okay, Scarlet and I are going on a picnic. Shelley's going to make chicken salad sandwiches. You could come along." When he didn't answer, she added, "We can take the golf cart so you don't have to walk far."

Seamus felt Bud hesitate. He wanted to be alone. Or maybe not. He recognized Brodie's offer was made out of an attempt to make him feel better. He stirred, as if banishing sadness with movement. "You know, Brodie, that might be the best thing for all of us. Thanks."

She smiled hesitantly and backed up a few steps before turning to run toward the house. Seamus guessed she was going to tell Scarlet and Shelley about the picnic they had no idea they were planning.

After a few minutes, Bud rose with a heavy sigh and started for the house. Seamus felt a new dread in his host's mind, a duty that was onerous but necessary. Inside, the air changed from hot and humid to cool and dry. Bud searched the rooms until he came to the den, where the door was closed. He knocked softly.

Arnold Wilk answered. Behind him, Arlis sat at a table, a

stack of cards before her. "I'm addressing envelopes for Arlis," Arnold said, "but if you need something—"

"I include a personal message in each card," Arlis said. "People want to know someone in the family took note of their gift."

"That's good of you, Aunt Arlis. I need Arnold for a minute."

He led the way to Gramps' office, where he closed the door. Arnold's pasty face revealed anxiety, but he tried to present a brave front. "I have those papers ready to file, Bud. As soon as Arlis and I finish, I intend to take them to the county courthouse."

"That won't be necessary," Bud replied. "Leave them here and I'll do it myself in the morning." He raised his chin slightly. "I saw my mother just now. She seems to know all about my accident yesterday."

"Really."

"It got me to thinking. When she found me on the Island last summer, I never figured out how she learned I was there. But I think I know now."

Arnold cleared his throat. "I suppose she heard it somewhere."

"I think you keep her informed. Wherever she was last weekend, she heard of Gramps' death and came hurrying home. Today, you told her about my accident, giving details of how it happened. No one in this house would give Callie the time of day except you."

"I don't know what you mean."

"How long have you been on her payroll? I suppose she's been waiting for Gramps to die for years, probably since that first stroke."

Faced with bald truths, Arnold seemed unable to concoct a decent lie. He glanced around the room as if looking for salvation. When nothing offered itself, his shoulders slumped, his chin dropped, and he clutched weakly at his throat as if something was choking him. "It didn't hurt anyone." He waited, but Bud didn't respond. "It won't happen again."

"Not to us. Pack your things tonight and leave in the morning. Provide an address, and I'll send you two weeks' pay and whatever Gramps left you in the will."

"Bud—"

"I'm sorry, Arnold. There's no more to discuss."

Bud watched impassively as Arnold groped for an argument to excuse his disloyalty. Finding none, the secretary turned and left the office without another word.

CHAPTER TWELVE

If Brodie had known of Seamus' deduction concerning the picnic, she'd have been forced to admit he was correct. Although she and Scarlet did plan to go spider hunting that afternoon, no plans had been made for a picnic lunch.

"Chicken salad sandwiches? I didn't even know you liked them, though Bud sure does. But I was going to make gazpacho." Shelley pronounced it "gapancho." The request was easy, though, and she soon went to work cutting last night's leftover chicken into small chunks, her strong hands guiding the knife to rhythmic chops against the cutting board.

Scarlet was a little more difficult. "You invited Bud along? He's just spent a night in hospital."

"He said he'd like to come." Brodie implied his interest came before her invitation.

"If I didn't know better—" Scarlet left the sentence unfinished, but Brodie got it. Was she trying to push the two of them together? Maybe. The why of it was fuzzy in her mind, and she didn't pause to clarify. She wanted Bud to like Scarlet so he'd keep paying her wages. That was all it really had to be.

Promptly at noon, they loaded the cooler into the golf cart and headed out. Scarlet fussed a little, sounding uncharacteristically maternal. "I'm not sure you should be doing this."

Bud grinned. "I'm just riding along. It's got to end better than our last trip, right?"

Brodie drove with unusual care, having a newly released

patient aboard as well as Scarlet, who had at times commented on the abandon with which she handled the golf cart. They chose an open space at the back of the property where Briggs had planted rape to attract deer so Gramps could sit and watch them. Brodie predicted they'd find lots of spiders nearby.

When they arrived, Bud took the cooler out of the back of the cart and looked around for a flat spot. Soon they had their meal spread out on a plastic tablecloth in the shade and were unwrapping the promised sandwiches along with a variety of extras.

"Shelley's a wonder," he commented, unpacking pickles, potato chips, cookies, and a plastic bag with three damp washcloths for post-meal clean-up. "She thinks of everything."

The mood warmed a little as they ate their meal. Scarlet spoke mostly to Brodie, but she smiled a few times when Bud said something amusing. When they finished Brodie announced, "I guess I'll start my spider search now." Taking a plastic cup with a lid, she headed into the open space. Scarlet looked uneasy, but Brodie figured it was a good time for them to talk about what happened on the Island. Maybe Bud would get to like Scarlet again and want her to stay around.

Through Bud's eyes, Seamus watched Brodie go. Hunched over like a goblin, she searched the ground for signs of arachnid movement. When she reached the center of the meadow, she sat down with her back to her companions and waited, cup ready.

The humidity had eased somewhat, but it was still very warm. Grass baked by the sun gave off a pleasant, grainy odor. The two adults watched Brodie and sat listening to the buzz of insect wings and the chatter of a squirrel unhappy with their presence.

"She forgot her hat." Scarlet took up the cap and trotted after Brodie. She stopped a few feet back and tossed the hat, apparently to avoid scaring any spiders in the area away. Brodie gave her a distracted smile, clapped the hat on her head, and went back to staring at the grass.

Seamus felt Bud's admiration as Scarlet walked back toward him. Though not beautiful, Scarlet was pretty enough to merit any man's attention. Today she wore khakis with an olive-green shirt over a lighter green tank. The colors highlighted her pale skin and complemented dark red hair that shone in the sunlight.

Scarlet sat down on the grass, far enough away from Bud to make him aware she was avoiding him. "I owe you a shirt."

Her look of surprise was quickly replaced with a polite smile. "It wasn't a favorite."

"Well, I'm glad you were with us," he went on. "I think Brodie would have done okay, but you were great." He paused. "It was nice of you to stay with me all night too."

"I'm told it's best to have an advocate when one is helpless in hospital," she replied. "Staff simply don't have the time to check on a patient as often as they should."

Bud was frustrated by Scarlet's practical responses to his attempts at gratitude. *She seemed worried about me then,*

Seamus heard.

Brodie approached, calling, "I got one!" Scarlet took a pad and pen from her bag as her student approached. There was a short discussion, and Brodie wrote down characteristics of the spider: color, size, markings. Once they'd agreed on the basics, Brodie took the paper and pen and went off to let Spider #1 go and find another.

"We never talked about the Island," Bud said when she was out of earshot.

The muscles around Scarlet's eyes tightened. "What is there to talk about?"

"I stood you up."

She shrugged, elaborately casual. "You found something better to do."

"That wasn't it, Scarlet."

"It doesn't matter." Her body language said differently.

"It matters to me. I'd like to tell you why I left so suddenly."

Scarlet busied herself with putting things into the cooler, even folding the tin foil flat before storing it at the bottom. "When I agreed to meet you that night, we were Scarlet and Bud. Now you're my employer. Things are quite different, so what happened then doesn't matter."

A shout from Brodie interrupted again. This time she brought two spiders, one such an odd yellow that even Bud had to admit it was interesting. Beneath it, though, Seamus felt his frustration. He wanted Scarlet to understand something, but she seemed to think their present relationship negated the past and any feelings they might have had then.

Seamus sensed in Bud no murderous guilt, no thought that William Dunbar's death was anything but a terrible accident. What he knew now was that Bud was head over heels in love with Brodie's tutor. He'd done everything in his power to get her this job so he could win back her respect, and after that, maybe her love.

It was fun finding the different kinds of spiders. Scarlet claimed there were hundreds of different kinds in any wooded area, and Brodie was soon convinced she was right. After a while she gave up taking the spiders to Scarlet. She could get more done if she simply documented them on the pad of paper and went back to looking.

After a few minutes, though, the sun became hot on the back of her neck. Waving to Scarlet and pointing toward the woods on the opposite side of the meadow, Brodie signaled she'd hunt in the shade for a while. Scarlet waved acknowledgement.

The coolness felt good, and she slipped the hat off and stuck the brim of it into the back waistband of her pants. She spotted a big old brown spider right away, but it darted under a fallen log, and she lost it as it blended in with its cover. A few steps farther on she found another, this one with stripes on its legs that made it look as if someone had decorated it with the world's tiniest paintbrush.

As she documented Spider #12, Brodie heard a faint noise up ahead. Cautiously, she moved toward the sound. It retreated, or it seemed to. Deer? Her experience with deer was that when you got too close, they panicked, raised their white tails like an alarm signal, and took off as fast as they could. The sound she heard wasn't headlong flight. It was scrabbling such as a creature might make if it was unaware of her presence. She liked seeing animals in the wild. Once she'd come upon some coyote pups playing and watched them for some time before they noticed her presence. That was cool.

When she was some distance into the woods, whatever it was began a plaintive cry. It reminded her of a time when she'd come upon a porcupine stuck in a tree. The creature had whimpered pitifully as it paced the length of a branch, trying to get up the courage to climb down. This sound was like that, repetitive and distressed.

Brodie moved quietly onward, hoping this experience would not be like the time she'd tracked down a rustling in the woods and come face to face with a skunk. She looked back to where Bud and Scarlet were waiting. She couldn't see them, but she wouldn't be gone long.

Two people in love but unwilling to admit it is all well and good, Seamus said to himself. *It doesn't do a thing for a murder investigation.*

Scarlet and Bud seemed destined to not say the right things to each other. "I don't care if you're my employee." Bud stretched a hand toward Scarlet in a classic gesture of entreaty.

"I do," she rejoined. "It would be a serious breach of professionalism to—" She struggled for a way to say it, "—have anything personal to do with my student's guardian."

"Then—" Bud struck a comic pose, "—you're fired."

The look of surprise on her face made him backpedal quickly. "I'm sorry! Bad joke." He ran a hand through his hair. "You're devoted to Brodie, and she depends on you. I get that, but I don't see why it has anything to do with how you and I feel about each other."

"As far as feelings go, I *feel* you are less than serious where women are concerned. I respect you as my employer, but that's all. If you fire me, there won't even be that."

Bud was hurt. Seamus was irritated. It was like watching Claudette Colbert in one of her brave-but-too-too-noble roles. Bud tried again. "I was serious about you, Scarlet. What took me away that night was unavoidable."

She met his eyes and said calmly, "You were with a woman."

"Well, yes."

Scarlet's careful reserve vanished, and her eyes glowed with anger. "You see? I'm not stupid."

Bud calmed in response to her fire. "After this morning, can't you guess who the woman I met that night was?"

There was a long pause, and Scarlet finally got it. "Do you mean—"

He sighed. "I was getting ready for our date. Another five minutes and I'd have been gone. A knock comes on the door. When I answer, Callie's standing there, looking gorgeous and caring and desperate. She says, 'Hi, Babe. I'm your mother.'

Just like that."

Bud took a long drink of the tea that was now tepid. "It was like something hit me in the gut. Before I knew it, she was inside my hotel room, talking. She's really good at that. She said she'd wanted to see me for years, but Gramps wouldn't let her. She said, with tears in her eyes, that he'd tricked her into giving him custody then totally shut her out of my life."

"You weren't aware of the details of how he came to adopt you?"

Bud shrugged. "I was a toddler when my dad died. All I knew was I spent more and more time with Gramps until my mother disappeared altogether. He never said a word against her. While that's to his credit, it meant that when Callie hit me with her pack of lies, I wasn't prepared. I had no idea what kind of person she is."

"You believed her story."

"Hook, line, and sinker. She said Gramps should never know she'd contacted me, because he had the wrong idea about her. Then somehow, we were talking about the fact that she needed money. Before I thought it through, I was promising things right and left." He counted the promises on his fingers. "I wouldn't tell anyone we'd met. I'd get her money to live on until she got back on her feet. I'd find her a place in Chicago so we'd be near each other." He paused. "I was shocked when she told me how much she needed, but I'd been saving to buy a piece of property up here." He added bitterly, "My mom needed help, and I thought I had to provide it."

Scarlet looked out across the grassy field to where a yellow and black bird flitted over the tops of the weeds. A grasshopper buzzed nearby. Finally she spoke. "It was all about the money."

"Yes. We left the Island together the next morning and drove to Chicago. The whole trip, she was charming and funny and affectionate. I went to my bank and withdrew everything I had." He sliced the air with an angry gesture. "As soon as I gave her the money, I started calling around, looking for an apartment she could afford. While I was doing that, Callie was making a reservation for a flight to Cancun."

Scarlet let that lie. "You didn't think to call me and explain?"

Bud's answer was oblique. "You have parents, right?"

"Yes."

"Then you can't know how it is. Your whole life, you're the one who is different. Even kids of divorced parents have one who shows up for important events. You hear them talk. 'My mom is so weird.' Or 'My dad won't let me,' and you think, 'What's that like?' You want it. You want to be able to say, 'My mom' in that offhand way. I never had that."

"You had Mr. Dunbar."

"And I thank God for him. I really do. But I always asked myself: did he want to start raising a kid at sixty, or did duty force him to do it?"

"It might have been duty at first, but anyone could see he loved you."

Bud touched the bandage on his head, gently rubbing a spot that itched. "Yeah."

"So now your mother has come back. What will you do?"

"I don't know." His voice was low. "She is my mother."

Scarlet's next question was timid, as if she thought it was none of her business. "You think her visit this morning had a selfish motive?"

"Oh, yeah." Bud grimaced. "I could see the dollar signs flashing in her eyes. I'm rich, and she's going to be my shadow from now on."

"What did you say to her?"

"I told her I needed time to think."

Scarlet looked as if she wanted to say something but pressed her lips together as if willing herself to be quiet. After a moment Bud went on, "When I realized what Callie is, I felt like I'd betrayed Gramps, believing for even a second that he'd have been unfair to me or to her."

"He'd have understood."

"You're probably right, but I was still ashamed. I tried to forget the whole thing." Bud's expression brightened. "I did do one thing to atone. You had told me you'd like to stay in the States for a while. When Gramps needed someone to help with Brodie, I suggested he contact you."

"You did that?"

"It didn't take much to convince him, and of course, he checked you out first. He is—was nothing if not careful." The recent loss seemed to catch him unaware. *Except on the ledge that morning.* Bud bent his head, gulping down a lump of sorrow.

Scarlet shifted her legs, apparently shifting her mood as well, and brushed some crumbs from her lap. "Bud, I'm sorry to have misjudged you. Still, it doesn't change the fact that you're Brodie's guardian, and I'm your employee. We must keep our relationship on a business level."

Bud nodded, but Seamus felt his spirits rise slightly. He'd gone from "Mr. Dunbar" to "Bud." It was, it seemed to both men, a step in the right direction.

Stopping to listen every few steps, Brodie followed the animal sound deeper into the woods. She didn't see the man, didn't know he was there until he grabbed her, stuck a strip of duct tape across her mouth, and pulled a stinky, person-sized bag over her head and shoulders. Like a big nylon stocking, it pulled snug as it stretched over her, pinning her arms to her sides.

Brodie fought back, but surprise hindered her defense. Before she knew it, she was thrown to the ground so hard the breath left her body. It was a struggle to breathe with tape over her mouth, and the fibers and dirt pulled into her nostrils with each inhalation made things worse. The man—she thought it was a man—touched her body roughly. She sobbed an objection, but he only took her hat and one shoe. Searching her pockets, he located her phone and took that too. Once he had those things, he pulled at the top as if putting a pillow into a pillowcase, jostling Brodie farther down into the bag's smelly confines. She tried to kick him away, but the motion hurt her cause and helped his. Once she was completely inside, the man jerked on a drawstring, closing it and trapping Brodie inside.

Helpless now, Brodie heard her attacker move away, scuffling through damp, dead leaves as he went. She lay on the forest floor, bruised and terrified. The bag smelled strongly of fish, and not fresh fish, either. It made her stomach heave and her throat constrict in waves of physical nausea that added to her fear.

She listened, wondering where he'd gone and what she could do to get away. She pushed against the bag, struggling to free herself, but the neck was tightly tied. Working one hand up to her face, she tried to peel the duct tape from around her head. There was no time. Footsteps approached. Grunting and wriggling, she tried to scoot away, but she didn't even know which direction to scoot. "I made a little trail," a voice told her. "Your stuff will lead them astray."

Brodie got it. The smelly bag hid her scent, and the things the man had taken from her would lead searchers in the wrong direction. Where was he taking her?

She felt hands under her body, heard a grunt of exertion, and felt herself lifted up. Soon they were moving, her gut bent painfully over the man's shoulder, her head dangling down his back. His breath grew labored as the heat and her weight taxed his abilities. He didn't let it stop him.

The fear that overtook Brodie wasn't regular fear. The craziness she'd always dreaded built inside her until it broke out in full cry. A voice screamed shrilly, though Brodie could hardly get enough air in to breathe. She heard the word "Help!" sounded over and over, like someone completely out of control lived in her head. There was more—something like "Shame us!" but that made no sense.

CHAPTER THIRTEEN

If Mildred's screams startled Seamus, they terrified Bud. When she started in, he jumped to his feet, looking around as if the jack pines had gathered to attack.

"What is it?" Scarlet asked.

"Where's Brodie?"

"Over there." Her expression was puzzled. "She won't get lost. She knows these woods well."

"I heard a scream. There! Did you hear it that time?"

"I don't hear anything." She rose and stepped into the sunlight, looking across the meadow into the trees opposite. "Brodie?" she called tentatively.

There was no answer, only the hums and chatters of non-human activity.

Bud tried it, a little louder. "Brodie, where are you?"

No answer.

"There it is again!" Scarlet shook her head to indicate she'd heard nothing. "I can't get a direction." Bud pointed. "You go that way. I'll come around and meet you." He started off before he'd finished speaking.

They circled the glade, calling from time to time and getting no response. When they came together on the opposite side, at the last place they'd seen Brodie, they entered the woods together. A short distance in, they found the plastic jar, set carefully on the ground alongside the pad of paper. Brodie had listed twelve spiders she'd found, sometimes adding a *2* to indicate a second find of the same type.

Bud peered ahead, where the thick foliage obscured their view and shut out most of the afternoon sunlight. "She went on from here without the jar."

"Maybe she saw a deer or something."

They separated again, heading into the woods at a widening angle. Bud called, "Anything?"

"No." Scarlet's voice held a note of fear as she returned to meet him. "Did you hear it again?"

"No. But there are leaves disturbed over there, like a struggle."

"You think someone dragged her off?"

"What other explanation is there?"

"But why?" Scarlet looked around anxiously.

Bud didn't say it, but Seamus heard his thought *Money*.

They returned to the picnic spot, hoping Brodie would be there waiting. When she was not, Bud called the house to ask Shelley if she'd returned there. Shelley went outside to ask Briggs if he'd seen the girl. As he waited, Bud's muscles were so tense Seamus felt constricted, like a bow string drawn to its maximum. The guy had been through a lot, and it seemed there was more.

"Who knew we were coming to this spot?"

Scarlet took a long time to reply. "Just the people in the house."

Bud took a mental step back, letting out a breath and trying to quell his rising panic. "Could she be hiding, trying to scare us?"

Scarlet brushed a hand over her forehead as if to banish such thoughts. "Never. Brodie is sad, and she's concerned about what will happen to her now Mr. Dunbar is gone. But she'd never worry m—us by running off."

Bud recalled a time when Brodie had stayed in a tree for hours because Arlis made her eat stewed carrots. This didn't feel like the time to bring that up. "Okay. Either she's badly hurt or someone took her." He turned, surveying the circle of trees. "Those are the only possibilities."

"Maybe she decided to—" Scarlet couldn't finish. She could think of no reason Brodie would go off without telling them. "What should we do?"

Bud pulled out his phone. "First, we get help to look for her."

At times, the man who carried Brodie like a sack of potatoes had to stop to rest. Once he even set her down on the ground, but she could do nothing, tied inside the bag like a cat about to be drowned. She could hear him panting, felt the dampness of his sweat as he labored through the heat. She sensed that when he set her down he stretched his muscles, easing the places where her weight rested. After a few minutes, he hefted her onto his shoulder again, and the trek continued. They were moving through woods, she could tell from the branches that smacked her legs and brushed against her head. Unable to raise her arms to protect herself, she burrowed her face into the man's back to keep from losing an eye.

It seemed like hours that they traveled this way, but the last part was the worst. Her captor started down an incline so steep that in no time he was sliding as much as he walked. Brodie felt even more helpless than before, certain he'd drop her in his struggle to remain on his feet. If he did, she would roll down the slope, banging into trees and ending up—where else but in the waters of the lake? There she would drown, unable to keep herself afloat in this stupid bag. And after days of thinking the opposite, Brodie realized she really didn't want to die.

While they waited for the police to come, Bud and Scarlet widened their search. Due east of their picnic location, Bud found Brodie's baseball cap on the ground, and a few yards farther, a clear footprint. Reiner and two other sheriff's officers arrived, covered with seed pods and with grasshopper juice on their uniform trousers from wading through the tall grass and weeds. Bud showed them where he'd found Brodie's hat, still trying to quell panic that lapped at his insides.

Although the deputy immediately called for search crews to begin combing the woods, Bud suspected Reiner thought Brodie was playing games with them. "A kid feels bad when somebody dies, but they also feel a little left out," he said, hitching up his pants in a way that brought Barney Fife to mind. "The focus isn't on them. Sometimes they do something to get back that attention they want."

"Brodie is not like that," Scarlet said firmly.

Reiner was unable to hide a sneer. "I've had a beer or two with Arnold Wilk, Miss McMorran, so I have an idea what Brodie's like." He went on with his description of what the search would entail, but Bud knew the deputy had come to his own conclusions. Again.

Reiner returned to making phone calls. Looking at Scarlet's white face, Bud saw his own fear reflected there. He led her aside, putting a comforting arm around her. Scarlet leaned into him as if needing support. "She's just a kid," she murmured.

"It's pretty obvious our local officer of the law thinks she's a brat."

"He's wrong. She had a bad reputation as a child, but she's outgrown all that."

"I don't think people around here know what Brodie went through before she came."

Scarlet apparently realized she was almost in Bud's arms and took a step back. "I know she had a difficult start, but I don't know the details."

Bud frowned. "Gramps didn't know Brodie existed for several years. When he learned about the child and went to see if she and her mother needed help, the way they were living made him sick."

"It was so bad that he took the child away from her mother?"

"He tried to get her to accept help, but she was using drugs pretty heavily. She practically sold him the child, and she died a few years after Gramps adopted Brodie."

Bud turned as a pair of deputies joined those already present. Reiner waved them over, still talking into his phone.

Scarlet continued, perhaps to keep both of them focused on something other than the search that didn't seem to require their help. "I wondered where she got her colorful vocabulary. She told me once, 'Gramps doesn't want me to swear, but it's hard when you know all the words.'" She shook her head slightly. "She really does try to be good."

"When Gramps first brought her home, she was like a wild thing." Bud ran a hand across the back of his neck. "Being a big, bad teenager by then and probably more than a little spoiled, I was pretty unhappy about having her around."

"I suppose it was difficult."

He rubbed his hands together. "She was a disaster at the dinner table. My friends made jokes about Gramps' little freak. I was ashamed of her—of how she acted. Once when she pulled some prank on me, I told Gramps I didn't want his little freak going into my room." The last words came out in a whisper.

Scarlet put her fingers against her lips. "That's why she

thinks you dislike her."

Bud shook his head. "It wasn't my finest moment, but at least I didn't say it in front of Brodie."

She gave him a look. "Come on, Bud. You must know Brodie is an A-number-one junior spy." She added more gently. "I think she heard. She's told me several times that you hate her."

"Oh, god." Bud seemed to deflate. "I didn't mean it. I was upset."

Scarlet tried to excuse his youthful mistake. "You were what, sixteen? Not a great age for self-control. When we find Brodie, you can make it up to her."

He glanced at the deputies clustered around a plat map. "First we have to find her."

"We will." Scarlet shifted back to Brodie's past. "How did Mr. Dunbar not know his daughter-in-law had a child and a drug habit?"

Bud looked at her in confusion for a second before realizing her mistake. "Brody isn't really Gramps' granddaughter. She's the child of a distant relative, a third cousin or something. She knows it, but he encouraged her to call him Gramps."

Scarlet sighed. "No wonder she feels she doesn't belong anywhere."

"I tried to make her understand she's part of this family," Bud said miserably. "I'm not very good with kids."

"But Bud, Brodie thinks you're good at everything. You're the perfect heir, and she is the one who is always wrong."

"Really?" Scarlet nodded, and Bud looked to where one the sheriff's men approached with a dog. "When we get her back, she and I have a lot to talk about."

The end of Brodie's unplanned journey was a hard wooden surface, where she was dumped with a great sigh of relief from the man who carried her. Unable to break her fall, she bumped her head painfully, letting out a muffled "Umph!" before her pride could withhold it. Sounds echoed, odd and hollow, and a dankness permeated the fishy bag's smell.

She felt a tug, heard a sawing sound, and the tension loosened around her feet. Soon the side seam of the bag was sliced open with a pocketknife, and she could see again.

She knew where she was immediately—an old boathouse on her grandfather's property. It sat below the bluff, a few hundred feet down from the viewing point, though the canopy of trees blocked sight of it from above. The original cabin had been here, on a little inlet the owner thought would provide shelter from the harsh winds off Lake Michigan. What those winds had done, however, was fill the inlet with sand so that it took constant effort to keep it clear. Gramps had chosen to build in the open, accepting the winds in return for a spectacular view.

The boathouse was the only structure left on the original home-site, and it was pretty much a wreck. Toward the back the roof was gone. The walls were filled with gaping holes where boards had fallen away. Thirty feet long and fifteen feet wide, the building's center was open so a boat could be brought inside, hoisted up on pulleys, and repaired or repainted. There were walkways on both sides, and Brodie had been dumped on the one on the right, which was in a little better shape than its counterpart. An ancient block and tackle once used to lift boats hung overhead. A few shapeless mounds in the corners suggested no-longer-useful tools, probably broken or obsolete. Below her, the water was greenish and murky.

Brodie had been here lots of times, though Gramps had talked about tearing the rickety structure down. It was far enough removed from the present house—and therefore from his notice—that he'd never gotten around to it. For Brodie, it was the perfect place to be alone. Getting to the old boathouse was inconvenient, so nobody bothered her there.

She wasn't alone now. Beside her crouched the bird watcher, smiling as if they'd bumped into each other at the post office. He removed the tape from her mouth, gently pulling strands of her hair away from the adhesive. She worked her lips and jaw, savoring the ability to breathe in clean air.

"Hey, Brodie." His voice echoed off the walls and water. He was a bigger man than he'd seemed at a distance two days ago, tall and wide-shouldered, with curly brown hair and a pleasant face. When she didn't return his greeting, he seem unoffended. "Can you walk?" He took her arm and helped her to her feet. "Let's get you inside."

She looked around to see what "inside" meant. In the water below them was a sailboat, a little bigger than the one she and Bud had taken out the day before. The bow was draped with a camouflage tarp. The boat looked old, maybe because it was made of wood, but perfectly seaworthy, t as it bobbed gently in the shallow water. The mast had been lowered and laid along the boat's length. This man was no birdwatcher. He'd sailed right onto Gramps' property and hidden his boat in the old boathouse. Why?

Glancing out the open doorway, she saw that a downed tree blocked the shallow channel from the boathouse to the lake. "It's not as permanent as it looks," her captor said with a casual gesture. Tracing the line of the tree's trunk Brodie saw the raw stump, bright among the darker wood around it. "The tree shields the view from the lake. The tarp hides what planes and helicopters might see from the air."

Her heart sank. He'd planned this, had known about the old boathouse, unused and obscured by years of neglect and overgrowth. He'd cleared the narrow channel that led into the trees, concealed himself and his boat here in the half-rotten boathouse, and waited to kidnap her. In other words, he'd gone to a lot of effort. She didn't know why, but it couldn't be anything good.

Responding to a gentle push, Brodie boarded the boat. It was a beauty, though not as well-maintained as Gramps would have required. Opening the hatch cover, the man gestured toward the companionway. Even more fearful than before,

Brodie regarded the steps down to the cabin. She knew why men kidnapped girls, knew what they suffered. Whatever he did to her, she told herself, she'd live through it. When she was able, she'd escape and go home, remembering every detail about the man. She'd tell the police all about him so they could put him in jail for a long, long, time.

When she reluctantly made her way down the four steps to the cabin, there was another surprise. A woman sat on one side of the tiny table, smoking a cigarette and working on something with a pen. As Brodie got closer, she saw it was a word-find puzzle.

The interior was a mess, with musty clothing in one corner, used paper plates and cups on every surface, and stale cigarette smoke hanging in the air like bitter fog. Brodie's presence seemed to make the man take note. "You could clean up a little down here, Cher."

Looking up, the woman looked Brodie over then stood, turning a cold glare on the man. "What is this?"

He seemed to shrink from large to medium. "It's the girl I told you about. Brodie."

Taking in Brodie's frightened demeanor and tousled appearance, the woman stepped toward him accusingly. "You kidnapped her."

Something in his reply reminded Brodie of one of her vocab words from the month before: *bravado*. "Cher, we'll talk about this later."

She took another step toward him, and Brodie felt the

man's body tense. "We already talked about it. I said it was a stupid idea."

He drew himself up. "It's done now. We need to get ready."

Cher rolled her eyes, gave Brodie a cold glance, and returned to her place at the table. She took up a pen and went back to the puzzle, making angry circles. The man's tone became pleading. "Cher, it will all work out, just like I said."

Brodie stood there, unsure what to do. Should she run? The woman obviously didn't want her there, so maybe she'd stop the man from chasing her. But he blocked the path of her retreat. She waited. Maybe Cher would insist he let her go.

What did the man mean about getting ready?

"I want to go home." Geez. She sounded like a little kid, but it was how she felt.

The birdwatcher seemed glad to have someone to talk to other than the angry Cher. Clapping a hand on her shoulder, he moved in front of her and squatted down until they were eye-to-eye. "That's exactly what we want for you, Brodie. You're going home."

That was some relief. Apparently he didn't plan to kill her. "But first I need to talk to you." He glanced at the woman, who glared at him briefly before returning to her puzzle. "I can explain all of this, but I had to get you away from Bud and his little girlfriend. You know they're screwing each other, right?"

That was a crock. She'd know if anything like that was

going on between Bud and Scarlet. Although—Brodie forced her mind off that topic. She needed to figure out what this guy wanted. They could be deceiving, the men who hurt kids.

"Sit down," he urged, indicating the bench opposite Cher. "We've got some things to do." Brodie obeyed, and the man began emptying his pockets. From the large side pocket of one pants leg he took her sneaker. "You can have this back now." She took the shoe and sat there, holding it and feeling lost. When the man unzipped his pants she froze, but he didn't even notice. She relaxed a little when she saw he had swim trunks under the jeans he'd been wearing. "Cher?" It was half an order, half a plea.

The woman sucked on her tongue then said in a tone of defeat, "You're nuts."

"We've got an hour, maybe a little more before the cops get involved. Once we're out of here, we're just another boat on the big lake."

"And slower than a turtle," Cher commented. "They could stop us anywhere along here."

"But they aren't thinking water. And who'd suspect this old tub of being a getaway vehicle?" The man grinned at his own genius but turned serious. "If we get going."

"It's supposed to storm. You said we'd take off in the morning, after it clears."

"That was the old plan. This is the new one. They'll be looking for her, and someone might remember this place and check it out. Besides, a storm is a perfect cover. They'll be busy helping boats in distress and won't even notice us." He spoke more forcefully. "We have to hurry to beat the weather, though, so let's move."

"Whatever you say, *Captain*." Slamming her pen down to underscore her objection, Cher rose and stomped up the steps.

The bird watcher seemed relieved that Cher complied, however unwillingly, with his request. "Stay down here, Brodie," he said. "I'll explain all this as soon as I can."

Brodie stared after his retreating figure until the hatch closed over her and she heard the latch click shut. Tears threatened as she surveyed the messy, cramped cabin. It contained the sort of down-sized table common to boats, with bench seats that folded out to make bunks for sleeping as well as providing storage underneath. A tiny sink off to her left looked unused except for a few beer cans set in it. If this boat was like others she'd seen, there was a commode under the steps. There was no way out.

She saw no hope of escape from the bird watcher, no possibility of kindness in the taciturn Cher. Despite her despair, she heard the crazy voice inside her head say, "Okay."

She was a kidnap victim. She was probably going to be raped, possibly murdered. And some odd segment of her mind wanted her to believe things would be all right? Now that was crazy.

Things had been going so well, Mildred thought to herself, then everything fell apart. She'd been trying to bolster

Brodie's self-confidence, and she really felt it had been working. The child had no idea how lovely she was, and Mildred could tell she was intelligent too. With Scarlet working from the outside and her own efforts, Mildred was sure the girl would become self-confident in no time, and all her experiences with that awful mother would be forgotten. It wasn't easy.

Most of the time Brodie seemed to be upset by the encouraging words she heard from inside her head. Seamus had cautioned that hosts might think they were losing their minds, but that was a warning they probably had to give every cross-back, like the admonition on hair color instructions that you HAD to do an allergy test forty-eight hours before dying, every single time. No one really did that. It was something manufacturers said, just in case. While she agreed that talking to a host should be done carefully, surely a young person so unsure of herself could benefit from the experience of someone older. And Seamus didn't understand how gentle Mildred could be. She wasn't pushy, not at all.

But when the kidnapper entered the picture, everything changed. It was the absolute worst thing for Brodie as well as a total surprise to Mildred. She'd panicked briefly. She admitted that. Now she was trying to remain calm. She had to find out exactly what this man had in mind. She hoped it wasn't more pain for poor little Brodie. All she could do right now was assure her that things were going to be okay. Even if they might not.

CHAPTER FOURTEEN

Determined not to give in to either despair or false hopefulness, Brodie looked for something that might help her escape. She could hear the two of them on deck, moving things. Even if she could open the hatch, it was unlikely she'd get past them. The boathouse wasn't easy to get to—or get away from. The bluff rose steeply behind it, and the lake was marshy and overgrown around the inlet. Any direction she took would be tough going, and the bird watcher had long, strong legs. He'd chase her down before she got anywhere.

As she sat there, still holding her shoe, he came down the steps with a garbage bag and began picking up the trash around the cabin, dropping empty beer cans and limp bits of bread into the bag. As he worked, he talked, apparently trying to put her at ease. Brodie noticed he spoke softly, as if he didn't want the woman to hear. "Go ahead and have something to eat while we get the boat ready." He took three sealed deli sandwiches and several kinds of pop from a cooler, laying them out before her on the table as proudly as if he'd made them himself. "They say kids are always hungry." Brodie took one that said "Ham/cheese" and a soda, though she had no appetite. Maybe if he thought she was cooperating, he'd lower his guard.

"Great," he said approvingly. "Now relax for a few, okay?" Taking his bag of trash, he went up the steps again. The hatch slid downward, ending with a wooden thud. It was like the Mad Hatter's Tea Party, because, like Alice, she'd been offered a friendly reception, even refreshments, but not a clue what was going on.

An hour after the police arrived, they were no closer to finding Brodie. The dog, shown her hat, puts its nose to the ground, trotted off through the trees, circled several times and came back, looking confused.

"Could she have climbed a tree?" Reiner asked the handler. Bud didn't hear the answer, but the man's body language suggested a negative response. "Well, keep looking."

The tenor of the search changed when Briggs came looking for them. "Shelley got this message a few minutes ago." He handed Bud a phone. The message read, "Gong 2 live w/ my dad. Dn't wrry abt me. Wll cll whn trn gts in2 Chcgo. Brodie"

Bud handed the phone to Reiner, who had a hard time concealing a smug expression at confirmation that Brodie's disappearance was voluntary. "At least now we've got an idea which direction to look." His brow furrowed. "Who's her dad?"

"I don't know," Bud said with a shrug. "I'm pretty sure Brodie doesn't know, either. At least she didn't yesterday."

The new developments led to Reiner making more phone calls. Bud and Scarlet moved away, standing close together as if to draw support from each other.

"If some man came along and said he was her father, would she stop to ask herself if he was telling the truth?" Bud asked.

"Brodie doesn't trust easily. Still—"

Bud thought of his mother, appearing at his door and

offering the one thing he'd never had, a parent. "If the guy knew which buttons to push, she might go for it."

Reiner closed his phone with a snap and approached. "I've called the state police. If she's on the train to Chicago with some man, they'll find them. I'll leave two men to continue the search here too, in case this was meant to throw us off."

Bud got Reiner's meaning, and apparently Scarlet did too. "Brodie did not do this to get attention," she said firmly. "If she sent that text, she thinks the man she is with is her father."

"Oh, she sent it. It's from her phone."

"Anyone who has a person's phone can send a message," Bud argued. "It doesn't have to be Brodie who did it."

"That might be true, but she has kind of a reputation, doesn't she." It wasn't a question, and Reiner didn't wait for an answer. "From the time she came here, she's played tricks on people. If I remember right, Bud, you didn't find them very amusing when we were in school."

"She's outgrown that." Bud hoped it was true.

"What was it, two years ago she drove her aunt's car into the woods and left it? We spent quite a while thinking it was stolen. That wasn't funny."

"That was before Scarlet came. Brodie's been a different kid the last few months."

Reiner's lips pulled inward, as if he wanted to say more. Instead, he turned away.

Half an hour later, one of the deputies reported finding a spot where someone had pulled a car off the road. Reiner was enthusiastic. "See? She planned to meet the guy out here. He waited in the car, and she went to him."

"Why bring us along if she was planning to run away?"

Reiner considered. "You have a set schedule for lessons?"

"Usually," Scarlet admitted. "Nine to noon for classroom studies and then something educational but not necessarily book-related in the afternoon."

"Who decided you'd come out here today?"

Scarlet hesitated before answering. "We've talked about doing it for some time, but it was Brodie who first suggested it be today." She raised her voice in unconscious defense of her pupil. "She needed to get her mind off what's happened."

"And who suggested Bud should come along?"

Scarlet glanced at Bud. "Well, Brodie did. But he needed to get away too."

"And having him here kept you occupied so she could get a head start."

Reiner's inference was obvious, and Bud couldn't meet Scarlet's eyes. How long had they ignored Brodie as they talked about themselves? He joined the argument, knowing it was useless. "Shouldn't the dog have been able to follow her scent to where the car was parked?"

Reiner sniffed. "Scent dogs aren't perfect."

The dog handler had come up beside them, and he rose to the defense of his animal, which sat down beside him, panting but alert and willing to obey a new search command. "Someone could have stopped in that spot to look at deer or take pictures. We don't know the girl left in that car."

Reiner turned on him, probably venting anger he wished he could direct at Bud. "How else did somebody get her away, carry her on his back?" Reiner turned to Bud again. "The state police are putting out an Amber Alert. They'll watch the train stations between here and Chicago. We'll get her back." He added, "It'll be up to you what to do with her then."

Seamus had no idea where Mildred was or what sort of trouble her host was in. It was exactly the sort of situation he'd feared, one where he had no control. Ruefully, he admitted he hadn't had control of Mildred from the start. If the abductor killed the girl, would Mildred realize his intention in time and jump to another host? If she didn't, if Brodie died, Mildred would become a lost soul. Being her mentor, Seamus knew it was his responsibility to see that didn't happen.

As Bud watched Reiner walk away, Seamus called out a single word, hoping Mildred would obey. "Ship!"

It was all he dared do. He tried to tell himself Mildred would do as he said and go back to the ship, realizing there was no more she could do for Brodie.

He tried to look on the bright side. William Dunbar could rest easily: his grandson had not pushed him to his death. Seamus had begun to suspect, however, that someone else had.

Through one of the boat's tiny windows, Brodie saw Cher and the bird watcher leave the boathouse. A few minutes later she felt the boat rock, heard the crack of branches and the swish of leaves through water. It seemed to get lighter outside. When the two returned, wet to their waists, she guessed they had cleared the channel of their makeshift screen. They were indeed getting ready to go somewhere.

What about the man's assurance that she could go home? If he meant it, they didn't need to go by water. It was less than a quarter mile down the beach to her house.

The sound of something brushing across the bow was next, and she saw the bird watcher gather up the tarp and roll it tightly, fastening it with an elastic cord before disappearing. When she heard a bin lid creak open and bang closed, she guessed he'd stowed the tarp.

Now the two adults moved from one end of the boat to the other, checking the engine, the gas tank, and the sails. They secured some things on deck and stowed others in bins. Brodie peered out the small, round portholes on either side of the cabin, straining to see as much as she could. Two pairs of legs, one hairy, one elephantine, went back and forth, at times quickly, at other times slowly as they lugged heavy items.

Something was about to happen, and she didn't think she was going to like it. Once again, she looked around the cabin for a means of escape. Among the things the man had set on the table while undressing was a roll of duct tape, some change, and the tape recorder he'd carried when she first saw him. She picked it up, wondering what its purpose was, since she knew now he wasn't really a bird watcher. Turning the volume dial to low, Brodie pushed "play" and held the recorder to her ear. She heard an animal whimpering, over and over again.

As she sat listening to the sounds of animal distress, Brodie realized how well the birdwatcher had thought things out ahead of time. Apparently he'd told Cher his plan to lure her away from Bud and Scarlet and she hadn't approved. Might she be willing to help Brodie escape? It was an idea worth pursuing.

Peering out the window again, she saw the bird watcher go by with one of several gas cans he'd lined up on deck. When he came into view again, the can seemed lighter. He was filling the boat motor from the cans, Brodie deduced. He handed Cher the empty one, and she disappeared around the entrance of the boathouse. In a few minutes she returned without it. Finished with that task, they each picked up two bulging trash bags that sat along the wall of the boathouse and disappeared again. The bird watcher stopped to pick up a small spade as he passed. She realized they were going to bury their garbage in the woods, hiding the fact they'd been here.

It seemed to Brodie that her captors were preparing for an extended trip. The boat was well-stocked and the gas tank was full, so there'd be no need to stop for some time. They had come from somewhere in secret and planned to return the same way.

The bird watcher's promise that she could go home was a lie.

Brodie searched the cabin again, looking for something she could leave behind as a clue that she'd been in the boathouse. There was nothing. She thought of leaving the uneaten sandwich, but some animal would undoubtedly carry it off long before anyone found it. Nothing else was unusual enough to signify her presence. Still fearful of the bird watcher's motives, she wasn't about to voluntarily give up one of the few articles of clothing she wore.

She probably only had a short time until they finished burying their trash. Her eyes darted around the tiny room. What could she leave behind?

The tape recorder! If someone found it, especially Bud or Scarlet, it would explain why she'd left them. Brodie opened the window latch and swore softly. "Shit!" A moment later she amended, "I mean, 'Shoot!' Sorry, Gramps."

The little window opened only a few inches before a hinged clasp stopped it. Grasping the tape recorder in one hand, she slid her arm out the opening as far as she could get it. Her position was unwieldy, and she had to twist her body to see where she was aiming. There was a clump of weeds at the entrance to the boathouse. If she could throw the tape recorder that far, the leaves would cushion the drop, and her captors might not hear it hit or see it as they passed. Finding it, though, would be a clear sign to Bud that someone had been here recently. It was the best she could do.

Brodie hesitated, fearing she'd miss and launch her clue into the water. She had to hurry, though. They'd return soon and there she'd be, her skinny arm stuck out like a monkey in a cage. Hefting the device gently once, twice, like the horseshoes Gramps had taught her to throw, Brodie let it go. There was a sharp crack followed by the rustle of leaves.

"What was that?" They were just outside the doorway. Brodie hurriedly pulled in her arm and closed the port. By the time the man entered the cabin, she was sitting innocently on the bench. "Did you hear something just now?"

"It sounded like a bird hit the wall," she told him calmly. "They do that—fly in here and then get scared when they can't find the way out."

He nodded. "Dumb birds."

Cher, who stood at the top of the hatchway, huffed in derision. "Guess that's where the term *birdbrain* comes from. Come on. Let's get this done." The man hesitated, looking at Brodie. She tried not to look toward the window, to the spot where the tape recorder had landed. She hoped contact with the doorpost hadn't broken the little machine beyond repair.

Turning, he gave her a friendly grin. "It won't be long now."

Soon she felt the boat bounce as the weight of the two adults left it again. Grunts and a swishing sound at the bow followed, along with some words Gramps wouldn't have approved of. After a couple of false starts, the boat began to move, water lapping against the sides as it slid through the shallow channel. She felt the boat's bottom bump a couple of times, heard the rustle of leaves and the scrape of branches moving and then snapping back into place. Light flowed in through the portholes, and they were out of the enclosing woods and onto the lake itself. One more push sent the boat scooting forward. It stopped with a jerk as the man pulled on the tow rope, bringing it to rest in a few feet of water.

It was quiet for a moment. Then the boat bobbed, and she heard two thumps hitting the deck. The captain and his helper were aboard. A period of activity followed that Brodie couldn't see, but from the movement, the man's impatient instructions, and the hum of a winch, she surmised they'd set the mast upright again.

A few minutes later the hatch opened and Cher came down the steps, wet and puffing with exertion. She glanced once at Brodie then sat down opposite her, lighting a cigarette and picking up her puzzle book and pen. Above them, the engine sputtered once, twice, and took off, and the boat moved smoothly forward. Brodie was on her way somewhere, unknowing and unwilling. She twisted around to get a last look at home. Would she ever see it again?

Once they were into deep water, the engine stopped. The bird watcher came below with a crank, inserted it into a spot near the steps, and turned it. A rumble sounded below their feet as the keel lowered to its full extension. That done, he disappeared up the steps again. Next Brodie heard the sounds of the mainsail being hauled up. When the wind caught it, they began to move again, but this time silently. After a few minutes, he shouted down, "You'll be able to come on deck as soon as we get a few miles north, Brodie."

It wasn't much comfort to know she'd been right. He wasn't taking her home. She looked around her prison, scaled-down furniture, tiny windows, and the smell of mold and cigarettes. The stone-faced Cher worked on, lips moving slightly and wet sneakers squishing as she shifted with the motion of the boat. She certainly didn't intend to explain the situation.

The crazy voice in her head started in again. At first it sounded like noise, but she thought after a while that someone was repeating, "Boat! Boat, boat!"

That made no sense, but what could she expect? *That's*

what crazy thinking is—nonsense. A burst of noise followed, none of it intelligible. It scared her, but then, Brodie thought, she was right to be scared. Sighing in defeat, she took up the Coke and popped it open. She didn't think there was any way to get a date-rape drug into a sealed can of pop, and she needed to keep her energy up so she'd be ready when a chance came along to escape and get back home.

"Seamus? Seamus, it's Mildred. I'm sorry to talk during their awake time. I know you don't like it, but I thought you should know. Brodie is on a boat and we're somewhere on Lake Michigan. I'm helping her remain calm, and I'll continue to protect her as best I can. Seamus? Seamus, can you hear me?"

In a few seconds she heard one word. "Understood."

Once the police focused their efforts on trains to Chicago, there wasn't much for the family to do. Bud was uneasy, aware Reiner didn't see Brodie as a victim and equally aware Scarlet thought the deputy was completely mishandling the situation. Bud was somewhere in the middle. He knew from experience that Brodie was capable of totally inappropriate action, but he also thought she had changed lately, becoming less likely to act out and more willing to fit in. Growing up, maybe. Because of that, and because he cared what Scarlet thought, he tried to look at the situation objectively.

He wished there was something he could contribute to the search, something to keep from feeling guilty about Brodie's disappearance. If she'd gone unwillingly, he wanted to get her back. If she had gone for some reason of her own, he wanted to make sure his attitude toward her, or at least her impression of it, hadn't contributed to that choice. An officer of the state police had called to promise, in a professional, detached way, that they would bring Brodie home. He heard in the man's voice—or thought he did—doubt. So many young people disappeared because they wanted to. They ran off with a relative or a boyfriend. They hid out to punish their families for some perceived slight. The police knew that kids like Brodie, kids with troubled pasts, were capable of all kinds of wrong decisions. Bud tried to believe things would turn out all right, but it didn't feel that way.

He paced the house for a while, unable to think of anything to say to Scarlet, who watched out the window as if she could summon the girl with pure vigilance. Scarlet believed Brodie had been taken against her will. If that was true, the text message was a false lead, as the footprint trail had been. Someone had deliberately tried to lead them in the wrong direction. Which path did that person want them to ignore?

"Let's go up to the viewing point," he said suddenly.

Scarlet turned to look at him, and the blinds thumped gently back into place. "Why?"

"Brodie's been drawn to that spot since Gramps' death. If she didn't run away, maybe she's up there hoping we'll come looking for her. Besides, it's high enough that we might see something we can't pick up from ground level."

Scarlet shrugged. "The sheriff's men have probably been up there already, but I guess it's better than doing nothing."

They took the golf cart, bumping across the open space

before picking up the two-track road that led up the hill. The heat clung to Bud's skin like woolen clothing. He smelled his own sweat, the combination of exertion, humidity, and fear.

When the ground smoothed and they were able to talk without their teeth chattering, Scarlet asked, "Had you noticed any change in your grandfather lately?"

It took Bud a while to decide how to answer. "What do you mean?" She waited, apparently aware he was avoiding the question. "Maybe."

"Tell me what you saw."

"He was forgetful, I guess." Bud tried to dodge a washout in the road and failed. The bump made Scarlet grab for a handhold. "Sorry!" He shook his head, arguing with his own thoughts. "Lots of older people forget things. Hell, I forget things, and I'm not old."

Scarlet seemed to sense there was more. "What else?"

He let out a long breath. "Two of our vendors said he'd called recently to place an order."

"Was that unusual?"

Bud smiled grimly. "Gramps hasn't phoned in orders for twenty years. It's done by computer, and we have an employee whose time is fully devoted to it."

"So what did these vendors do?"

"One took the order then called me to see what he should do about it. The other tried to explain to Gramps that he was mistaken. He got very upset and hung up. Then she called me."

"I see."

Bud sighed again. "I hoped it was some kind of aberration. Medication or even an infection can make an older person act weird, can mimic the symptoms of—"

"Dementia?"

"Yeah." After a pause he asked, "You noticed it too?"

"He drove Brodie and me to town a month ago and forgot the way home. She directed him, and when we got here, he insisted he'd been joking. She accepted his explanation, but I saw the fear in his eyes. I noticed he'd begun writing down things he should have been able to remember, like what time the evening news comes on." She wiped her forehead with the back of her hand. "I've only known him for a year, but I know the signs. My gran had Alzheimer's."

"Did anyone else notice?"

"Who'd say anything? If they knew he was having trouble, Shelley and Briggs would simply watch him more carefully. Arnold wants—wanted to keep his job, so I suppose he'd cover when he could."

Bud had told the police about terminating Arnold Wilk's employment. They'd found his room empty and his car gone, but Bud couldn't imagine Arnold kidnapping Brodie. Thinking he might know something, Reiner wanted to speak with him. So far he hadn't been found. His parents in Indiana hadn't heard from him, nor had any of his friends they'd contacted.

Bud didn't comment on Arnold but asked instead, "What about Arlis?"

Scarlet replied in an even voice, "I don't think she'd want to upset the apple cart."

"Yeah." Bud thought Arlis might not have noticed a thing, being pretty much wrapped up in herself. As long as Will was there to pay the bills, she'd been content.

"She wouldn't have confided in me, anyhow." Bud heard a tinge of bitterness in Scarlet's tone and wondered what it was like for her, living even partially under Arlis' thumb.

He returned to the point. "Well, I noticed. It's why I proposed selling the business." The golf cart slowed, chugging as they began the steepest part of the incline. "Gramps didn't want to, so all my arguing did was make Reiner suspicious that I killed him."

They fell silent then, each with his own thoughts. Soon they caught glimpses of Lake Michigan through the trees. The lake sparkled in the late-day sun, its surface a million tiny mirrors that caught the dying light and magnified it. Bud parked the cart on the trail and followed Scarlet along the narrow wooded path to the open space.

There was nothing to see, at least nothing unusual. On the lake a small boat traveled north, a vintage model that was all wood. Seeing it reminded Bud of their trip two days ago. Brodie hadn't seemed likely to run away. And he had reassured her, hadn't he? Had his promise that her situation would be unchanged been enough, or had she feared he would—What? What could he have said that would cause her to run off with a stranger?

Scarlet stopped several feet back from the fence. "I haven't been up here since—"

Bud turned away from the lake. "Yeah."

She met his gaze directly. "It wasn't your fault, Bud."

"I guess."

"No," she said firmly. "That isn't a guess. It's a fact."

He smiled weakly. "Okay. I'll try to believe you." Taking up the binoculars he'd brought along, he surveyed the area. The little boat was sweet, like the Alden Gramps had owned when Bud was a kid. White oak frame with mahogany, and bronze everywhere. Together they'd polished that old boat until it shone.

As the sail receded, Bud turned to survey the trees around them. "If Brodie was hiding up here, would she be more likely to come out if you were alone?"

Scarlet's lips pursed briefly. "She isn't hiding."

"Sorry. She's kind of famous for pranking people."

"Was." His words seemed to spur a thought, however. "Bud, I think Brodie knew your grandfather's mind was failing."

"What do you mean?"

"Twice in the last month or so she confessed to playing pranks. I was surprised, because I was pretty sure she'd outgrown such things."

"What sort of pranks?"

"That's just it. They seemed pointless. From what I understand, her actions in the past were in retaliation for something she felt was an insult or unfair. Is that right?"

Bud chuckled. "Yeah. A few years back, Arlis browbeat Gramps into hiring a Brunhilde type who should have worn army boots and carried a riding crop. The woman—Ms. Pickerel, I think her name was—insisted that a new lock be installed on the door to her room, insinuating strongly that Brodie might sneak in and rifle through her things. Her method of dealing with Brodie was to report every picayune misdeed to Gramps, from daydreaming during math lessons to wearing her swimsuit to bed instead of pajamas."

"What did he do?"

"He generally listened, promised to talk to Brodie, and ignored it, but it irritated both Gramps and Brodie. Soon Ms. Pickerel began to find each evening that the key to her room wouldn't go into the lock. Briggs would have to be called in to fix it while she stewed in the hallway. After four days of it, Briggs appealed to Brodie's sense of fairness. She was punishing Ms. Pickerel, but he was the one who had to keep digging pencil lead out of the lock."

Scarlet chuckled. "That's the sort of thing I've heard, though I saw little of it." A lock of hair played against her face as the breeze caught it, and Bud felt an urge to brush it away, touching her cheek as he did so. "The pranks she confessed to recently were strange. One day no one could find the keys to the four-wheeler. We searched everywhere and finally found them in a potted plant. Brodie said she'd hidden them there. Another time, we found several windows open after a cold night. The furnace was on full, attempting to heat the house despite the March winds. Brodie insisted she'd opened them, but she wouldn't explain why."

"You think she was covering for Gramps."

"I do. I wondered about it at the time, but with what you've told me and what I saw myself, I think she realized he was failing and tried to prevent the rest of us from seeing it."

"Poor kid. He was her rock, and he was starting to crumble." Bud looked around, hoping to spot a flicker of movement among the trees that might be Brodie. A crow called from a tree branch to their right, and a memory stirred. "She met a guy up here the other day, a bird watcher."

"She mentioned it."

Bud scanned the trees again. "Hard to miss that this is private property. It's posted."

"Do you think it could have been a kidnapper?"

"There's been no ransom demand."

Scarlet checked her watch. "It's only been a few hours."

Bud massaged the bridge of his nose, trying to ease a frown that wouldn't stop. "I wish there was something we could do other than wait."

Inside Bud's head, a word sounded over and over. *Boat,* his mind whispered. *Boat. Boat.*

Bud looked up the north shore of the lake. The wooden boat was almost out of sight, sailing slowly and peacefully away from them, a postcard-perfect image.

CHAPTER FIFTEEN

"Where are you taking me?" Brodie asked the woman. She'd been silent for what seemed like hours, but her fear finally spilled into words.

Cher didn't even look up. "He'll tell you when he's ready." With a glance upward she added, "Idiot." Brodie thought the word was for the bird watcher, not her, but she decided further conversation was a bad idea, at least until the word-finds ran out. Cher did one after another, stopping only to stub out one cigarette and light the next one. Sometimes they smoldered in the tuna can she used for an ashtray, filling the air with acrid smoke. Brodie was tempted to finish them off with a splash of her soda.

She saw the Sleeping Bear Dunes pass and recalled Gramps telling her the story. "Chippewa legend claims that once an enormous forest fire on the western shore of Lake Michigan drove a mother bear and her two cubs into the lake. After swimming many miles, the two cubs fell behind. The mother bear reached the shore and turned to wait for them at the top of a high bluff. The exhausted cubs drowned, but the mother stayed on in hopes her children would finally appear. Impressed by her faith, the Great Spirit created North and South Manitou Island to commemorate the cubs. The winds buried the sleeping bear under the sands of the dunes, where she waits to this day.

He added that a small, tree-covered knoll at the top edge of the bluff had once had the appearance of a sleeping bear when viewed from the water. Wind and erosion had greatly reduced its size over the years, but she thought now of the loving mother bear, waiting for her cubs. No mother waited for her to return on the shore. Maybe no one cared that she was gone. They might all be glad to be rid of their problem child.

Though she didn't know why, Brodie counted on Bud. His loyalty and affection for Gramps would make him do what he could to rescue her. From the time she first came to the Dunbar house, she'd believed Bud could do anything. She told herself she had to continue to believe it now.

Finally the hatch slid open, and the bird watcher's face appeared. "I guess you can come out now." Glad at least to leave the smoky cabin, Brodie climbed to the deck, noting the shoreline far to her right. Nothing was familiar. The compass indicated a westerly direction, and a group of islands lay outlined against dark clouds that rolled toward them like angry waves. "We're going to get some weather, but I know where we can ride it out," the man said confidently.

He slouched against the transom, the tiller held loosely in one hand and a beer in the other. "You didn't get sick down there, did you?" He peered down the stairs suspiciously.

Despite the situation, Brodie was offended at the suggestion. "I'm a good sailor."

"That's a relief, 'cause we're going to be stuck down there until the storm passes. In the morning, we'll take off early. We've got a ways to go." Watching her face, he added with a grin, "C-eh?-N-eh?-D-eh? Get it? Canada!"

The word hit Brodie like a blow, but oddly, her first thought was entry requirements. "I haven't got a passport."

He gave her a knowing look. "You won't need one the way we're gonna do it."

She got the idea. There was a lot of shoreline between the two nations. Patrols couldn't cover the comings and goings of every small pleasure craft. "They'll be watching for me."

He huffed in disagreement. "Why should they?" He ticked off his points on his fingers. "They think you went south, not north. They don't know you're on a boat. And nobody knows I left Canada. I plan to slip back in and pretend I didn't."

"You're Canadian?" Why would someone come from Canada to take her back there with him?

"Yeah," he said with an odd smile, "I'm Canadian. And so are you."

He pointed ahead. "There's our spot for the night." Adjusting the tiller, he maneuvered the boat toward the islands. On one of the larger ones was a lighthouse with a building next to it, both shuttered and dead-looking. "I promise, I'll explain everything soon," he said, watching the lake ahead for hazards. "I'm not your enemy, Brodie. I'm trying to protect you."

Yeah, right, she thought. *People always kidnap other people to protect them.*

He seemed to sense her objection. "Bud wants to control the money your grandfather left you. I'll bet he's been real nice, hasn't he? Taking you sailing and stuff. Did he ever do that before?"

She didn't answer, but her doubts about Bud re-surfaced. He had pretty much ignored her until she became an heiress.

The man was watching, so she kept her face impassive. He didn't seem bothered, though. "When you know the facts, you'll thank me for coming to get you."

I doubt that, she thought. He turned the tiller sharply, and she sat down rather than fight the pull of it as she surveyed the unfamiliar territory ahead. The sun had disappeared into the clouds, but the air was warm and heavy. The bird watcher dropped sail, turning a corkscrew-shaped anchor into the lakebed near shore. The smallest island in the group, their sheltering land appeared to be deserted, not even a boat ramp or a dock. What it did have was a crescent shape that hugged the boat like a contour pillow, protecting it on three sides. "Just like home." The man cheerfully popped open another beer. "We can lay up for the night without anyone getting nosy."

The sky grew darker, the clouds leaned lower, as if their weight was pulling them down. Securing the boat with brisk efficiency, the man indicated Brodie should return to the cabin. "We're in for some rain, and we can't show any lights, so we might as well get some sleep."

As if to underscore his prediction, thunder grumbled to the west, and the sky flickered once with accompanying lightning.

They went below, where Cher had stowed the table and readied the two benches to serve as bunks. There were sleeping bags on either side, and her puzzle book lay atop the one on the left. The man started to close the hatch and paused. "Do you have to pee?"

She did. In fact, she'd felt the urge for some time but was

unwilling to mention it.

"Go with Cher," he ordered, and the two women went on deck. Brodie had an idea how the process would go. Although there were toilets on these small boats, most people used them as little as possible, since they tended to smell. Instead they would add to the waters of the lake.

Raindrops began to fall, not frequent but large and heavy. When they finished, neither looking at the other, Cher gestured for Brodie to precede her down the steps. The rain came harder all at once, slapping her arms and making wet spots on her scalp where it penetrated her thick hair.

Once they were inside, the man padlocked the hatch and put the key in his pocket. He shook himself, wiping moisture from his face with a good-natured, "Whooh!" Rain tattooed against the wood above them, and he said loudly, "I'll see you girls in the morning." He disappeared aft, to where there must have been some kind of berth. Brodie heard bumps for a few seconds as he settled in. The storm began to rage, coming in swells that rocked the boat and roared over their heads. The cabin seemed to grow smaller, as if the weather outside compressed its space.

Cher used a small flashlight as she prepared for bed. She plumped up her pillow, releasing a musty, damp smell that made Brodie's nose itch. Then she plopped herself down on the bed with a long sigh, her face not two feet from where Brodie lay. Smacking her lips, Cher closed her eyes, shutting out everything but sleep. When the rain eased slightly a few moments later, Brodie heard them both breathing, Cher softly and the man snuffling like the bears at the Detroit Zoo.

She rolled over, putting her back to the woman. She felt like crying, but she would not. If she couldn't cry for Gramps, she would not cry for herself.

The storm was nasty, loud, and scary. For perhaps fifteen minutes Brodie lay awake, listening to the rain and wind and thinking she'd never be able to sleep. How much worse could things get? Would the boat swamp and leave them all floating in the lake? Would the bird watcher be too slow opening the padlocked hatch and drown them all? She was trapped, exhausted, and terrified, so much so that even the crazy voice in her head was silent. For a while she thought the storm would last forever, but finally the winds died, the drum of rain slowed, and the boat stopped rolling. The peace that followed seemed like the greatest gift ever. Despite everything else that was wrong with her life, Brodie relaxed a little with the cessation of foul weather. And she slept.

There was no further word from the police, and the household fell into an uneasy silence. Even Arlis could think of nothing to say, though she made pathetic attempts: "Brodie is probably at a friend's house and forgot to call us." No one bothered to say that Brodie did not have any friends outside the house they inhabited. Later she tried again. "I saw the pastor speaking with her before the funeral the other day. I'll bet she's gone to see him, to try to find some comfort." Again, no one commented, and Arlis lapsed into nervous silence.

They went to their rooms just after midnight, each pretending for the benefit of the others that sleep was an option. Thunder rolled outside the window, and lightning lit the sky so often it looked like some mischievous child was flipping a heavenly light switch on and off, on and off. Seamus heard Bud fret over whether Brodie had a place to get inside when the storm came. He almost hoped she was on a train to Chicago with her dad. It was better than the alternatives that kept cropping up in his mind.

After pacing for a while, paging through a magazine with no idea what it contained, and staring out the window at the darkness, Bud threw himself across the bed and fell into a fitful sleep sometime after two. By that time Seamus was a wreck. "Millie?"

"Seamus?" Her voice came through clearly, and he felt some relief. She was okay, so far.

"Millie! I've been nuts here."

"Brodie is asleep. I'm trying to encourage her, but she's very upset, and she seems to get rattled when I speak to her."

"I told you—"

"She's plotting an escape," she interrupted, "right up to when she drifted off. She's a very strong young lady, but I gather she's had to be."

Seamus chose to stick to practical matters. "I heard you say 'boat', but where are you?"

"On a sailboat, headed north. The man says our destination is the eastern shore of Lake Huron."

"Huron! The eastern shore of Huron is—"

"I know my geography, Seamus. He's Canadian."

"He's taking her to Canada!" Bud moaned and rolled over, disturbed by the noise in his head.

"Try to calm down. You're no help to Brodie if you get upset."

Realizing she was right for once, he paused to gather his thoughts. "Tell me what happened."

"The man—she calls him the bird watcher—forced Brodie onto a boat."

"I figured that much from your message. I tried to make Bud notice it, but he was distracted and didn't pay attention."

"It's a little claustrophobic. This man has a woman with him, and the cabin is really too small for four people." Seamus noted wryly that Millie included herself in the count. *As if we exist.*

"Can you jump to the guy, see what his plan is?"

He felt Mildred's resistance, as if she'd taken an actual step back. "I can't leave Brodie."

"But we need to know what this is about."

"She's very fragile right now."

"It won't take ten minutes."

"What if I can't get back to her? And what could I learn while he's asleep, anyway? He told Brodie he'd explain in the morning."

"So in the morning, you jump to him."

Mildred was having none of that. "Whatever his plan is, Brodie will need me to help her get through it. I've been encouraging her, and I think she's beginning to get used to me."

"Millie, will you listen, for pete's sake?"

"No, Seamus, I won't. And it's Mildred. You might know a lot about investigating, but what do you know about young women? I'm telling you, Brodie needs me."

Seamus could have punched the wall—if he had fists. "Our job is to find out what happened to William Dunbar, not to fix what's wrong with that kid."

Her tone turned regretful. "I knew you wouldn't understand."

He counted to ten. "Okay. Where are you? I'll see what I can do to get Bud there."

"We anchored at a small island for the night to ride out the storm. He plans to reach the Straits of Mackinac sometime tomorrow. He said passing through the straits will be easy with all the racers and sightseers around the area."

"I thought the race would be over by now."

"It is, but apparently there are activities afterward: shorter races, parties, that sort of thing. There'll be lots of boats up there, and no way for the authorities to keep track of them all."

"So if I can get Bud to drive north, he might catch this guy in the straits?"

"How would Bud find one boat among the others at night with all the commotion up there?"

"I don't know, but the cops are looking to the south. A text message sent from the girl's phone said she was going to Chicago with her father."

"He took her phone, and I haven't seen it since. He probably sent the message then tossed it." Mildred paused as Brodie moaned softly in her sleep. "He thought this out very carefully. Do you think Bud is up to stopping him, with a concussion and all?"

"I don't know."

"But he's the only chance we have of getting Brodie back to her family."

"Yeah," Seamus said reluctantly, "It wasn't supposed to be part of the job, but I think that's what our client would want us to do."

When Brodie woke, for a few seconds she couldn't remember where she was. The unfamiliar, thin cushion with a hard surface under it. Someone snoring. The boat bobbing gently at anchor.

Her mind kicked in and she remembered. Gramps was dead, and she was the prisoner of a crazy guy who claimed he was saving her from the people she called her family.

Muffled noises came from the back of the boat. The woman in the bunk opposite Brodie moaned softly in her sleep but didn't wake. The noises came closer, and Brodie saw a dark shape enter the cabin. She froze, all her fears about child molesters returning, but the man ignored her and climbed the steps, where he unlocked the hatch.

The beers he'd drunk that afternoon had caught up with the bird watcher. Brodie lay very still, waiting to see if he left the hatch open. If she could get to the island, she might be able to find a place to hide. If he caught her, she wouldn't be any worse off than she was now.

When she heard water hitting water, she climbed noiselessly from the bunk and crept up the steps, praying they wouldn't squeak.

Once on deck, she could see better. The sky had cleared to the northwest, and a tiny slit of moon shone above them. The man's back was to her as he emptied his bladder into the water below. He stood on the bow, so Brodie moved aft, staying near the center so the boat didn't tilt. Reaching the ladder, she climbed nimbly over the side, hoping the bird watcher wouldn't finish too soon. If it was too dark for her to see him, she hoped the opposite was true.

The snap of elastic signaled his imminent return to the cabin. As soon as she heard his feet on the steps, Brodie lowered herself into the water and let go of the ladder. The lake was cold, but she'd expected that. Worse was the darkness, the feeling of being in unknown territory without a clear idea of what to do next. She almost wanted to return to the safety of the boat, but she forced herself to resist the urge.

Behind the boat, the island was only a dark blot against the clouded sky. The crazy voice kicked in. "Swim!" it said. "Swim!"

Like I've got another choice! she would have answered if it wasn't her own head talking. *They say you aren't crazy if you talk to yourself. You're only crazy if you answer.*

Leaning back in the water, Brodie pulled herself away from the boat, watching and listening for a reaction on board. It wasn't long in coming. She heard the bird watcher swear as he came back up on deck, ran fore and aft several times, and finally called out to her. "Brodie? Brodie, honey, you have to come back. There's no place for you to go."

A powerful flashlight came on, pointed in the opposite direction, toward the land. The beam moved across the water, rising and falling as the man tried to gauge how far away she'd gotten. He was on the port side. Soon he'd move starboard. Where could she hide?

"Brodie. That island? There's no one there. It's a little hunk of nothing." She knew he was telling the truth. The island was merely a lump in the lake, protection from the storm but unpopulated, overgrown and, if others she'd seen were any indication, swampy. "You might as well come back. Where can you go?"

The light moved toward her. She ducked underwater, but fear shortened her breath and she was only able to stay under for a few seconds. When she came up, he heard her gasp for air and turned the light toward her. Pinned in its beam, she found a new sense of determination. She would not climb meekly back into this guy's boat and sail off to Canada!

Grabbing a huge breath of air, she dived and swam under the boat. Using reeds and other vegetation as a guide, she headed toward where she hoped the island lay. When she emerged, gasping for air, on the inland side, she heard Leland's bare feet scuffling across the deck, trying to see where she'd gone. As quietly as possible, she waded toward the shore, hoping to disappear into the trees before he saw her again. Once there, she'd hide until he gave up looking for her. Maybe she could swim to another island, one with more places to hide.

Cher's muffled voice echoed off the water, her tone questioning. "She took off," the man called back. Brodie couldn't hear Cher's response, but the tone was definitely accusing. "I thought she was asleep." His voice carried easily across the water. "I will. It won't take long."

"Brodie," he called again. "Listen, honey, I'm doing this for you." There was a pause, and when she didn't answer, he added, "Brodie, I'm your dad."

That stopped her, being about as unexpected as anything he might have said. The guy was nuts, maybe worse than she was herself. If he *was* her father, why hadn't he knocked on the front door of Gramps' house and said so? If he was *not* her father, why did he think he was, and what did he have planned for her?

The shore loomed before her, a black spot in the graying darkness. She dragged herself through the mucky shallows, feeling the rotting vegetation sliding beneath her shoes. At the waterline there was a lip she had to climb, and she reached for nearby plants to pull herself up. One foot found solid purchase, and she reached farther in to get a better handhold. Either the plants she grasped weren't firmly embedded or her grip was too far from the roots. They came out of the earth as she transferred her full weight to them. Brodie fell back into the lake with a splash.

That wasn't the end of it. Scrabbling desperately, she made it over the lip on the second try, but the noise she made alerted her captors. Cher came on deck with a second flashlight, which she focused on Brodie. "Keep it on her!" the man called, jumping into the water and wading ashore.

Throwing herself into the underbrush in a frantic attempt to hide, Brodie ignored the scratches inflicted by sharp branches as she burrowed as far down as possible. She crouched in the darkness, trying to make herself smaller, struggling to quiet her breathing, and hoping her pursuer would pass by. She dared not look up, dared not move. It was hardly any time at all before his voice came from above her. "Come out of there before I drag you out."

Would he kill her now? Something told her he wouldn't. Whatever he planned required that she remain alive. It didn't lessen her fears one iota, because he could hurt her in a hundred ways without killing her. Resigned, she stood, facing him as defiantly as she could manage. "Let's go." He sounded more frustrated than angry.

They boarded the boat again, and Brodie descended, dripping, to the cabin with her tormenters right behind her. "Okay," the man said, securing the padlock. "I thought our talk could wait till later, but I guess not." Setting the flashlight on the floor, where its light showed mainly on their feet, he seated himself on the bunk Cher had occupied, indicating Brodie should sit on her own bunk. She did, feeling her wet shorts spread their moisture onto the sleeping bag. Cher leaned against the countertop, arms folded in disapproval.

"You want to know what's going on," he began.

She'd already figured out that he didn't need the encouragement of a verbal response. She met his gaze expectantly, and he went on. "I am your dad. You probably don't believe that, but I can prove it." He shifted his feet, kicking her without realizing it. Brodie pulled her feet back till they were up against the wooden bin under the bench.

"Your mother was Jeannie Brooks. She was a real—" He glanced at Cher. "She was pretty. I knew you were her kid as soon as I saw you. You look just like her, wild hair and all." He seemed to drift into the past. "We had some good times, Jeannie and me."

Cher shifted impatiently, and he pulled himself back to the present. "You gotta believe this. I didn't know you existed. Mom said Gramps had taken in another kid, but I guess he never told her why. I'll say one thing for the old man. He knew how to keep his mouth shut. I don't think he ever told Ma that I stole this boat. Didn't tell the police, either."

Brodie was beginning to comprehend, though the explanation was, so far, anything but clear. Her possible father chuckled, rubbing his bare chest absently. "My mother tells me all the time, 'Leland, you're every bit as close to him in blood as Bud is. You should get consideration when it comes time to divide things up.' But Uncle Will didn't see it that way."

Brodie sat stunned, looking at the bird watcher/kidnapper/sailor. This was the man Bud jokingly called Saint Leland, Arlis' wayward son. And he claimed to be her father.

Leland leaned back, resting his arm along the bench and crossing one hairy leg over the other. "Now that you're here, I guess I'll get consideration after all."

CHAPTER SIXTEEN

Seamus started as soon as Bud awoke, repeating, "Boat. Boat." He whispered, since hosts were likely to regard a whisper as their own thoughts, whereas a fully voiced message seemed alien and frightening. He wished Mildred had taken that piece of information more to heart. She was probably scaring the kid to death with her "encouragement."

Bud showered and changed into fresh clothes, having slept in the ones from yesterday. He'd rested uneasily, partly due to the conversation Mildred and Seamus held inside his head. In addition, he was tortured by thoughts of what might be happening to Brodie. *Is she dead? Has she been harmed? Molested? Abandoned somewhere in a dark basement or even a shallow grave?* Horrors passed through his mind, stories of children who'd suffered terrible deaths. *I'm sorry, Gramps,* Seamus heard in Bud's thoughts. *Not only was I not there when you needed me, but while I wasn't paying attention, Brodie got grabbed by some lunatic.*

He examined the cut on his head in the mirror. It didn't look bad, but he had a fierce headache that Seamus shared with him. Before leaving his room, Bud took a couple of the pills the doctor had prescribed, swallowing them with effort and hoping there'd be coffee downstairs to speed them on their way.

Seamus felt a little guilty, knowing his presence made it harder for his host to recuperate from his injury. However, he was also able to be a little optimistic, knowing the girl was alive. He had to get Bud to remember what he'd seen from the ridge yesterday. "Boat."

Bud shook his head in response to the word that seemed to buzz inside it like a fly. "Boat?" he finally said aloud to the mirror. "What boat?" With a shrug, he started downstairs.

Scarlet stood inside the dining room doorway, her eyes even darker than they'd been the night before. She stared without interest at a breakfast table laden with food. Shelley apparently counted on the police continuing their search today and intended no one would go away hungry. What was there could have fed the 101st Airborne Division.

Bud poured two cups of coffee and handed one to Scarlet, who sipped it absently before starting as if they'd never left off yesterday's conversation. "Something isn't right, Bud. Brodie would not go off to Chicago with a man she doesn't know."

After considering the situation for most of the night, Bud was inclined to agree. Brodie was standoffish with everyone, including him. More and more, he doubted she'd leave home with a stranger, no matter what story the guy told her.

"Boat," his mind prompted, and he shook his head slightly, hoping the pills would kick in soon.

"Maybe the man had something that convinced her he was her dad." Scarlet was at the window again, as if hoping Brodie might walk up the drive.

"Yeah." He stopped, doubting that. "No. I think she'd have brought whatever proof he offered to you."

"If we knew who her father was, it might help." Scarlet turned away from the window to look at him. "Do you think Mr. Dunbar left that information somewhere?"

"We can look through his things and see. I haven't—" Bud

cleared his throat. "I haven't done much in there yet."

"It might be important." Her hands fluttered as she added, "It will give us something to do while we wait for word from the police."

Bud led the way to the office, where the copy of his grandfather's will he'd been given lay folded on the desktop. Together they perused the document, Bud tracing the sections with a finger and Scarlet following along.

"Small bequests to Shelley and Briggs, nothing to kill for, even if you could imagine them harming Gramps. You get the car you've been driving, and Arnold gets his. Brodie's money is in trust until she's eighteen, with me as trustee. Some bequests to charity. The rest comes to me." He shook his head. "That's why Reiner suspects that I—" He stopped, unable to finish the sentence. "Money seems like a motive, but I'd never hurt Gramps."

"I know that, Bud." Scarlet put a hand on Bud's arm. "Even when I tried to convince myself you liked breaking the hearts of innocent Irish girls, I knew you loved your grandfather."

There was a pause, an insignificant moment in time's eons. To Seamus, however, it felt as if centuries passed. *There are crimes to solve, you two!*

Bud finally got back to the subject at hand. "Someone, possibly Brodie's father but not necessarily, hears that Gramps died and she inherited a lot of money. This person contacts Brodie and arranges to meet her, where he either convinces her to go with him or abducts her."

"If that's the case, he must either be her father or have convincing evidence that he is. Even if he got Brodie to accept him, he'd have to get legal custody to access her money."

"Right. I'm not sure what the courts would do about trusteeship if an immediate family member showed up to contest my right to it."

"Is it possible this person really is Brodie's father?"

Bud turned back to the will for a few seconds. "Here's something." He read aloud. "'If Brodie Dunbar should, upon her majority, want to know the events that led to her adoption into this family, she may at that time be given a video recording kept in my safe. Though I do not recommend the second and third segments, I leave it to Brodie's judgment. Whatever she decides, she must understand that I love her as much as if she were my own.'"

Bud looked in the direction of a small safe in a corner behind the desk. Scarlet asked, "Do you think it would help us to know the story?"

He laid the will on the desk and took in a deep breath. "I think we need to know everything we can." Opening a drawer, Bud rummaged until he found a slip of paper with the combination to the safe, and after only two unsuccessful attempts, opened it. From its depths he took a stack of items: a coin collection book, envelopes marked with identifiers such as "Deed to House" and "Life Insurance", and a vinyl sleeve marked "Brodie" that held a DVD.

They looked around the office, devoid of machinery. A self-proclaimed technophobe, Gramps had been unable to fathom why others spent so much time "facing screens instead of people.”

“The next task is to find a DVD player where we can have a little privacy.”

Blushing a little, Scarlet said, “There’s one in my room.”

“Great,” he replied, and headed up the stairs, assuming she would follow.

Scarlet’s room was actually a small suite: a sitting room with an open doorway that looked in on a mauve-and-cream bedroom. The whole place had a feel of neatness, though there were signs of the resident’s recent preoccupation: the slightly crooked bedspread and a pair of mud-caked pants hung over a chair to dry. Seamus noted the scent of apples, shampoo or body wash or whatever women used to make themselves smell like fruit.

“Maybe you should watch it alone,” Scarlet offered.

Bud looked surprised. “I need all the help I can get if we’re going to find Brodie ali—so we can get her back safely.”

Nodding agreement, Scarlet put the DVD into the player and started it.

Seamus felt the momentary shock that went through Bud at the sight of his grandfather, apparently alive and well, on the mid-sized TV screen. The William Dunbar they saw was ten years younger, a vital older man. Tears stung Bud’s eyes. *Gramps before the strokes, before the dementia, before he was a pitiful old man.*

“Brodie, my dear,” Dunbar began, “I am making this video for you with the help of a clever young man from the local cable company. It is in three segments. The first part, this one, is basic information I feel you need to know. The second explains how you came to be adopted, should you want to hear it. Since you undoubtedly remember some of your early years, it might help you cope with the dreams—" His expression hardened briefly "—the nightmares you have on occasion. When you're ready, it's here."

Dunbar looked slightly uncomfortable as he continued. "The third part was problematic for me. It is my final interview with your mother, Jeannie Brooks. I do not believe you should watch it; in fact, I advise against it. Still, I won't pretend to understand what you might want or need to know in the future. Instead of two loving parents, you had only an old man who very possibly did things all wrong. However, I've always encouraged informed decisions, so I won't withhold information you might require to make decisions later in life. I don't know if it will help or hurt you to see your mother and understand why I took you from her. I leave that decision to you."

There followed a brief recitation of biological facts: Brodie's birth weight, blood type, the hospital and county where her birth was registered, and genetic factors she might need to know. Dunbar read from a sheet before him, commenting in the way of older people who feel compelled to give warnings that will go unheeded by their listeners. He noted that Jeannie's feet caused her trouble. "You should always wear good, supportive shoes," he directed, looking up at the camera to emphasize his point.

"I've tried for months to get Brodie to wear something besides flip-flops," Scarlet murmured.

"Good luck with that," Bud replied. Recalling at the same

moment that they might never see Brodie again, they quickly returned their attention to the screen.

The first segment ended with Gramps telling Brodie, "You have a generally healthy family in terms of bodily constitution. You were slightly malnourished when you came to me, but you recovered quickly and show no signs of permanent disability or physical harm."

Bud glanced at Scarlet when the screen went blank for a few seconds. "Part one gave her information many adopted people don't have. 'Will I get Parkinson's? Should I watch for aneurisms?' That sort of thing."

"The next part might be what we need," Scarlet said. They watched the blank screen for a few seconds, anxious to hear the story of how Brodie had come to the Dunbar home.

There was a muted beep as screen lit again, and Dunbar reappeared. "Here's what happened in 2001." He folded his hands on the desk and spoke directly to the camera. "I received a phone call from a woman who said a relative of mine was living in poverty in Muskegon. She was the child's mother, and she claimed she needed $3000 to pay her bills and get back on her feet.

"Not being born yesterday, I did some checking through a private investigator. There was indeed a woman named Jeannie Brooks living in North Muskegon in what the investigator called a 'rat-hole'. She had a three-year-old daughter. The investigator interviewed the woman and was told the child's father was Leland Voorhies, my nephew. Leland had left the country a few months before your birth, and Jeannie didn't think he knew he had a child. She had no way to reach him, so she'd contacted me, hoping I would be willing to help.

"Armed with that information, I went to see Ms. Brooks. What I found was beyond my imagination. You, Brodie, were pitiful, afraid of everything and everyone. Believing you could not thrive in that atmosphere, I took you home with me that day. Once you were safe, I tried to get your mother to change her lifestyle, offering whatever help she needed to do so. When it was obvious that she would not, I began negotiations to adopt you."

Dunbar's voice took on a slightly harder tone. "It took some persuasion, but I was eventually successful. I believe your mother realized her life would not be a long one." He frowned slightly. "While I'm not certain I did her justice, I was focused on your welfare. Everything I've done since learning of your existence I did in hopes it was best for you."

He shifted in his chair before beginning again. "Once more, I suggest you leave your personal history at this point. You need know no more, and I fear further explanation will hurt more than it helps. Trust me, Brodie, and live your life looking forward, not back."

The screen went blank again, and Bud pressed the PAUSE button. "Wow."

"You didn't know this?"

"That Brodie was Leland's kid? No."

"Would Mr. Dunbar have contacted Leland to tell him he had a daughter?"

"I doubt it. Leland cheated his own mother, stole one of

our boats, and ran away with the cash Gramps kept in his desk drawer."

"Does Arlis know Brodie is Leland's daughter?"

"No way. She was not happy about Brodie coming to live with us. And Leland would hardly have shared the news of a pregnant girlfriend with her."

"If he even knew this Jeannie was pregnant."

Scarlet picked up the will Bud had brought along. "Leland gets the old family property in Canada."

"Yeah. Arlis talked Gramps into that. She claimed he'd need a place to live when he's too old to do disaster relief anymore. She said it was as much hers as Gramps', since it belonged to their parents."

Scarlet seemed to be only half listening. "If Leland knew Brodie was his daughter and Mr. Dunbar's heir, might he come here, abduct her, and take her back to Canada?"

Bud looked incredulous. "You mean in order to get his hands on her money?"

Scarlet shrugged. "You know him. I don't."

He looked around the room as if trying to escape the conclusion he was forced to accept. "Leland sees nothing but what he wants. I think the term for people like him is *sociopath*."

"A sociopath might do what I said. He wouldn't care what was best for Brodie."

"It's hard to apply that term to someone you once knew well, but it fits." He paced the room, trying to assimilate the new information. Stopping, he asked, "If Leland is the bird watcher Brodie saw, he was here the day of the funeral. Why didn't he just show up, hug his mother, and say, 'I'm back'? The statute of limitations has got to have run out on what he did a decade ago."

"But would he know how you'd react to his return?"

"I suppose not. I certainly wouldn't have let Brodie go with him until I'd done some investigating."

Scarlet smiled grimly. "You don't believe in St. Leland?"

Bud's smile was equally grim. "I was the guy below him in the pecking order, the kid Leland could take advantage of. I always found it hard to believe all that stuff about his philanthropic rebirth." He tapped the will with a finger. "The place in Canada is a perfect place to hide out, though."

"You think he's headed there?"

"That might be where he's been the whole time."

"Of course. He could easily have driven here after Arlis reported Mr. Dunbar's death."

Bud's face took on a faraway look. "Or sailed."

"What?"

"The boat we saw last evening seemed familiar, and now I know why. It was exactly like Gramps' wooden sailboat that Leland stole. It's been re-painted, that's all."

"And it was heading north."

"He takes Brodie and leaves evidence to throw off the search for her." Bud turned off the TV.

"Wait." Scarlet seemed to need time to absorb the conclusions they'd come to in the last few minutes. "So the man on the boat and the bird watcher are the same person, Arlis' son?"

"What exactly did Brodie say about him?"

Scarlet looked up as she recalled. "She said that he was taping bird calls with a small recorder." She frowned, searching her memory. "And that he didn't look the nature boy type."

He spread his hands. "Because he wasn't after birds."

"But he could have taken Brodie then. Why wait?"

"Maybe he didn't have time." Bud started down the stairs. Scarlet followed, hurrying to keep up.

"Where could he have hidden a boat where the police wouldn't find it?"

"A place I'd forgotten about, but I'll bet Leland hadn't."

Breakfast was still laid out in the dining room, and different aromas arose as Bud peered into warming trays. "Have you ever seen the old boathouse?"

"I didn't know there was one."

Bud found scrambled eggs and set the cover aside. "A guy could hide a boat there."

Arlis came in, and Bud shot a warning glance at Scarlet. "Good morning, Aunt Arlis."

"Bud. Miss McMorran." Arlis went to the sideboard, poured some hot water into a cup, and began thumbing through the choices of tea available.

"Arlis," Bud's tone was casual. "Did you talk to Leland yesterday?"

She looked at Bud quizzically. "No. Why?"

Taking some toast from the warmer, Bud fashioned two portable breakfasts: toast, egg, and bacon sandwiches. "I wondered how he'd taken the news of Brodie's disappearance."

"He doesn't know yet, poor thing, but he will be devastated. I tried to phone, but it's often difficult to get through, and of course he's very busy with his work. Still, he's always interested in what goes on here." She gave Bud a beaming smile. "You are all very important to him."

"Even Brodie?"

Arlis removed the teabag and laid it on a small plate. "Of course, Leland doesn't *know* Brodie. I've told him—" She backed up and went a different route. "Lately he's taken some interest in her, I think. Only a day or two ago he asked me all sorts of questions."

"About her studies, things like that?"

"Oh, yes. Now that William has passed, he is interested in how Brodie will adjust. Of course we all feel sorry for the girl, who lost the only person in the world who—" She thought better of that sentence as well and switched gears again. "I told Leland about Miss McMorran's plan to take Brodie out to look for insects yesterday. I thought it was a bit too adventurous, but Leland said it was just the thing to take her mind off her troubles."

"So he was interested in the spider hunt."

"Yes. He even asked me where you expected to find these insects."

Bud noted Scarlet's averted eyes and guessed she found it hard to ignore Arlis' repeated reference to spiders as insects. A teacher is a teacher, even in the midst of a crisis.

"We've got some things to do, this morning, Aunt Arlis, so please excuse us. Handing one of the sandwiches to Scarlet, he said, "Here. We can eat on the way."

Exhausted from stress, lack of sleep, and trying to decide what she did and did not believe of Leland's story, Brodie dozed. Her last waking thought was that it might be nice if Leland was her dad. Wouldn't it?

"Jeannie, the kid looks hungry. What can I give her to eat?" A man Brodie had never seen before leaned over her as she sat on the tattered couch that served as her bed. He backed away, nose twitching, when her odor registered.

The answering voice was muffled. "There's some Doritos on the counter."

"Shouldn't she have cereal or something?"

Jeannie's face did not turn from the pillow. "She likes Doritos."

"But kids need milk and stuff." A snuffle was all the response Jeannie gave. The man leaned toward Brodie again, his whiskered face curious. She held herself very still, not knowing what would happen next. Some of them were

nice. Others threatened her when she cried, and still others joined Jeannie in tormenting her in small ways, finding a three-year-old's anger hilarious.

This guy seemed okay. Turning, he went to the kitchen. "There's some dried cherries in the fridge and some little cans of apple juice."

"Yeah, my neighbor bought her that."

"Why?"

"I don't know. The old guy gives me the creeps, watchin' what I do and shit. But he'll always babysit her if I need to go somewhere, so I'm nice to him."

"Think she can eat those cherries? I wouldn't want her to choke or nothing."

"Go ahead and give 'em to her." Jeannie's tone was flat, as if her daughter choking was of no concern at all. The man handed Brodie a plastic bowl half-filled with dried fruit then opened a juice box by stabbing the foil seal with the attached straw. "Here, kid," he said gruffly. He left her there with the food and went into the bedroom, closing the door. Brodie concentrated on her breakfast of cherries, Doritos, and juice, ignoring the sounds from the room where her mother and this week's lover lay together.

CHAPTER SEVENTEEN

"Seamus! Seamus!" Mildred's voice was like an ice cube running down his spine. Actually, Bud's spine.

"Quiet!" Bud stopped dead, and Scarlet looked at him in concern. Seamus knew his host could not decipher Mildred's words, but he reacted with shock at the commotion inside his head.

"I know, Bud's probably awake," Mildred continued, "but you have to know that the guy who has Brodie is her father, Leland Voorhies."

Seamus didn't answer, unwilling to upset his host any further. He'd been trying to absorb that very fact, wondering why Dunbar hadn't seen fit to mention it.

"Go to Leland." He kept it short, trying to minimize the effect on Bud, whose brain struggled to cope with what sounded like bursts of static between his ears.

"I can't," Mildred answered. "Brodie's very upset, and I need to help her through this."

Her self-righteous tone made Seamus want to shout, *What happened to the woman who promised to do whatever I said? What happened to her agreement we were here to gather information, not to interfere with the living?* For that matter, he added bitterly, what had been so attractive about Mildred that he'd ignored his instincts in the first place and brought her along?

After Leland's revelations, Brodie returned to her bunk and

feigned sleep, trying to make sense of the present situation in terms of what she knew of the past. Memories of her earliest years came mostly in her nightmares, with Jeannie playing the starring, scary lead. Jeannie had hated having a kid. Jeannie had blamed Brodie for all sorts of things the child didn't understand. Crying was bad. Talking was bad. Calling Jeannie "Mommy" was forbidden. Life with Jeannie had been far beyond her understanding. She'd learned early to keep quiet when possible and to attack when keeping quiet didn't work. For some reason, her childish rage amused her mother, and the worst of Jeannie's moods dissipated if Brodie threw a fit.

Jeannie had had good acting skills. She could fake motherly concern when the occasion demanded, toting her daughter around on one hip and crooning endearments when she went out on the streets to beg. Brodie knew better than to believe those times were real.

She'd known kindness from a few people: a neighbor called Amos with a bushy beard and a raspy voice called her "sweetie" and made sure she had something to eat most days. Even some of Jeannie's boyfriends had been good to her, though the nice ones never stayed long. She didn't recall anyone called Daddy, and she was sure she'd never seen the bird watcher before a few days ago.

She must have dozed for a while but woke with the feeling someone had said something to her. Cher was still asleep, though, her mouth slightly open and one ham-shaped leg hanging off the narrow bench. Someone was moving on deck. Leland must be getting ready to cast off.

The hatch was open, so she went on deck. All sign of the previous night's storm was gone, and the lake seemed welcoming and serene.

"Hey, Brodie." Leland sounded almost shy. She gave him a weak smile and sat down to watch him get under way. He unscrewed the anchor from the lakebed and motored briefly to get to deep water. Then he set the sails, moving efficiently from the tiller to the bow, bare feet sure under him despite the movement of the boat. Once they were on the course he'd charted with a GPS, he took a relaxed stand, holding the tiller extension in one hand and looking at the expanse of water ahead. After a few minutes he removed his cap, ran a hand through his hair, and slapped the cap back into place, screwing it slightly to settle it.

"You wonder why I wasn't there for you." Brodie said nothing. She hated people who talked about being "there for" someone or knowing "where you're coming from," making emotions into rooms a person could walk in and out of. Leland scratched at the stubble on his chin. "Here's the thing. I ran into some trouble and had to leave Michigan. I couldn't let anybody know where I went, not even Jeannie. I guess you came along after that. She didn't know what to do, so she gave you to Uncle Will to raise. Because the old—" He stopped to choose a different word than the one he'd almost used. "—man never told Mother who you were, I never knew I had a kid." He smiled. "But when I saw you on the ledge, everything got clear. I knew why he took you in. Just like with Bud, he couldn't stand to let a relative of his suffer."

Leland's expression grew serious and his voice took on a teaching tone. "Bud's all about money, Brodie. Well, money and women. That girlfriend of his will find herself out on her ear someday." He looked up at the wind indicator, adjusted the tiller slightly, and turned back to her. "He's going to want to control you, Brodie, and I don't think that's right. Shouldn't your dad help you decide what to do, not some guy you hardly know?"

When Brodie didn't speak her thought—*I don't know you, either*—he said, "Cher didn't like my idea when I went back that first day and told her about you. She said you'd never see my side of things. But I think blood is thicker than water, you know? I think you're smart enough to figure out that your dad is the person you should be with, not some guy who lives in Chicago and doesn't even care about you or the house and all that."

She tried to look agreeable, knowing her only chance for escape was to lull these people into believing she was on their side. At her forced smile, Leland grinned reassuringly and turned his face forward. At least he was smart enough not to pressure her for an immediate answer.

As Brodie watched Leland's confident movements, she compared her image of Saint Leland to the real version. Arlis' misunderstood son had been the old woman's main topic of conversation since she could remember. "Leland is working with AIDS babies in Ethiopia," she would announce, or "Leland plans to go to Sri Lanka again and work for Doctors without Borders." Brodie had noticed a distinct lack of enthusiasm from Gramps when the subject of Leland arose, but Arlis never seemed to get it. She updated the family on her son's activities as if everyone waited breathlessly to hear his latest exploits for Truth, Justice, and the American Way.

According to Arlis, Leland had made one mistake and spent the last decade making up for it. His only purpose now, she insisted, was doing good in the world.

This guy didn't strike Brodie as that type. Not only did Leland not have the air of serenity she expected from a holy man, Cher seemed unlikely to associate with a do-gooder of any sort. Neither did Leland strike a chord in her, the way she'd always thought a parent would. Brodie had often imagined her dad, who would be a lot like Gramps. His eyes would light with affection when he looked at her, his long-lost daughter. Leland had a definite air of selfishness about him, the same air she'd always sensed in Arlis.

And Bud? Was what Leland said about Bud true? Shelley often shook her head when she spoke of his many girlfriends, the model from Denmark, the assistant district attorney, the Channel Ten reporter, but she never seemed really disapproving. Actually, Brodie didn't recall any stories about Bud's conquests in the last year or so. Maybe he was starting to settle down, as Gramps had always said he would someday.

Bud had never paid much attention to Brodie; that was true. But as she considered the cause, she found it might have been a lot of things: their age difference, Bud's busy life in Chicago, even the small army of crawling things she'd put into his bed when he returned home from college all those years ago. She knew, looking back, that she'd acted from jealousy. Bud was the one person in the world Gramps loved as much as he loved her, and Brodie had wanted to punish him for it. For that and also for being smarter, more attractive, and less crazy than she was.

Bud had offered to help with her money, but he'd made it sound like something they'd do together. Still, she reminded herself, being nice to someone who just inherited a ton of money was very likely to come from selfish motives.

But then, here was her supposed father, being nice after ignoring her all her life. Had he really not known she existed? Despite his charm, Brodie didn't trust the guy. Whether he was really her dad or not, she suspected that more than having his daughter with him, Leland wanted to get his hands on the money Gramps left her. Maybe Bud's motives were the same, but Gramps had trusted Bud. On the subject of Leland he'd been silent, which for Gramps meant he disapproved.

Bud and Scarlet took the golf cart as far down the shore as they could. Past the viewing point, the sandy beach gave way to a swampy spot with dense foliage that grew right to the waterline: birch, jack pine, and cedar so tightly packed they choked each other, resulting in spindly, ragged-looking trees. Equally dense undergrowth had sprung up between them, hardy weeds and bushes that grew waist high, sporting thorns, burrs, and plenty of tiny, intertwined branches.

"No way to get through this stuff without a machete," he told her, "but we can wade around it." He slipped off his shoes and stuffed his socks inside, tying the laces and hanging them around his neck. "It's kind of mucky, but easier going."

Scarlet did as he did but was soon wet to the knees as she tried to avoid trees that leaned out over the water, catching her hair and scraping her arms. He tried to ease her way, holding branches up so that she could pass under them. Some way down, the trees receded and a shallow channel led inland. Bud led the way up the channel, feet sucked downward by the soft muck under the water. The branches of the leaning trees often met overhead, making a tunnel of their passage. He walked in the center, where the water reached their thighs but was clear of snags. He pointed out several places where branches were broken off. "Something's been through here recently."

About thirty yards in, a small stretch of sand gave way to an open space that elevated gradually for a few dozen feet then turned to forest and rose abruptly. They sat down to put their shoes and socks back on. "The original cabin was there," Bud said, pointing. "See the foundation?"

When she located a square of badly cracked concrete and the base of a fieldstone fireplace on their right Scarlet said, "That's all that's left?"

"It burned back in the twenties." He glanced around at the trees that canopied the spot. "Seventy or so years of vegetation overcame most of what the owners cleared."

She looked around. "I don't see a boathouse."

Bud pointed. "There."

Barely visible through the canopy of trees before them was a building so dilapidated as to hardly merit the term. It straddled the far end of narrow inlet they followed, tilting to one side as if it were dizzy. The back section of the roof was caved in, and moss coated the rest. The forest was reclaiming the place, dead though its wood might be.

Bud moved cautiously forward. The structure was built of plank lumber, and a platform ran along the front with stairs at each side that led up to floor level. Ignoring the steps, which appeared too rotten to chance, Bud turned his back to the platform and hefted his rear onto it. Once he was up, he stepped cautiously into the gaping doorway. Assuring himself there was no one inside, he beckoned for Scarlet and helped her up onto the walkway. He led the way inside, stepping carefully on each floorboard before trusting his full weight to it.

"Not exactly welcoming." Scarlet wiped her hands on the rear of her jeans.

"We used to come here as kids," Bud said, his voice echoing off the walls. "I remember being scared of the place but fascinated by it too."

"Ghosts?"

"I guess. Leland liked to scare me with stories about pirates and dead men's chests." He turned in a circle, looking up. "It seemed a lot bigger then."

"Look!" Scarlet said, pointing at the inner edge of the walkway. A fresh scrape marked the wood. "From the hull of a boat?"

Kneeling, Bud examined the scrape. "Leland hid the boat in here, stayed long enough to catch Brodie alone, and took her away." He pressed a hand to his forehead. "And I watched him go."

"We need to get the police in here."

She was right. He had to stop thinking of what he hadn't done and concentrate on what must be done. "And you and I need to look at the rest of that DVD. Leland wants control of Brodie's money. That's why he took her instead of coming forward openly."

"He figures you won't stop him if Brodie chooses to stay with him." Scarlet bit her lip. "All he has to do is give her what she lost when Mr. Dunbar died."

Bud nodded. "The feeling that she belongs somewhere."

"Not!" Mildred told Brodie firmly. "Not!" She could not believe the girl would even consider that Leland was telling the truth.

Brodie shook her head as if trying to shake something loose. "What are you doing?" Cher asked, irritation in her voice.

"Nothing."

Mildred reminded herself not to be too forceful. "Not," she whispered. "He's not your friend."

He might be her father, Mildred thought, *but Leland is a bad man. I can feel it.*

Reiner responded quickly to Bud's phone call, and Bud met him on the beach and led the way to the boathouse. Warned about the location, Reiner had brought waders, and he clomped ashore clumsily, peeling off the high boots and leaving them standing on the shore like half a man.

The two entered the old boathouse, where Scarlet waited impatiently. "I found something, but I didn't want to touch it until someone in authority was present." Avoiding rotted and uneven boards, she led the two men to a spot at the front corner of the boathouse. Weeds grew against the lichen-covered wall, but a man-made something shone among the leaves.

Reiner knelt to examine the object. "What is it?" Bud asked, peering over the deputy's shoulder.

"It's a mini-cassette player." Taking a camera from his pocket, Reiner took two pictures of the item in place. Pulling a rubber glove onto his right hand, he picked it up and took it out into the light so he could see the instructions on the buttons. He pressed "play" and started slightly when the noise of an animal in pain came from the small device.

"That's the sound I heard the day Gramps died!" Bud said. "It's what led me into the woods."

Reiner slid the recorder into a plastic bag from his pocket. "I think I know what happened." His expression warned they wouldn't like what he had to say. "Brodie likes pranks. You know that."

Scarlet opened her mouth to disagree, but Reiner put up a hand. "Everyone around here's heard about them, so listen for a minute. Suppose she thought she'd pull a trick on Bud and her grandfather." He turned to Bud. "She plants this thing in the woods and draws you away from the bluff. She thinks it's real funny, you climbing through the jack pines looking for a hurt animal. But in the meantime, Mr. Dunbar gets dizzy and falls over the edge." He raised both hands. "How is a kid going to feel about that? She knows her stupid trick is responsible for her grandfather's death. That's why she ran away."

"We don't think she ran away," Scarlet said, but her tone was for once uncertain. The scenario the deputy outlined was possible.

Reiner's jaw set, but he didn't argue. "Whether she ran away or not, we'll find her. We've got a lot of people looking."

"To the south. But the boat I saw was heading north." On the walk in, Bud had explained his theory that Leland had been on the property, but Reiner seemed doubtful. "You saw a boat on Lake Michigan, Bud. That's not exactly a unique experience around here in July. You don't know for sure it was the boat that was here, or that any boat was here, for that matter."

"There's a mark on the timbers, there." Scarlet pointed to the scrape they'd found.

"And there's a freshly cut tree over there," Bud said, pointing out the raw stump. "He used it to block visibility from the lake."

"Okay, so somebody stayed in here. There was a storm coming, and you know what docking fees are at the marina. The guy was trying to save himself a few bucks."

"But how would anyone know there was a boathouse here?"

"Luck. He sees the inlet, comes in, and gets a free night's rest, out of the storm." Reiner's voice took on a reasoning-with-overwrought-relatives tone. "Bud, Lake Michigan is a big area to search. We have to go with what's most likely. Brodie's message said Chicago and mentioned a train." He relented slightly as he began climbing into his waders. "I'll talk to the state police, tell them what you've told me. They'll decide what to do. They've got more experience with these things than either you or me."

Bud's shoulders slumped. "Thanks, Frank. I appreciate that."

Reiner took a few steps away then returned. "Listen, I gave you a hard time earlier. I—" His lips worked as he sought the right words. "I'm sorry about your grandfather's accident."

Bud got the message. "Forget it."

Rolling his shoulders, Reiner assured them, "If Brodie took off alone, we'll find her. If she went with some guy, we'll find the two of them." He pressed his lips together briefly before finishing with what sounded like a warning. "And if the man is her father, we'll see what happens once we're all in the same room."

The little boat continued northward. The day was perfect for sailing, with a brisk wind, a remnant of last night's storm, that sent them flying across the waters of the lake. For the first hour or so, Cher worked on word-finds as if the fate of the world depended on them. Brodie ate some potato chips and drank a Sprite, which made her stomach feel queasy. She winced to think what Shelley would say about a breakfast like that, but there was nothing else. Cher apparently didn't eat breakfast, and Leland popped open a Red Bull and drank it all at once.

Brodie was staring out the window, watching the shoreline, when Cher closed the book with a sigh and an air of finality. "You like puzzles?"

Brodie shrugged. "Sometimes."

"Keep you from gettin' Old Timers', eh?" She tapped the book with a blunt finger. Brodie tried to form an interested expression so the woman would keep talking.

Cher seemed willing now that she had no other entertainment. "So you're Lee's kid, huh?"

Brodie shrugged again. No sense mentioning that she had her doubts.

"He sure got excited after he saw you. Kept tellin' me how you look like your mother." After a pause, she added, "Guess Lee likes his women raven-haired, like the romance novels call it." She touched her own lank black hair, pushing it back behind her ears.

Inside Brodie's head, a voice said, "Talk!" The word repeated until she felt like screaming in despair. The crazy voice was back—exactly what she didn't need. It repeated, "Talk! Talk!"

She had to admit that talking wasn't a bad idea. Cher might tell her things she needed to know.

"How did you meet him?"

It was Cher's turn to shrug. "He came to the town where I grew up. I was working in a bar. He seemed like the best thing I ever seen." Her face softened, and she almost smiled. "That guy can charm the pants right off a girl, eh?"

"Hmm."

Cher shifted on the plastic seat, making a coming-unstuck sound with her bare thighs. "Of course, that was a long time ago. I learned since then to look past the charm. We do okay together most of the time, 'cept when he gets these dumb ideas."

"Like coming to Michigan?"

"Oh, that wasn't a bad idea." Cher's expression said there was more she could have added but would not. "Snatching you? That was a bad idea."

"Why?"

"For one thing, it puts us in the state at a particular time, which we were not supposed to let anyone know about. People at home think we went camping for a few days."

"Where do you live?"

"Lee has a place, a lodge. We get hunters, fishermen, a few leaf-lookers in the fall." She pushed the hair behind her ears again. "If you can make 'em think it's cool to sleep in a cabin with no electricity and a pump in one corner, you can make a living."

"He doesn't go all over the world helping with disasters and stuff?"

Cher gave a knowing snicker. "You've been listening to his mother." She rubbed her nose with the back of one hand. "We get a kick out of her—so thrilled at Leland's good deeds."

Brodie was putting what Cher described together with things she'd heard from Gramps. "The place you come from. Is it north of Horn-something?"

"Hornpayne. Yeah." Cher looked at her sideways, as if spying into her mind. "Okay, so it isn't his place yet. But it will be, now the old man is dead."

"Leland moved into Gramps' lodge?"

Cher's lip curled. "Nobody here cared about it, did they? He needed a place when they chased him out of Michigan." She sounded as if Leland's troubles had been her own even before they met.

"When him and me got together, I moved in. It was a real dump back then, but neither of us had any money, so it was better than nothing. Then I said, 'Why don't we sell the timber, eh?' Up there, if you're willing to sell trees and you look like you might own the rights, there are guys who'll buy 'em. With the money we got for that, we fixed the place up some so we could rent out the cabins." She tapped her cigarette ashes onto the floor. "I do the cooking and cleaning, Lee does the guiding and schmoozing." She huffed a half-admiring, half-disgusted sound. "A musty old lodge, a buggy trek through the woods, and Lee telling stories over a few beers in the evening. The guests always leave feeling like they've been treated special. He's got a knack for that."

Brodie didn't know where to start with her questions. "But is he Canadian?"

"Lee's mother is, so he's got dual citizenship."

Brodie guessed that had paved the way for a lot of what Leland had subsequently done. Once he'd lived on the property for a year or two, people would assume he owned it. He could prove he was Canadian, he could prove he was a member of the Dunbar family. Being an experienced criminal, he'd probably forged any other documents he needed.

She asked Cher the question that mattered most to her. "So we're going to the lodge?"

"For a while anyway, till we can sell it. Prospecting is up

since the price of gold went so high, and there are all kinds of people looking to buy land in the area. We plan to cash in, but we gotta do it now, before the prices go down again. That's why—" Cher abandoned that thought and frowned at Brodie. "Only Lee thinks he's got something better, now he knows about you."

So it was about the money. Brodie tried not to be hurt that yet another person didn't really care about her. *You knew better*, she told herself. *Only Gramps cared, and Gramps is dead.*

The crazy voice started up then. "Okay," it whispered. "Okay. Okay."

It was more than she could take at this point. Even her slim hope that Leland, her possible father, might actually want her around—her, not her money—was obviously not true. And now her mind, which was all she really had, was acting crazy again, whispering things that were not, could not be true. It was not okay. Nothing was okay. Nothing would ever be okay again.

Leaving Cher fishing for yet another cigarette, Brodie went up on deck, anger deeper than any she'd ever known boiling inside her. She dared not speak, dared not let either of her captors know how upset she was. She loosed all of her anger on herself and on the voice that kept trying to tell her the opposite of what she knew to be true.

Tensing her whole body, she concentrated with every ounce of her being. *Leave!* She ordered. *I don't want voices in my head. I want to be like everybody else, and I—want—you—gone!*

To her shock, she felt an easing of her mind, a lightening of her body. The nausea she'd felt for several days seemed to dissipate, and she stood a little straighter. Worst—or best—of all, she couldn't have said which, something hovered beside her, a vague form that seemed unwilling to leave but unable to stay in the face of her rage. It almost had a face, and the face looked sad.

Then it was gone. A few feet away, Leland grasped his stomach, looking a little green. "I guess I shouldn't have had that Red Bull for breakfast," he said. "It isn't sitting very well."

CHAPTER EIGHTEEN

Bud was drawn to the lakeshore. He stood staring northward, unconsciously revealing a desire to follow the boat he was certain had taken Brodie away. His mind conjured pictures of her in different phases of her life, the wild-haired three-year-old, the silent, solemn-faced child, the girl who seemed always to be nearby when he came home to visit. She'd said little, so he'd done no more than make the obligatory conversational overtures: "How are your studies going?" and "What's your favorite subject?" He often got only a shrug in answer, but Gramps would step in, asking specifics. He got answers, though Brodie had always seemed nervous. Still, she hadn't avoided his company. When he was home, she'd curl up with a book in a corner of whichever room he and Gramps were in. She'd appeared to be reading, but Bud often thought she wasn't. Arlis said she was a sneak who liked to eavesdrop on adult conversations. It dawned on him now that Brodie might have wanted to be part of those conversations.

Hearing steps behind him, he turned to find Scarlet, who stopped beside him, looking in the same direction. "How will they find her?" she asked softly. "Reiner's right. The lake is big."

"If Leland gets through the Straits of Mackinac, it will be even harder. He'll be in Canada by tomorrow noon."

"The Coast Guard patrols the straits. They must have radar or something."

"Leland's a good sailor, and radar isn't good at picking up a wooden boat. If he passes through at night, who'll see him?"

His eyes narrowed as he stared at the water. "Gramps took us all over up there when we were kids. I know where Leland might go better than anyone else." He looked toward the boathouse, where Briggs banged on something with what might have been a sledge hammer. "The storm last night must have set him back. He'll be off his schedule."

Scarlet's head turned slightly as she regarded Bud. "I know what you're thinking.

Bud nodded. "We've got the Starcraft. It's fast and it's ready to go. I could catch him."

Inside Bud's head, Seamus reacted with distress. A boat? What normal person would choose a boat under his feet when he could have four tires on solid pavement? *Drive!* he whispered urgently. *Drive!* Bud ignored him, mentally making a list of what he'd need for a couple of nights on a boat.

"—a huge head start," Scarlet was saying.

Bud's lips tightened. Seamus was considering a jump when she said, "—we might catch them."

"We?" Bud sounded surprised. Seamus was stricken. It seemed he was going for a boat ride, no matter what.

"You know it's dangerous to do this alone. You're recovering from a head injury, and I'll bet you got almost no sleep last night." She looked at him, ready to meet whatever argument he posed. "You know I can handle a boat." Sensing his indecision, she added, "We're going to locate them, call the Coast Guard, and report where they are, right? There's no danger involved."

Bud considered it. "All right. I could use the help, and

Briggs is no sailor."

"You're the boss," Scarlet promised. "I'll be like a ghost, hovering nearby and following orders."

Bud seemed convinced. "Let's get ready to go."

"Wait," Scarlet said, taking his arm. "We need to see the end of the video Mr. Dunbar made."

Bud made an impatient gesture. "Why? He said it was about Brodie's past."

"We need to know everything we can about the situation. If Leland is Brodie's father, and if she did go willingly, we might not have any legal right to stop them."

Bud raised his eyebrows at her. "But you were sure Brodie wouldn't have done that."

Scarlet's lower lip set firmly against the upper one. "There's no telling what that man has told her. It's best we learn what we can. Between a story Leland might have told and what's on that video, I'd definitely lean toward your grandfather's version."

"Good point. I'll ask Briggs to get the boat ready. Pack a few things and we'll watch the rest of what Gramps had to say before we take off."

In only a few minutes, they were again in Scarlet's room. She'd put some things in a gym bag, and Bud set a similar one on the floor beside hers with a soft thud. "Ready?" she asked. When he nodded, she pressed some buttons on the remote.

William Dunbar appeared for a third time on the screen. The video was grainier than the earlier segments had been, and Dunbar was dressed differently. He wasn't alone. "That's our lawyer at the time, Collin Marks' father Ben," Bud told Scarlet.

Across a table from them sat a woman and a man. The man had the same professional demeanor as Marks, and Bud deduced he was a lawyer representing the woman's interest. She had to be Jeannie, Brodie's mother. It was possible to see that she had once been attractive, but her looks were ruined by sores on her face, circles under her eyes, and a general aura of decline.

Marks spoke first. "We are here with Ms. Jean Brooks and her attorney to discuss the formal adoption of her daughter Brodie by my client, William Dunbar. Mr. Dunbar asked that the proceedings be videotaped so all parties are aware of the parameters and there is no confusion about them in the future." He cleared his throat.

"In other words," Bud put in, "they didn't want Ms. Brooks coming back later and claiming they stole her child."

"Ms. Brooks," Marks said in a tone devoid of emotion. "Would you please explain what you propose to Mr. Dunbar?"

Jeannie looked at her lawyer, who nodded slightly. "He wants to adopt my kid. It's okay with me as long as I get something out of it."

"And what amount have you agreed to?"

"Fifty thousand." Anger flared briefly, and she said, "That ain't much for me to give up my kid. I agreed 'cause I know I can't care for her like I should." She attempted a pitiful look that didn't quite form before going on. "And I get the money today, right?"

William Dunbar nodded, his face blank.

"If your nephew wasn't a crook, I'da been okay." The woman leaned toward Dunbar accusingly. "He took off and left me without a pot to piss in!"

Dunbar made as if to say something, but Marks silenced him with a gesture. "Ms. Brooks, you understand that you are giving up custody of your daughter permanently."

Jeannie didn't hesitate. "Yeah. I got it."

"All right, then. Mr. Winters, will you step out with me and look over the documents before we ask our clients to sign them?"

The two lawyers left the room, which seemed odd to Bud. After a moment, he realized it was purposeful, at least on Gramps' part. Jeannie Brooks had apparently forgotten the video camera was there.

"So now you got a pretty little girl to show off to all your rich friends," she said after a brief silence. "What if I need more money later?"

"There won't be any more." Dunbar's tone was flat and cold.

"Not even if I clean up my act?"

"You had that chance. I won't offer again."

"So Brodie grows up rich, and I'm s'pose to get lost!" She seemed jealous of her own child.

"You're the one who threw away your life, young woman. If you don't sign the papers today, I'll work through the court system and get custody of Brodie anyway. It's only because I never want her to return to that hellhole you live in that I offer this settlement."

"It ain't enough."

Gramps shrugged. "Refuse it. You'll get nothing when the state takes her away from you."

"I can't help it if I'm sick!"

Dunbar seemed genuinely sad as he nodded agreement. "You are sick, but I see no sign that you want to get well. I can't help you, but I will help Brodie."

The door opened then, and the two lawyers returned. The camera recorded a final statement by Jeannie's lawyer warning that her signature meant she relinquished all rights to the child. With a last squint of anger at Dunbar, Jeannie scrawled her name in the required spaces. The rest of it took only a minute or two: signatures from the others present, the presentation of a check to Jeannie. No one offered to shake hands with her, though the lawyers shook hands with each other and with Gramps. Jeannie stared at the check as if mesmerized.

After the lawyers left, Dunbar remained behind. He seemed torn, and Bud wondered if he might make another offer of help. If that was his inclination, Jeannie ruined it.

"I shoulda got more money," she cried, tucking the check into the pocket of her jeans. "She's my kid! Mine and your nephew's!"

"Actually, Brodie is not Leland's child," Gramps said calmly.

Jeannie's face revealed anger rather than surprise. "You don't know that."

"I had DNA tests run. Brodie is unrelated to him." He leaned toward her, resting his fists on the polished surface of the table. "You were seeing another man at the time of Brodie's conception, only days after Leland left the country."

Jean made a dismissive gesture. "He was just some guy I met at a club."

"It apparently didn't take him long to discover that you were addicted to drugs."

"Jerry was a jerk." She seemed to like the sound of it. "Jerry the Jerk."

Dunbar opened a file near his hand, looked briefly at the top sheet, and closed it again. "You know him better than I, of course, but my investigator believes him to be an honest man. He might have done right by you if you'd told him you were expecting."

"Yeah, right. And spend my life with a guy who installs satellite dishes for a living!"

Dunbar eyed her with distaste. "He has a wife and a child now, with another on the way. From what I'm told, his wife is not the type who would—" He didn't finish, but his concern was obvious. Good old Jerry was a nice guy who picked the wrong sort of women. "I've decided, arbitrarily, I admit, that Brodie is better off with me. I'll treat her as a member of the family." He paused before adding, "Despite your lies."

Jeannie didn't have an answer for that, and for a moment even seemed ashamed. Then she rallied, rising and pulling her selfishness around her like a protective cloak. "Well, you got what you want, and I did too." Holding her head so high that the chords in her neck stood out, she left the room. Dunbar held the door then followed her out, and the camera saw nothing more.

As the screen went blank, Scarlet turned to Bud, her eyes wide. "Brodie isn't related to Mr. Dunbar at all, but he took her in anyway."

"That was Gramps," Bud said, swallowing a lump in his throat. "Quite a guy."

As they went down the stairs they met Arlis, apparently headed for an appointment. Her silver hair lay in soft waves around her face, and Bud noted, as he often did, her resemblance to her brother. That brought a question to mind.

"Arlis, you said Leland takes an interest in the family."

She was checking the contents of her purse, her lips moving as she cataloged what was there. She snapped it shut, satisfied, and looked at Bud, her face glowing with pride. "He says the world is his family, but a person can't help but care about the one he was born into, as well."

"Did he know I planned to take Gramps up to watch the race?"

Her expression turned questioning, but she answered willingly enough. "Yes, I think we did talk about it once or twice. He knew of William's interest, and I mentioned last spring that you intended to come home as usual and take him up to the viewing point to watch the boats pass."

"What did he say to that?"

Arlis took a step back, as if Bud planned to attack her. "What are all these questions about?"

"Aunt Arlis, it's very important that you answer me as honestly as you can. I'll explain everything later, but I need to know what Leland said about Gramps watching the race."

"Not much, really. He said it was good of you to come home to do that. He asked if I went up with you." She tittered. "Of course I said that was not my idea of a day's entertainment. Especially in this heat!" Apparently sensing Bud was waiting for more, she drummed her fingertips against her lips, trying to remember. "He asked if anyone else went along. I said no, that I thought you two liked the idea of going on your own. Will looked forward to the time with you, and the rest of us knew it."

"Thank you."

Arlis hesitated, glanced at Scarlet, and started for the door. Sensing there was something she wanted to say, Bud walked with her. Scarlet hung back, apparently sensing the same thing.

Outside, Arlis stopped and faced him, though she didn't meet his eyes, looking instead at her age-spotted hands. "My appointment this morning is about moving into Bliss Senior Living."

Bud was surprised by the news, but relieved too.

Arlis didn't wait for him to respond. "I've thought about it, and it seems best for everyone if I move out. I'm sorry I won't be able to stay and help Miss McMorran with Brodie, but to be honest, I'm too old for teenagers. You have your work in Chicago, and I don't want to be the one responsible for her." She bustled slightly, glad to have disposed of an uncomfortable topic. "I have friends at Bliss, and the apartments there are lovely." She added one more item to her list. "They have a choir."

Bud paused, not wanting to appear too eager at her news or so devastated that she reconsidered. "If that's really what you want, Aunt Arlis, I'll see that your financial needs are met."

"Thank you, Bud." She looked at the driveway surface. "It's a nice place." Her gaze returned to him. "And you can always come and visit."

Bud took his aunt into his arms and planted a kiss on her forehead. "I know you loved William. I'm sorry things can't be as you'd like them to be."

Arlis' eyes filled with tears. "I did wish William could have forgiven Leland for the foolishness from before. He's a different man, now, but William could never see it."

Bud walked Arlis to her car and helped her inside as Scarlet hung back. The old woman seemed pleased at the attention, but he felt like a Judas goat leading a lamb to destruction. Arlis' answers to his questions had convinced him that Gramps had been right to mistrust Leland. He wasn't only a con man. He was very likely a murderer as well.

Seamus, learning along with Bud where Brodie had come from, had a lot to think about. First, if Leland had killed once, he might kill again. He apparently thought he was Brodie's father. It was hard to predict what he would do if he learned the truth, especially under pressure.

He paused to ponder the morality of Dunbar's choice. Had the guy been wrong to buy the child from her drug-impaired mother? Using money to circumvent the law was probably bad, but the courts would have taken months, perhaps years, to achieve what Brodie needed: a permanent, loving home. Maybe money was good in the hands of good people.

Bud's condition worried Seamus. Not yet fully recovered from his head injury, his thoughts were even slower than usual for the living. Bud was on the right path now, though Seamus would have preferred a land route to Mackinac. He vowed he wouldn't overload his host's already aching head if he could avoid it.

William Dunbar had asked Seamus to determine if he'd been pushed and if so, who'd done it. Seamus now had in Leland a suspect with motive, means, and opportunity. He could go back to the ship and report the matter closed, but Seamus couldn't do that. He felt compelled to do two things before he went back: help Bud rescue Brodie, and in the process, achieve justice for Dunbar.

Neither of those things would be easy. Bud might not be able to find Leland's boat, despite his optimism. It was unlikely the Coast Guard could do it either, given the amount of traffic at the Straits and Leland's familiarity with the area. The best option, Seamus decided, was to mobilize a force already in place. With a mental sigh of resignation at having to burden his wounded host with more nagging, he whispered for the first of many times, "Racers."

When Cher came up on deck with a sunhat and a romance novel, Brodie decided it was a good time to go below and rest. She wasn't usually one for naps, but her sleep the night before had been fitful at best. Besides, she had a strong desire to be wherever Cher was not.

She stretched out on the bunk, but it was really close down there. Cigarette smoke hung over her head, waiting to choke her if she sat upright. Holding her breath, she opened both ports. That was a little better, but unfortunately, getting rid of the smoke meant she could hear Cher, who was sitting right next to the window, talking to Leland. She didn't hear it all, but what she heard was enough.

It started when Leland said something to Cher. Brodie heard her own name but no more. The tone, however, was coaxing.

"Look, Lee. I told you not to do this, but you did it anyway. That was stupid."

His reply was unintelligible.

"They're gonna know you were in Frankfort." At his reply, she made a rude sound. "Yeah, right. You just happened to be there. Who's gonna believe that?"

Again he said something Brodie couldn't make out, but Cher's smoky voice was clear. "You'd better have a plan, that's all I'm saying. You need to think about how we can cover our tracks if things don't go the way you want."

Seamus found it hard not to shout aloud when Bud finally got the message he'd repeated over and over. After several hours of motoring at almost top speed, Seamus was at least as nauseated as his host, but he kept repeating, "Racers."

Finally, it sunk in. Scarlet, who was piloting the boat, watched the water ahead while Bud made several phone calls. Her expression revealed curiosity, but true to her word, she remained quiet.

"I talked to the sheriff's department at the Straits," he said, closing the phone. "Reiner called them, and they're on the lookout for Leland's boat."

"But you said he'll slip through at night, when it's dark. Can they cover the whole area?"

"Probably not. For one thing, they're dealing with the aftermath of the storm. Some boats suffered damage, and there's a kayaker missing over on the Cheboygan side." He slid the phone into the zippered pocket of his shorts. "I called a buddy from Chicago who sailed in the race. He says quite a few people I know are still up there, and he volunteered to round up some help."

Scarlet looked doubtful. "What can a bunch of celebrating yachtsmen do?"

"Help the Coast Guard and the sheriff's department with their patrols."

"All night?"

"If that's what it takes."

Her doubt turned to approval. "That's really good of them."

"They're good people." Bud rolled the tension from his shoulders. "Looking back, it was mostly Leland and his dad who took the fun out of racing for me. Most of the guys who are up there right now are great. They'll take finding Leland and stopping him as a challenge."

"You've got quite a challenge yourself." Scarlet frowned at the bandaged spot on Bud's scalp. "There isn't much you can do right now. You should get some rest."

Seamus felt Bud's brief inner battle between doing what he felt he should do and doing what made sense. "Four hours," he finally told Scarlet. "Then it's your turn. You're as sleep-deprived as I am." He hesitated, looking at the darkening sky. "Sure you're all right?"

She chuckled. "How hard is it to keep going straight ahead? Now off with you!"

Bud gave Scarlet a comical salute and moved to the bench seat that spanned the boat's stern. No sooner had he made himself comfortable than his phone rang, vibrating the pocket of his shorts.

"Hello?"

"Buddy, it's me."

"Callie."

"I heard about Brodie going missing. That's terrible."

"Is Arnold still providing inside information?"

"Buddy, don't be mad at Arnold. I wanted to know about you, about what you were like and what you were doing. He didn't really do anything wrong."

Seamus agreed with Bud's unspoken thought: *That's your opinion.* What Bud said was, "I'm sort of in the middle of things right now, Callie."

"I understand, Babe, and I wouldn't bother you for anything, but it's kind of important. What we were talking about before. Have you thought about it?"

"Honestly, no."

"Look, Buddy. I'm your mother. I loved your father very, very much, and if he hadn't died, we would have been a perfect little family. I was a wreck for a while, I admit that, and I let that old coot talk me into things I should never have agreed to. Now that he's out of the picture, you and I need to get to know each other. Start over."

Bud had reacted to "old coot" and "out of the picture." Seamus felt his anger, but his voice was even as he asked, "What exactly do you need right away?"

Callie's pleased tone easily crossed miles of lake water. "I need twenty thousand right away, Babe. I mean, as soon as you've dealt with this Brodie thing. Maybe Monday?"

Her phrasing, her repeated fake endearments, and her confidence turned Bud cold. This woman, as close to him in blood as a person can be, was using their relationship in the most calculating way possible. Her reference to "this Brodie thing" was offhand and dismissive. Brodie's life was in danger, and Callie's concern was that it delayed her acquisition of a share of the Dunbar fortune, a share she'd given up along with her only child two decades ago.

Bud massaged the back of his neck with his free hand,

trying to ease the knots. "I'll call Collin right away and tell him to arrange it. He won't get the message till morning, but he'll contact you. Is this the number he should call?"

There was a pause, as if she hadn't expected it to be quite that easy. "Well, yes."

"Good. Here's the deal. Collin will send you twenty thousand. Then he'll set up a monthly stipend."

"Babe, that's so—"

"Wait until you hear the rest. The stipend will be enough to keep you in a modest apartment with reasonable expenses. It continues until you remarry. In return, you agree to never contact me again."

"Buddy—"

"That's what you have to do to get a share of my money, Callie. You have to give me up, like you did all those years ago."

"But I'm your mother!"

"That's something I'll always have to deal with. But I don't have to deal with you."

He almost hung up, because there was no response for some time. When Callie finally spoke, her voice was different. "I'll take fifty, in a lump sum." The odd streak of honesty showed up again. "That will catch me up, and I'll marry Nick. He's a bore, but he'll give me more than a 'modest' apartment with 'reasonable' expenses." Her voice was bitter as she emphasized the words she objected to.

"That's the deal, then. I hope it works out well for you,

Callie," Bud said. "I really do."

After that call, Seamus didn't think Bud would ever go to sleep. He lay back on the bench seat and watched the stars for some time, his mind a twisted skein of tension. However, the rhythmic movement, the drone of the engine, and exhaustion from last twenty-four hours at last combined to lull him into slumber. Seamus waited impatiently for him to drop into real sleep. It was after ten, and he hoped Brodie might also be asleep by now. He needed to know what was happening on that sailboat.

"Millie!" he called out softly.

"Seamus? Where are you?"

The answer was terse. "Boat."

"A boat? I thought you hated boats."

"Sometimes a guy doesn't get a choice."

"You got Bud to come after us?"

"Not quite the way I planned it. Bud and Scarlet and I are behind you in Dunbar's powerboat. They plan to travel all night and catch Leland before he reaches the Straits. Coast Guard is out looking for you, along with the sheriff's department and some boaters from the race."

"That's good, but we have to be careful. I'm worried about Cher—" her voice faded for a moment, and then he heard, "could be violent."

"Share? Share what?"

"Cher! C-H-E—. She's Leland's—friend."

He tried to piece together what he was hearing. "You

never said there was someone else there."

"Well, it's a little—icult to keep every—straight."

There was a pause that went on a little too long, and Seamus said, "Mildred? Are you there?"

Her voice came faintly. "Yes.—Leland—awake, and—conversa—is upset—him."

"Leland? You're with Leland?"

Mildred's voice crackled and faded, and all he got of her response was, "—thrown out." After that was silence. Seamus wanted badly to speak to her again but concluded an answer was unlikely. With a wakeful host, there could be all sorts of bad results. They didn't want Leland in a frantic state where he might do something foolish.

Mildred had said "thrown out." He guessed she had "encouraged" Brodie to a point where the girl rejected her. He'd heard it could be done. Free will meant no one could be forced to serve as a host. They simply didn't know they were hosts most of the time. Aware of Mildred's voice in her head, Brodie might have asserted her will and expelled the interloper.

If the situation hadn't been otherwise desperate, Seamus might have enjoyed the fact that Mildred now understood from real world experience the advice she'd refused to accept from an expert.

CHAPTER NINETEEN

It was dark when Brodie woke with the feeling that something had changed. She sensed a slowing of forward progress and realized Leland had shut down the motor. Everything went silent. A sharp pull to the right tipped her sideways in the bunk. The boat had turned toward shore.

His voice came down the hatch, low-pitched and tight. "Something wrong up there, Cher. Gotta heave to and see what's up. Brod, you stay out of sight, hon."

Apparently satisfied when Brodie didn't actively deny their relationship, Leland had taken to acting as if the two of them were of the same mind. He called her "Brod" in an apparent attempt at casual familiarity. Cher's stare was hostile, though, and she took a serrated knife from a drawer and held it at her side, ready.

As the boat swung to the south, Brodie peered out the porthole. There wasn't much to see. Not only was it the middle of the night, but lights ahead of them were cloaked in mist. South of their position was a town, but its lights were mere blurs. Ahead was the Mackinac Bridge. A graceful arc of amber bulbs illuminated its highest points, but below that, a low-lying bank of fog clung to the bridge deck, leaving the massive towers exposed above it as if they floated unsupported in the air.

Struck by the odd effect, Brodie almost failed to notice what Leland had referred to as something wrong. Under the bridge was a second, different line of lights, some high over the waterline, some just above it. Definitely not part of the bridge, these lights were obscured but not invisible in the fog. In several places a dozen lights clustered together, in other spots, only one or two penetrated dimly. It added up to an irregular string that stretched all the way along the bridge, thin in places and thick in others, but definitely in the way of anyone passing through.

Brodie stared, unable to figure it out. Finally she heard Leland mutter, "They're boats."

He was right. Boats of differing sizes and shapes had lined up along the bridge. Each one had whatever lights it possessed focused ahead: running lights, searchlights, floodlights. It was clear those on board intended to make passage under the bridge without notice impossible.

Someone knew they were coming and planned to stop Leland from getting to Canada. What would he do now?

The answer became obvious as the boat continued southward. They were heading for land.

Bud took the helm at midnight, insisting Scarlet retreat to the bench seat and rest. He traveled as fast as he dared, careful to watch the charts, the instruments, and the water ahead in order to steer clear of hazards they might encounter in the dark: floating debris, sandbars, even other boats.

With several hours' time to himself, he thought again of Brodie. He tried to concentrate on what he'd do once she was safe again rather than what might happen or might have happened to her already. The long trip gave him a chance to think, really think, about things, and he realized Brodie had grown up while he was focused on other things.

He knew she was intelligent. He could see she was turning into a real beauty. And he trusted Scarlet's judgment that she was a good person. Brodie had seen that Gramps' mind was failing and protected him the best way she could, taking the heat rather than have others find out what Gramps hadn't wanted them to know—what he hadn't been able to admit, even to himself.

With Gramps' love and Scarlet's help, Brodie had overcome the early neglect of her so-called mother. He knew how it felt to be the kid with no parents, the kid whose grandfather showed up for Parents' Night and the Little League picnic. Brodie'd had it worse, though. The wounds her mother had inflicted were beginning to heal, if such wounds ever really healed. He should have seen their likenesses, should have been more help to her. Bud hoped he'd get the chance to let Brodie know he was proud of her. Despite her odd ways and her stubborn refusal to conform, she was by far the best of the family he had left.

His phone tingled its cue that a text message had arrived. Digging it out of his pocket, Bud read a note from Reiner. "Found Arnold at LR casino. Knows nothing. No sign of B on trains." Bud grimaced. He should have thought to tell them to check at Little River. Arnold's love of the slots was well-known, and he was no doubt consoling himself on the loss of his job by gambling he'd strike it big and never have to look for another one.

As the night passed and the lights on the shore slid by, Bud's thoughts returned to what lay ahead and the fears those thoughts created. Brodie was in danger, and thoughts of what might happen to her if he was wrong, if he was too late, if he was too rash, rattled in his head like tennis shoes in a dryer. He tried to push worry to the back of his mind so he could think about how to do this right, but it took constant effort. Fears leaked around the edges of the walls he erected to keep them out. His head hurt worse than he'd ever experienced before, the combination of physical pain and mental agony.

Mildred did not like being part of Leland Voorhies' thoughts. The man was completely unprincipled, unable to imagine that anything he did to get what he wanted could ever be wrong.

Leland's attitude toward Brodie seemed somewhat affectionate. He liked the idea of having a daughter, a pretty young woman with eyes like her mother's. He hoped to win the girl over to his side. *Poor kid needs somebody,* Leland thought more than once as he piloted the boat through the night. *Now that the old man is gone, she'll be grateful to have a real home and somebody to help her handle her money.* He didn't dwell on how William Dunbar had been removed from the earth, but Mildred heard enough to confirm her suspicions.

When Leland spotted the line of boats under the bridge

and turned aside, Cher came on deck, her expression determined. Leland tensed for confrontation. *Cher doesn't get it, doesn't understand how easily I can charm the girl now that Bud is out of the picture.* He marshaled his arguments. Because of this little snag at the bridge, Cher was going to be difficult.

"We gotta talk, Lee."

"Cher, I've got it covered. Help me with this, and we'll be right back on track. Think of the money. It isn't just the hundred thousand we could get for selling the lodge. It's millions."

She waved a palm in front of him as if trying to wake him from a dream. "You're never gonna get your hands on it. She don't like you, no matter what you think. And that Bud guy will figure out how to charge you with international kidnapping or something. Then where will you be?"

"I'm her father, Cher. It will take some time, but she'll come around."

"Maybe, but if she don't, you'd better have a plan. If they catch us before you get her on our side, she's poison." Cher paused. "There won't be anything to do except dump her."

Mildred felt the shockwave go through Leland at Cher's proposal. "Look," she went on, "with the kid aboard, we're kidnappers. Without her, we're a couple of dumb, lost Canucks who should have turned around when we got to this bridge." She watched him for a few seconds, her dark eyes intent. "Think about it. There might not be any other choice."

With that she retreated, leaving Leland to come to his own conclusions. Mildred heard most of them, and she did not like them one bit.

Brodie felt the bottom skiff against the sand and felt the jolt as the boat stopped. It was still afloat, but the stern swung inward. Leland's face appeared in the hatchway, his manner jerky and his eyes like fireflies, darting here and there without apparent purpose. He seemed scarier now, as if a switch had been turned too high.

He had to crouch to make his way down the stairs, and that brought something to mind. Brodie knew for certain Leland wasn't her dad, whatever he thought.

His eyes narrowed as he glanced around the cabin. "You don't have another phone or something, do you?" She shook her head, raising her hands to show their emptiness. "I didn't think so, but I gotta believe that line of boats is there to stop us getting through the straits."

Brodie's heart gave a hopeful lurch, but she said, "Maybe it's something to do with the race."

"I don't remember anything like this from when I raced with Uncle Will and Dad."

Cher spoke. "What I said before. We gotta do it."

"No."

"Lee, she can't talk to the police. She'll tell them you forced her."

"I'm her father."

"Says who?"

He straightened, offended. "I do. Jeannie and me—"

"Look at her! She don't look nothing like you." She turned to Brodie. "When's your birthday?"

"Um, September second."

Cher did some figuring. "You came to Hornpayne just before Christmas that year. I'd say your girlfriend replaced you as soon as you left." She pointed a finger at Brodie. "She's some other guy's brat, but he prob'ly didn't have a rich uncle."

Leland's head twitched toward Brodie. "But Dunbar adopted her. He must have thought she was family."

"So Jeannie pulled her own scam. Good for her." Cher put a hand on his arm. "Lee, if they do DNA, and she ain't your kid, you're gonna go to prison for the rest of your life."

"But if she *is* mine—"

"Your cousin or whatever he is will fight you in the courts for the next twenty years. You'll be lucky to live long enough to see a penny of that money." She glanced at Brodie, who stood white-faced as they argued. "You got, what, five years before she comes of age? And then it won't matter, 'cause the money will be hers. You'll get nothing." She ran her hand up Leland's arm, caressing it, and her voice softened. "You had a real nice dream, Lee, but that's all it was. Now we're in trouble, and we cannot get caught with this kid."

Leland's whole body slumped as he accepted Cher's view. "What should we do?"

"Knock a hole in the boat, put it on autopilot, and send it out into the lake. We swim to Mackinaw City and find another boat. Once this antique is gone, they got no way to prove we were here."

Leland raised his eyes to Cher's face. "What about Brodie?"

Cher kept her eyes fixed on his. "She goes down with the boat."

Straining to see as far as possible through Bud's eyes, Seamus was doubly shocked by Mildred's cry, like a siren going off next to his ear. "They're going to kill her!"

Bud reacted too, wincing and bringing his free hand up to touch the bandage on his head.

"What is it?" Scarlet asked.

"We're almost there!" It was all Seamus dared say, for Bud reeled slightly, causing the boat to weave in response. Scarlet stepped up and took the wheel, watching him with concern as he sank down on the seat, looking sick and confused.

"I'm okay," Bud said, but he didn't offer to retake control of the boat. Scarlet turned her attention to the water ahead, probably wondering if her ashy-faced employer was in any shape to continue the pursuit of Brodie's abductor.

"There!" she said excitedly. "It's the bridge, banked in fog. Bud, we made it!"

Ghostly lights showed dimly below the fog bank, and above it, the lights on the bridge towers shone brightly. Bud took heart at having their goal in sight, but Seamus was less hopeful. If what Mildred had said was true, they might stop Leland at the bridge but be too late to save Brodie.

Brodie thought she might be sick. Leland and Cher stood toe to toe, arguing the prospect of murdering her and sending her body to the bottom of Lake Michigan. She tried to think of something to say. "Please, Dad, don't kill me?" She could not say it.

After what seemed like an hour, Leland said, "No."

Both Brodie and Cher knew what he meant immediately. Brodie breathed a sigh of relief, Cher growled a curse word and turned away.

"I'm not giving up my daughter," Leland gave Brodie a sick-looking grin. "Don't worry, hon. Bud isn't going to win this one."

Cher opened her mouth to say something, but Leland raised a hand, palm out. "We'll do like you said, sink this boat, walk to the other side of the bridge along the shore, and find another boat on the Lake Huron side." He tried a charming smile. "That's a good idea you had, ditching this old tub."

Cher didn't bother to answer, but looking at her

expression, Brodie realized that Leland, crazy and crooked as he might be, was now her only protection.

He tried to pretend they were all in agreement on what would happen next. "Okay. I'll get the boat set up for its final voyage. Brodie, you can come up on deck and help. Cher, pack up what we'll need to get across the lake."

Brodie tried to picture what lay ahead. They were off the shore of Mackinaw City, the town at the northern tip of Lower Michigan. Toll booths for vehicles crossing the Mackinac Bridge were five miles away, in the Upper Peninsula town of St. Ignace. Next to the bridge on the side nearest them sat an old fort called Michilimackinac, open for tours during the day but deserted at this time of night. Directly under the bridge was the Visitors Center, which would also be closed.

What lay on the opposite side of the bridge-way? It was hard to remember. She thought there were some historic buildings, a park, and then the marina. At this time of night, or rather, morning, there would be few, maybe no, people around. Getting help wouldn't be easy.

If they could circumvent the blockade, Leland and Cher would steal a boat and cross Lake Huron to Ontario, where she'd be their prisoner. Alone with those two in the wilds of Canada was not where Brodie wanted to be.

Leland began rooting through a storage bin, grunting and clanging metal objects together. "Here we go!" he said triumphantly, pulling out the corkscrew anchor. "A perfect hole-maker."

Setting the anchor aside, Leland prepared the boat for disaster. Starting the outboard motor, he turned the wheel until they were headed away from the shore and into Lake Michigan. He fastened the tiller in place so the boat would continue in that direction for as long as it stayed afloat.

When Cher came on deck with a duffle bag, he ordered, "You and Brodie get into the water. I'll finish this."

Cher turned, blocking Leland's view with her body as she showed Brodie the knife she still carried. "Don't try anything."

Brodie's insides felt like they'd spill onto the deck if she opened her mouth. She went to the ladder and climbed down, letting her body into the chilly, choppy waters of the straits. Cher was right behind her, and Brodie felt a hand in her hair as they waited for Leland.

They saw only his head and shoulders as he moved about, but Brodie could fill in what she couldn't see. He checked the tiller and the motor once more to be sure they were where he wanted them to be. Then he picked up the corkscrew anchor and looked around, trying to decide where to begin. After some thought he muttered, "The cabin floor, I think." He disappeared from view, and they heard several sharp blows and the splintering of wood. Coming back up on deck, he jammed the anchor into the side of the boat nearest them, just below the waterline. It took several attempts to break through, but a satisfied grunt from Leland signaled a second success.

He moved to the transom and put the engine into gear. The boat, already filling with water, moved sluggishly forward. Brodie thought, *It's dying, bleeding in instead of out, but dying nonetheless.*

Leland stepped onto the tow-rail, balanced easily for a moment, and dived, pushing off from the foundering boat with strong legs. Making a watery chuggle, the boat went on alone, its bow cutting the water at a very low angle. Leland looked back briefly when he reached the two women. "There she goes!" He turned toward the shore. "Let's see if we can find something better."

They waded to dry land and stood, listening as distressed sounds from the boat went on. The motor coughed, coughed again, and died. Brodie felt a movement beside her and turned to see Leland with one hand raised in a salute. "She was a good old girl." Cher snorted derisively in response.

Before them was a stretch of beach, then some scrubby grass, then a wall of very old upright posts. The fort. *Got to act soon,* Brodie thought. If Leland had his way, she'd soon be permanently missing from the United States. If Cher had her way, it could be much, much worse.

Listening to the radio traffic, Bud tried to piece together what was happening up ahead. Fog obscured the view, not unusual for the straits, where fronts often collided and temperatures differed sharply. Being unable to see more than a few feet ahead slowed their progress, which was almost more than he could stand this close to their goal.

There was a lot of chatter, and he could at times pick out

Jim Ecker's voice, giving commands. "Okay, *Beach Girl*. Keep an eye out," and later, "I hear you, *Charlevoix Beauty*, nothing under the north tower." He wasn't sure what it meant, but he felt a rush of gratitude for the boaters ready to help him find Brodie.

As they got closer, lights penetrated the soup of fog, more lights than he'd expected. Some of them were random, not neatly spaced like the lights on the bridge. As he peered ahead, Bud realized what those extra lights were and what the radio traffic meant. His friends were doing more than patrolling. They had formed a chain across the narrowest spot, on the far side of the bridge. Even in fog, Leland wouldn't be able to slip through with dozens of brightly-lit boats in his path. Calling to Scarlet, Bud made for the bridge's center, where he guessed Jim was overseeing the impromptu blockade.

"What is it?" Scarlet asked, peering ahead.

"The end of Leland's run, I hope."

The line of boats was a festive sight despite its serious purpose. Boats large and small bobbed quietly in the choppy water. As the Starcraft neared the line and Bud idled the engine down, sounds of music and conversation wafted across the water. Bud turned and paralleled the line, looking for a familiar shape. The first two boats he passed were unknown to him, but then he sighted *The Gull*, a trim little sloop belonging to his friend Ecker.

"Ahoy, *Gull*!" he called, and someone rose from a chair on deck.

"Dunbar, is that you?"

"It's me, Jimmy. Any sign of the boat I described to you?"

"Not yet, but come aboard and we'll wait for Leland together. I want to see you kick his ass."

Leland led Brodie and Cher along the shoreline, past the buildings of the fort. The grounds were vaguely familiar. Gramps had brought her there to see the displays and watch the re-enactments of daily life in the olden days. Now it was empty and silent, a faintly spooky place where it seemed ghosts might walk. Brodie didn't want to think about ghosts. Her companions were scary enough, without worrying about what evil the spirits of Indians, trappers, soldiers and the rest of the dead might intend for her.

Soon the bridge pylons loomed ahead. The fog hovered above, cloaking the heads of the street lamps. A cyclone fence separated the grounds of the fort from the bridge area. There was a gateway, a porcupine-like turnstile that moved in only one direction, allowing exit but no entry. She thought Leland would head there, but he didn't, and she soon saw why. The fence ended at the lake edge. Leland waded around it, leading the way under the bridge.

Ahead of them was a short stretch between the water and a windowed wall. This was the Visitors' Center, nestled under the bridge to allow tourists to see the underside of the impressive structure. They passed unseen, since there was no one inside at four a.m. Over their heads was I-75, the freeway that connected Michigan's Lower and Upper Peninsulas. Occasional rumbles signaled traffic on four lanes of echoing steel and concrete.

"Wait here a minute." Leland's voice echoed against the concrete above them. Cher stopped, pulling Brodie to a halt beside her and holding her arm tightly as he moved ahead. He peered around the edge of the building, keeping well in the shadows.

In a few seconds he was back. "There's a couple of teenagers on the grass. I think they're sleeping, but even if they aren't, we'll just be a family passing by."

"At this hour?" Cher scoffed. "What if she hollers or something?"

"She won't, will you, Brod? She knows it's important for us to get away."

Brodie was indeed desperate to get away. How could she do it? She couldn't fight them both. Cher wanted to drown her. Leland wanted to get her to Canada, convinced he'd be rich if he had her with him—

An idea struck. If Leland knew the truth, maybe he'd leave her here and go back to Canada with Cher. "You aren't my dad."

It took him a second to process what she'd said. "What?"

"You're not my dad. Gramps told me." Though reluctant to discuss her background, Gramps had always answered when Brodie asked a specific question.

"He lied." Leland's voice sounded funny.

Stirrings of unease arose, but Brodie went on, hoping for the best. "When I asked if I'll always be short, he said the chances were good, since both my parents were." She looked up at Leland, whose shoulders were several inches higher than the top of her head. Her voice began to wobble, but the words came out in a rush. "Leave me here. I'll tell them I ran away. You can go back to Canada, and I'll keep quiet." To be sure he got it she added, "Gramps said my dad was five eight. That isn't you."

Mildred couldn't believe Brodie said what she did to Leland. His frustration grew as he absorbed her words, moving toward a great and towering anger. The man had built himself a dream. He'd committed terrible crimes to achieve it. He'd faced opposition from his girlfriend. Now he was marooned in a place where he might be arrested and imprisoned. And Brodie had just told him it was all for nothing.

"Calm!" Mildred ordered. "Stay calm."

"Arrrgh!" Leland responded, slapping himself on the forehead. "Arrgh!" He sounded like a madman, and she realized her encouragement would not work in this instance. Mildred lapsed into silence. Maybe Seamus was right about some things.

CHAPTER TWENTY

"I told you." There was a sneer in Cher's voice. Brodie didn't look at her but watched Leland, still hoping he'd give up and let her go. Instead he seemed to be losing control. Her idea had backfired, and Leland was barely hanging on to sanity.

Cher's next words made Brodie's stomach sink. "I told you, we gotta get rid of her."

"No. She's confused. She—"

"You had the guts to get rid of the old man. What is your problem with the kid?"

"Shut up!" The ferocity of his reaction made Brodie jump. Cher also reacted, loosening her grip on Brodie's arm. It was only for a second, but instinct took over. Leland was in front of her; the lake was on the other side. Pulling herself free of Cher's hand, Brodie took off, skirting the fence and heading back onto the grounds of the fort.

Her first idea was to escape by the turnstile gate, maybe jam it with something so they couldn't follow her through. That would put her in the Visitors' Center parking lot. Beyond it was Mackinaw City, where there were people, businesses, and residences. Help.

Behind her, however, she heard Leland call to Cher, "Follow her. I'll go around." Thoughts of Cher with her long, jagged-edged knife made Brodie's heart pound. She could almost feel the blade entering her back. But Leland was coming around the other side of the building. If she came out the turnstile he'd be there, waiting.

Where else could she go? Into the lake? She hesitated, aware of Cher's grunts as she maneuvered around the fence and started up the rise. What should she do? Hide among the buildings of the fort? Huddle there until someone came to work, hours from now?

There was only one answer. She'd go up. The turnstile could be used as a ladder, and from the top she could pull herself onto the roof of the Visitors' Center. If she was quick, she could disappear into the thick blanket of fog that hovered above her.

It almost worked. By the time Cher puffed her way up the incline, Brodie was above her line of sight. Cher stood peering toward the buildings inside the fort, unsure which direction to go.

Leland, however, came from the opposite side, along the front of the building. The tiniest squeak of the turnstile as Brodie's weight left it caused him to turn and look up. He peered through the fog. "There!" he called softly. Cher looked up but didn't seem able to see her.

"Get down here!" she called. Brodie backed into the shadows, looking around her. She was on the flat roof of the building, a sheer drop at her back and her pursuers watching the front and sides. Where could she go now?

It took only a few seconds for Leland to set one foot on the turnstile. Brodie could see only parts of him through the moving mist, but she watched helplessly. She was trapped with nowhere to go. He could kill her simply by throwing her off the roof. She backed away until she was stopped by an elevated section that blocked further retreat. It was a metal box, some kind of housing. Seeing no other option, she climbed up onto it. Maybe the fog would hide her and Leland would think she'd jumped off the other side. It wasn't the greatest plan, but there was nowhere else to go.

Unless she continued to go up. As she crouched on top of the box, holding still to prevent a *thunk* of flexing metal, she could see the underside of the bridge above her. Within reach, a catwalk for maintenance workers' use ran below the bridge. She couldn't see how far it went, since it was shrouded in fog. She might elude Leland and maybe even make her way to the opposite side. The toll booths at the St. Ignace end were manned all the time. Help was there.

It wouldn't be easy. The metal was wet and visibility was bad. Would she slip and fall getting onto the catwalk? If she did, would she hit the ground or the roof or land in Leland's waiting arms? If she didn't fall, would she end up trapped under the bridge with nowhere to go but down, into the water? Brodie thought of the days before, when she'd hung off the fence at the viewing platform, tempting death. Knowing now she didn't want her life to end, it was hard to decide how best to stay alive. Choosing to live was harder than simply waiting to die.

She heard a grunt below her. Leland had stepped onto the roof of the building. He would skirt the box first, but sooner or later he'd think of looking up. The climb onto the catwalk was all she had.

It wasn't as difficult as she'd thought. Once on the walkway, she hurried along its narrow space, forcing herself not to turn to see if Leland was behind her. It was slippery, and she forced herself to move more slowly than she wanted to, both for safety and to keep from making noise. Fog obscured the view before and to the sides, but she could see the waters below. Forty feet, maybe. Not a fall a person was likely to survive. Still, she had handholds and a firm pathway beneath her. Height wasn't the problem. Leland was.

She'd begun to hope things had turned her way when the catwalk ended. Brodie almost cried aloud in frustration. Now what?

Once she stopped, she heard metallic clanging behind her. Leland was coming. Her hopes that he'd give up, return to Canada, and pretend he'd never left were futile. He'd accepted Cher's argument that his only hope of staying out of prison was for Brodie to die. And now that she'd convinced him he wasn't her father, he had no reason to want her around.

No time to think about that. She had to keep going, had to do what she could to stay alive. Before her a ladder stretched upward. To what? Another catwalk? To the bridge deck? No way to know. She couldn't even see the top. Brodie had never felt so alone. No one knew she was out here. No one was coming to save her. Whatever she did, she must do it by herself. She set her feet on the rungs of the ladder.

When she got close to the top, Brodie saw a hatch that she guessed must open onto the bridge-way. Would it be fastened shut? Was she strong enough to open it? Having no choice, she continued upward. Reaching the hatch, she put her shoulder against it and pushed. It didn't move easily, and she almost concluded it was locked, but she pushed again, and it moved a little. It wasn't locked, but it was heavy. Going up another rung, she put her whole back against the hatch and pushed again, using her legs and gritting her teeth with the effort. The hatch squealed, shifted, and then opened with a metallic clang. She was on the Mackinac Bridge.

"You gotta do like I said," Cher told Leland when he reported that Brodie had disappeared into the guts of the bridge. "We got no choice now."

"If she gets up there, someone will stop and help her." He was torn between anger and despair.

Mildred whispered, "Canada!" She hoped he'd be susceptible to suggestion, but her urging seemed to drive him further into his own anger.

"I would have been good to her."

Looking around to be certain no one was near, Cher called in a stage whisper, "Listen to me. You came home for your uncle's funeral, but we got here too late. The kid stowed away in your boat. We found her on board tonight, and you told her she had to go home. She didn't want to, so she ran away and climbed onto the bridge. You're going to go after her, to try to talk sense to her, but she's going to fall." Cher waved a hand at the fog. "It shouldn't be hard to make that happen in this mess. Nobody can see ten feet in front of them."

Leland put both hands on his head as if it hurt. "She's just a kid, Cher."

"A kid who's gonna tell the police you kidnapped her if you don't shut her up."

Frightened by Leland's deteriorating condition, Mildred tried again: "Canada!"

Leland scrubbed his face distractedly. "My head feels like it's full of bees!"

Cher looked up at him, her expression worried. "Calm down. All they got is the kid's word against ours. If she ain't around to tell her side, they gotta accept yours." Sensing Leland's reluctant agreement, she added, "Now go! She's got a head start on you."

With a sigh, he turned away and climbed onto the metal housing, where he grasped the rail of the catwalk and began to make his way along it. His dream of wealth, his plan of escape, even his apparent relish at the idea of having a daughter, all those things were gone, and Mildred heard his thoughts with increasing distress. *Cher's right. She was right all along.*

Mildred did everything she could think of to disturb her host's thoughts and slow his progress, from expanding her presence inside his head to shouting for Seamus to singing at the top of her voice. Despite her efforts, Leland continued doggedly onward. He'd made up his mind, and when she finally gave up and lapsed into silence, she heard: *Brodie isn't what I needed after all. It's not my fault she has to die.*

Brodie climbed onto the bridge deck, her foot slipping a little when her sneaker lost traction on the final rung of the ladder. She sat for a second on the edge, breathing heavily, but she couldn't delay. She was at the side of the bridge, on a railed pathway meant to protect workers from traffic as they performed maintenance. Far below her, choppy little waves slapped the towers noisily. They seemed to be waiting, patient as Time itself. What difference would it make if one half-grown girl was thrown to her death tonight? The world would go on.

Still, there were people who would care, people like Scarlet and Shelley and Briggs, who might even miss her. And there were things she wanted to do. Help kids. Go to culinary school. Work with Bud, if he'd meant what he said that day. Her life might not be the most important one on the planet, but it was hers, and she wanted it.

The deck of the bridge was where the fog seemed thickest, and the security lights above looked like candles behind a curtain. She'd hoped to stop a passing car, but under these conditions, she might well be hit by one instead. There wouldn't be many chances at this hour, either. As she listened, a lone car approached from the St. Ignace side. It came slowly, as conditions and the speed limit required. Turning, Brodie saw a flash of movement. Leland's head and shoulders appeared above the railing. Her hope he would give up died.

The car's headlights finally showed in the grayness, and Brodie stepped in front of it, waving her arms frantically. The driver, a lone woman, didn't see her at first, and Brodie had to jump out of the way at the last moment. The woman turned, surprise and confusion on her face. She slowed, seemed about to stop, then her confused expression gave way to an angry frown, and she sped away.

Brodie sobbed aloud, imagining the woman's thoughts. Seeing no reason for a kid to be flagging down cars on the bridge, the driver concluded it was some kind of prank. *I'm not that kind of girl!* Brodie wanted to shout after her. *I used to be, but not anymore.*

Once the car was gone, Leland stepped onto the bridge, appearing out of the fog like a creature from another world. His face was different now, not friendly, not coaxing. "Get over here!" he called. "Or you're gonna be sorry."

Mildred was at a loss. As badly as she wanted to keep Leland from chasing Brodie onto the bridge, she'd begun to consider the consequences for herself. The man's thoughts were less and less rational, and she had no idea what she might say that would have an effect.

When Leland came to the end of the catwalk, Mildred whispered, "Back. Back."

He paid no attention whatsoever but stopped, listening. Above him he heard a grunt of exertion followed by a metallic clank. "She's above me."

Mildred tried again to stop him. "No!" she cried. "Back! Canada! Home!"

Leland's response was a sound an animal in a trap might make: uncomprehending fear and unreasoning anger.

Brodie stood on the bridge deck, unsure what to do. Leland blocked a return to Mackinaw City. She heard no more cars coming. With no other choice, she started running toward the town of St. Ignace. Pounding footsteps soon alerted her that Leland was following. It was five miles to the other side. She'd never outrun him. There was no help ahead, only four empty lanes stretching before her. Below was the line of boats, possibly waiting to save her, but she doubted they could see the road from the water, especially in this fog. Should she jump and hope one of them would fish her out of the water? There was little chance she'd survive such a fall.

Lacking other options, she continued along the bridge-way, shouting for help when breath permitted. At least the next vehicle she met—if there was one—would see the man chasing her and have reason to stop.

The bridge deck was well-maintained and smooth. Brodie ran as she'd never run before, the veils of mist parting and closing around her. She stayed as far as possible to the right in case a car came up behind unheard, but she dared not take the time to jump the railing and get back on the walkway. Her lungs ached, and her breath came in ragged gasps. Hope faded as her energy did. Ahead she saw no vehicles, and behind she heard nothing mechanical. What she did hear was Leland, also breathing in labored huffs. He hadn't yet reached her, but in the end he would win. He was bigger, he had longer legs, and he was, Brodie now believed, much crazier than she could ever be.

As she searched her brain for a way to escape, the mist parted slightly, revealing one of the huge cables that rose along either side of the bridge. Although they looked like extra-large tubes, they consisted of tons of wire, wound together and wrapped to prevent corrosion. She'd seen workers walking up those cables, and she and Gramps had watched the episode of *Dirty Jobs* where Mike, who was as brave as anyone she could imagine, changed light bulbs 550 feet above the Straits. The cables supported the weight of the bridge, suspending its million tons of weight from its two massive towers. The one she could see was a few feet ahead on her right.

What if she climbed up there, like the guy on *Dirty Jobs* had done? Would Leland follow, or would he be afraid? There wasn't a lot of time to make a decision. The cable rose sharply, and if she didn't climb on now, she'd pass the point where she could reach it. Ahead was miles of empty space, shrouded in fog that blinded the safety cameras stationed along the bridge-way. Leland would catch her on the flat. If she went up, there was hope he would not, maybe even could not, follow. Almost anyone would hesitate before making that climb. If she was lucky, he wouldn't see her leave the deck. He'd think she was still running ahead of him. In that case she'd simply wait until he passed by and head back to Mackinaw City. Making her decision, Brodie veered sharply to her right, jumped the railing, grasped the metal hand-rope, and hoisted herself onto the cable.

Leland's mind was a frightening coil of anger, hatred, and confusion, and Mildred quailed at what she heard. His plans were in ruins, and he focused the blame not on himself, but on the girl who raced along, out of sight at some times but appearing briefly when the mist swirled aside. Brodie was running ahead of him, when he had done so much for her! He'd offered her kindness, protection, and a family. *Just like her mother*, Leland thought. *Only thinks of herself.*

As he raced along the bridge, Leland caught a glimpse of something on his right. He slowed, peering into the fog. Before his eyes, Brodie's feet disappeared into what appeared to be thin air. She was climbing up the cable.

He stopped, cowed by the steep incline. Peering up into the fog, he tried to decide what Brodie thought she was going to accomplish. Did the kid plan to climb to the top of the bridge? Then what? "Is she crazy?" he muttered aloud. "Where's she gonna go from there?" He chuckled grimly. "She thinks she'll get away. She doesn't think I've got the nerve to follow."

To Mildred's horror, Leland hauled himself up onto the cable, a surface barely two feet wide. There were strong hand-ropes, and he gripped them firmly, first one hand, then the other, as he started upward. Brodie had ruined his plan to control millions of dollars, but she was not going to put him in prison for the rest of his life to boot. *Cher's right*, Mildred heard in his thoughts. *The kid has to die, and she's got no one but herself to blame.*

Mildred realized her own situation was as dire as Brodie's. If her host died before she could jump to someone else, she'd become a lost soul with no way to return to the ship. Seamus couldn't save her, even if he knew where she was. If Leland got close enough to Brodie, Mildred might jump to her, but who could say if Brodie would live through this nightmare? She and Leland might both fall to their deaths.

Fear clouded Mildred's mind like fog clouded the bridge, and she had trouble seeing the way ahead. Why had she wanted to come back anyway? Life was uncomfortable, and returning wasn't at all what she'd imagined. People were difficult and unappreciative of what she tried to do to help them. And there was really nothing here on earth she missed, now that she'd seen it all again.

As Leland climbed higher, the cold mist settled on his skin

and clothing. Soon his hands would become stiff, and the damp would make the climb slippery. The mists parted, and she saw how far down it was to the water. Mildred became very quiet, fearful of doing anything that would cause Leland distress. She couldn't even call out to Seamus to let him know where she was. All she could do was wish she'd never asked to return to Life. No way was it worth the pain, the trouble, and the chance that this time, she wouldn't be able to go on to something better.

Brodie stopped about fifty feet up and looked behind her. At first she saw nothing, but the mist shifted and she saw Leland, standing at the spot where she had begun her climb. He was looking up, aware of her detour. Doggedly, she continued upward. If she couldn't fool him, she'd have to out-climb him.

"Brodie, don't go up there!" Leland called. "You'll fall." His voice was loud, and the tone struck her as false, like a public announcement.

Then she got it. He was setting up a scenario that would get him out of trouble. Leland meant to see that she did fall, and he would pretend he'd tried to save her.

Brodie watched as he hesitated, uncertain he could do it, then made his decision. She had a good head start, but her hope he would chicken out was in vain. As she ascended, the wind picked up, growing stronger with each step. It whipped at her hair and her clothing. Brodie kept climbing. Maybe it was a question of how high Leland could make himself go.

The mist began to dispel around five a.m. At first Bud could see only the boat nearest the *Gull*. Then other shapes emerged like ghosts on a Hollywood set. Wisps of white hung in odd places, as if reluctant to leave, but the sky began to lighten. The sun would soon rise. The fog was doomed.

"What's that on the bridge?" someone shouted, and Bud turned to look. The angle was steep, but he detected movement above the dissipating fog bank. Snatching up a pair of binoculars, he focused them. Brodie was climbing the suspension cable, alternating hands as she put one foot carefully in front of the other. With determination evident in her posture, she kept her face turned upward to where the cable attached to the tower, five hundred feet above the water. As Bud watched, Leland appeared from a cloud of mist far below her, his face yellow in the amber glow of a nearby bulb. His climb was jerkier, and he stopped periodically as if uncertain he wanted to continue. Still, he too climbed on.

Scarlet appeared at his side, peering upward. "There's someone on the bridge?"

"Call the bridge authority," Bud told Ecker. "Tell them Brodie's up there, and Leland is right behind her." As his friend turned to comply Bud added, "Have you got a better pair of shoes than these?"

Without a word, Ecker took off the sneakers he wore and handed them over. Bud kicked off his sandals and pulled Ecker's shoes on, quickly tightening the laces.

"What are you going to do?" Scarlet asked.

"I'm going up there. I'll talk to Leland, get him to give it up. Then I'll get Brodie."

Scarlet looked at the small figure ascending slowly but steadily above them. "I'll start the boat and get you as close as I can."

Without waiting for Bud to agree, she stepped to the back of the Gull, pulled the *Lila*'s tow rope to bring it toward them, and jumped aboard. Within seconds she'd started the boat's engine. "Coming through!" she called out, passing the *Gull*'s stern and pulling alongside. Bud dropped into the smaller boat, and Scarlet took off, veering toward Mackinaw City at a clip that caused him to flail for few seconds before he found something to hold onto.

In less than three minutes, they neared the park on the east side of the bridge. Scarlet didn't slow until the last possible second, running the craft right up on shore. The boat stopped suddenly as its bottom hit sand, causing Bud to grab the side rail again. He fought a wave of nausea in his gut. The cumulative effect of the last few days seemed to be gathering in the front of his skull, like little men with hammers were inside trying to get out. Grief combined with shock and apprehension, not to mention the pain of a minor crack in his head. *Have to get to Brodie. Have to.*

Bud looked back at the bridge. Brodie was still climbing. Leland was still behind her. Both of them labored hard. Their progress seemed snail-like from the ground. He'd have to be faster.

Scarlet seemed about to say something but apparently thought better of it. "Call the police," he said. Nodding, she reached in her pocket and pulled out her phone. Bud stepped onto the hull of the boat and jumped as far as he could onto the dry part of the beach. No sense climbing with wet, slippery shoes.

The bridge-deck was high above, and he saw immediately that there was no way to reach it from the ground. He took the slope up to the Visitor's Center at a dead run then stopped, looking for a quick way up to the bridge deck. Hearing a voice behind him, he turned to see Scarlet, ten steps behind, speaking softly but urgently into her phone. "And a fire truck, with the longest ladder they have. And hurry." She closed the phone and joined him.

"You shouldn't be here."

"Where should I be, then?" Scarlet wet her lips. "I have to do what I can for Brodie."

Bud wondered if either of them could do anything. He knew he was in no shape to be launching a rescue, but somehow, with Scarlet at his side, he knew he'd try. He heard something that sounded like, "Roof. Roof." Was there a dog nearby? Then he felt a surge of something, possibly hope, and suddenly felt a little better. The roof! That was his way up. Beside the building were several metal boxes that probably housed the electrical system. He climbed onto the tallest one, which put him high enough to hoist himself onto the building's roof. Unaware that Brodie had recently done the same thing from the other side, he surveyed the bridge's underbelly. He could reach it if he stood on the roof's highest point. From there he would somehow make his way onto the bridge deck, get to the cable, and stop Leland.

Seamus settled into Scarlet's mind, hoping he'd made the correct decision. Bud needed all his resources to have any chance of success. If help arrived soon, Bud would be able to retreat to safety and let the authorities capture Leland. There were other possibilities, but Seamus didn't want to consider them. Whatever the situation, he was a hindrance Bud couldn't afford.

Looking through Scarlet's eyes, he gauged the situation. From this vantage point the scene unfolding before them was chillingly clear. Brodie kept pulling herself upward, her exhaustion obvious and her feet splayed as she sought a firm hold as the incline steepened.

Some distance behind her Leland did the same, but he was having a harder time with it. The mists had parted, and seeing the treacherous drop below was unavoidable. Whenever he looked down, he faltered and had to stop, clinging to the hand-rope for a few seconds while he gathered his courage. It slowed his progress considerably. Above him, Brodie looked only ahead. Seamus picked up Scarlet's thought—*Not afraid of heights, but this is different.*

Scarlet backed away from the Visitors' Center, trying to see Bud. He had disappeared for a few minutes, but now he appeared on the bridge deck, running full tilt down the highway. It was some distance to where the cable met the railing, maybe as much as a mile. Through Scarlet's eyes, Seamus could only see Bud's head and shoulders as he raced along. Then he saw headlights, and a car stopped beside him. Bud leaned into the window, telling the driver something. In seconds he was in the car. Seamus felt a glimmer of hope. There hadn't been much chance Bud could catch up with Leland after a mile-long run down the bridge-way, but a ride to the cable would save him time and energy. He would need both.

Seamus sensed Scarlet's uncertainty, and he shared it. Could Bud climb the bridge cable and face a desperate Leland? And if he did, what would the result be?

Voices from the boats below the bridge sounded. The words were garbled, but fear vibrated in the tones. A few called out encouragement to Brodie; others shouted to Leland to leave the girl alone. Neither paid them any attention. Seamus guessed Leland was beyond reason. His only goal now seemed to be to make Brodie pay the highest price possible for ruining his plans.

Scarlet took out her phone and began dialing 9-1-1 again, but two things happened at once. Sirens sounded in the distance, and she noticed a woman at the prow of Bud's boat, trying to push it into the water.

Seamus saw what Scarlet saw and knew immediately the woman was Leland's girlfriend. Concluding his case was hopeless, she was going to save herself.

Scarlet was down the slope in seconds. "Stop!"

The woman turned, her manner unhurried and calm. "Don't get in my way, honey. You ain't up to it." To stress her resolve, she brandished a large knife, meant for bread but daunting in the hands of someone desperate to escape.

"You're with him." Scarlet glanced up to where Leland clung to the bridge, unaware that Bud had climbed onto the cable behind him.

"I was. Now I'm on my own. Let me go, and you won't get hurt."

"The police are coming." She paused so the sound of sirens could come through. "Hear that?"

"Then I'd best be going." The woman gave another push, and the boat slid free of the sand. The sudden release unbalanced her, and she stumbled into the water. Before she could recover, Scarlet rushed forward and kicked her hard in the ribs. The woman doubled over, gasping for breath. Seamus wanted to cheer Scarlet's courage. Instead he urged her to finish the job. "Push!"

Scarlet either obeyed or had the same thought. As the woman crouched, holding her side, Scarlet pushed her, sending her into the water. She came up dripping but still holding the knife. Anger distorted her face. "You bitch!" She lunged at Scarlet, but the knee-deep water slowed her. Scarlet stepped back, and the knife met only air.

With a snarl, the woman came at her. Scarlet retreated up the sloping beach, eyes focused on the knife. Seamus felt her fear. "Stand!" he ordered. If she turned to run, she was likely to get stabbed in the back. Her best chance was to stay where she was. He guessed her opponent would opt for escape rather than revenge.

She did. Seeing that Scarlet didn't retreat, the woman backed into the water, her eyes never wavering. "See ya," she said, putting one foot on the ladder at the stern of the *Lila*. Her face registered surprise when a voice behind her said, "I don't think you're going anywhere."

A hand grasped her wrist and twisted it sharply, causing her to drop the knife. Another hand grabbed her other wrist and pulled it behind her body. On the other side of Bud's boat,

Seamus caught a glimpse of a rubber dinghy that had come silently up behind them.

"She tried to steal my boat," the woman cried. "I was trying to get away from her."

"That's funny," Jim Ecker said. "Scarlet came here in this boat with my friend Bud. Did you buy the *Lila* from him in the last ten minutes?"

CHAPTER TWENTY-ONE

"Leland!"

Mildred saw what Leland saw as he turned—Bud coming up the cable behind him. Leland's surprise turned quickly to anger. "Go away, Bud!" His voice was little more than a pant, and his thought showed how far he was from sanity. *How can I claim she fell when he's watching?*

"Leland, there's nowhere to go. The police are on the way, and there's no sense in what you're doing. Let Brodie come down before she falls."

"I'm trying to save her, Bud. She says she's going to jump." Mildred heard Leland's plan shift. *You'll have to fall now too, Buddy. I'll be the only family member who survives this tragic event.*

"Your scheme didn't work, Leland, but it's not Brodie's fault." Bud spoke as he continued his climb. "I'm the one who called the police. Come after me."

Leland looked up at Brodie. *If I can reach her before she gets to the tower, it'll be easy.*

"She's a kid, Leland."

He turned to look down. "But not my kid."

Mildred saw Bud's expression and knew he understood. Leland had no reason to spare Brodie and every reason to want her dead. Bud apparently decided that talking further was useless. Grasping the suspension cables even more tightly, he continued onward, his expression grim.

Brodie left the fog bank and climbed into the stars, or so it seemed. The wind was strong up here, stronger than she'd imagined. She'd heard about the stress on bridges and knew that the Straits of Mackinac was an area of weird air currents. Feeling it was much more convincing than reading it on an informative plaque.

She heard voices behind her, but they didn't penetrate, so focused was she on reaching the massive tower that loomed above her. Her feet hurt. Her hands burned from the friction of the stark metal against her palms. Her breath wheezed through clenched teeth. Her hair beat against her face like a thousand tiny whips. She had to keep twisting her head to blow the hair back so she could see ahead of her. Far below, the waters of the straits rolled, mixing Lake Huron's water with Lake Michigan's, ceaselessly moving, always cold. She kept on, prayed she'd gained on Leland, who she hoped was more afraid than she was.

Bud climbed quickly. Leland kept turning to look at him, unable, it seemed, to stop himself. As Bud gained on him, Leland's head moved almost constantly, looking first ahead at Brodie, then down at the water, then back at Bud. Finally, he made his decision. He stopped, put both hands on the hand-rope to his right, and turned to face his adversary. Mildred heard his thought. *Don't think about the drop. Think about getting it done.*

"Leland—" Bud hesitated, trying to think of an enticement to make him give up. Leland paused too, using the time to catch his breath and plan how to send Bud to his death. *I'm above him. One good kick to his chest and he'll go spinning off the bridge.* Aloud he said, "Little Buddy. Grandpa's favorite boy."

Bud looked tired, but his voice was angry. "You killed him."

Leland supported his weight with his arms, resting his legs so they'd be ready when the time came. "Yeah."

"For money."

"At first I just wanted the land in Canada. Then I saw the kid."

"You thought if you had Brodie, you'd control her share of the estate."

"I thought she was my kid. Honest. But she busted that bubble."

"Let's go back down. If you leave Brodie alone, I'll give you my boat and you can head for Canada."

The sound of sirens and the flashing lights below made that offer all but useless. "How about this?" Leland countered. "I tell the story my way. You get to be the bad guy, and I get to be the one who tried to protect Brodie from you after you killed her beloved Gramps."

"They'll never believe—" Bud didn't finish, for Leland lunged forward a step, aiming a forceful kick at his chest. If it had connected fully, Bud would surely have lost his hold on the hand-ropes, but he ducked out of the way. He swayed drunkenly for a few seconds before regaining his balance.

Mildred felt a sickening sensation as Leland also struggled to keep his hold. The misplaced kick almost sent him headlong into space. He recovered, however, swearing at his failure. Bud straightened, commenting through clenched teeth, "I expected that. You never did fight fair."

One of these men was very likely to fall to his death. Which one would it be? If Mildred made the wrong choice, she'd be lost. And she didn't have much time.

"I never gave up, either." Leland braced himself for another kick at Bud. Without a thought for Bud or Brodie or even Seamus, Mildred succumbed to panic and, using Leland's strength, launched herself toward the ship. Toward safety, security, and peace.

A police car responded to Ecker's call for help, and Cher was placed under arrest. The officer agreed to take Scarlet up onto the bridge, which meant a brief ride in the squad car into Mackinaw City and onto the freeway via the ramp. Leaving Ecker to secure the *Lila*, Scarlet promised to keep him informed by phone.

Ambulances, a fire truck and several police cars were parked along the bridge-way at the spot where Bud had begun his climb. The officers stood outside their vehicles, looking up at the scene above. Firemen were at work, maneuvering the truck into place in order to extend the ladder. Bridge workers hurried to launch their own rescue.

Above them, Bud and Leland struggled. Bud was unable to mount much of an offense from his awkward position below his opponent. Mostly, he ducked Leland's attacks. Bracing himself with his arms on the railing, Leland launched kick after kick, first with one foot, then with the other. Bud leaned left and right, avoiding some of the blows, absorbing others. Seamus felt Scarlet's heart pound as she watched.

"Hey, look up there!" a fireman shouted. All eyes had been on the two men, but there was Brodie, standing on the bridge tower. "The kid went all the way to the top!"

A man in a Bridge Authority uniform started for his car. "There's an elevator," he said. "I can get her down that way if she stays put until we get there."

"Is there room for me?" Scarlet asked. "She'll need a familiar face."

"Sure," the man replied. "We call 'em two-man elevators, but we'll make the three of us fit."

As the bridge patrol car made its way to the tower, Scarlet stuck her head out the window, watching the two men locked in a struggle that one of them meant to take to the death. A part of her didn't want to look away. *If I keep my eyes on him, Bud will be safe.* She knew it wasn't true, and that the police would help Bud more than she could. Her responsibility was to Brodie. Listening to her thoughts, Seamus wasn't sure if Scarlet's heart agreed with her head.

From her spot atop the bridge tower, Brodie saw everything. The space at the top of the tower was wide and smooth with sturdy railings, no more frightening than the viewing point. Tiny fire trucks and patrol cars below indicated rescuers would soon come for her. She knew from *Dirty Jobs* that there was an elevator somewhere below where she now stood. Her danger was over. She would survive.

Bud was not so well off. It must have been Bud who arranged the boat blockade, and now he had climbed the cable to stop Leland from catching and killing her. But he was stuck on the bridge, with Leland doing his best to knock him off.

Brodie knew little about fighting, but it seemed like Leland was winning. Bud simply held on, absorbing the force of Leland's kicks as best he could. There was blood on his face, but he watched Leland constantly, guessing—usually correctly—where the next kick would be aimed and avoiding it.

Maybe Leland would tire, and Bud would be able to retreat. Looking below, she saw two workers start up the cable, wearing safety harnesses with double lanyards that fastened to the hand-ropes. Each man carried a second harness slung over his shoulder. If Bud could hold on a few minutes longer, they'd reach him, put a harness on him, and attach him to the bridge. He'd be safe. Their progress was slowed by the constant clipping and unclipping of their harnesses so they were never without a safety line.

"Hurry!" she urged, whispering the words into the gusts that buffeted her. The tears in her eyes were swept away before they wet her cheeks. Bud had put his life on the line for her. Family or not, he was something.

Suddenly Bud seemed to lose strength. He sagged backward, his arms supporting his weight and his head lolling forward. Brodie whimpered in terror. Help was almost there, but Bud didn't know it. "Hold on!" she called, but the wind took her voice. She hardly heard it herself.

Leland saw Bud's weakness. He gathered his strength, repositioning his hands securely on the hand-ropes and his left foot on the cable surface. His shoulder muscles tensed as he raised his right leg for a mighty kick, aiming at Bud's defenseless head. Brodie screamed, "Noooo!" unable to watch but more unable to look away.

At the last second, Bud's face came up, and she saw his attack. Bud ducked to one side, lowering his head almost to the cable's surface while his hands gripped the hand-ropes tightly. He'd gambled that Leland would put all of his energy into expression clearly. He'd faked weakness, goading Leland into an all-out one mighty blow, and he'd been right. It was a desperate move. If Leland recovered, Bud would be vulnerable, with his head low and his arms pulled back behind him. If Leland could manage a second kick in good time, Bud would almost certainly fall.

Bud had figured correctly, though. Sure of his opponent's weakness, Leland put everything he had into the kick, raising his knee high and bringing his foot down toward Bud's head. When Bud collapsed on the cable, Leland's foot passed completely over him. The force he'd exerted carried Leland forward, and his hands, already weary from the climb and the struggle, could not bear the strain. First one, then the other released its grip on the railing. Leland rolled over Bud's prone body and continued forward onto the cable, where his head struck the twisted metal. His feet followed the trajectory his body had taken, and the trailing foot caught Bud's shoulder briefly before following in a clumsy somersault. Without a sound, Leland slid under the hand-rope and was gone. Brodie turned away.

At almost the same time, a trap door banged open behind her. Turning, Brodie saw a man's head emerge through the opening. In only a few more seconds, she was in Scarlet's arms.

Bud came down from the bridge harnessed and positioned between two men who watched his every step. Scarlet met him as he touched the solid surface of the deck, her hands reaching out unconsciously before she remembered herself and folded her arms. "Are you all right?"

"Shoulder hurts like mad," he said, grimacing. "Brodie?"

"An EMT is looking her over. She has some cuts from bolts and rivets." Scarlet gave a half-hearted chuckle. "You know what she told them? That the view up there is something else."

Bud shook his head. "Wouldn't know. I was trying not to look down." His tone was light, but she noted strain on his face. "Things got a lot better once that harness was clipped to the hand-rope."

An EMT interrupted, insisting Bud be examined. Scarlet said, "I'll wait with Brodie." Hesitantly she added, "I'm glad you're okay."

Understatement, Seamus thought. *The woman is a master of understatement.*

Seamus knew what Scarlet was feeling, even if she hadn't yet admitted it. He wasn't sure what he was feeling. Relief, certainly. Pleasure at the outcome, which he considered just. An eye for an eye, a fall for a fall. What he didn't feel was Mildred's presence. It was hard to believe she'd kept quiet through all that had happened. At some point she must have gone back to the ship.

After all that talking I didn't want, she leaves without a word?

Brodie sat in a sheriff's patrol car, wrapped in a blanket and looking miserable. While Scarlet assured her that Bud was okay, Seamus jumped to the girl. It wasn't fair, after what she'd been through, but he had to know it all.

He felt a difference between his first hosting with Brodie and this one. The girl's mind wasn't so closed. A hundred thoughts chased through it, and Seamus had to work to pick up on them. First, he sensed relief that Bud was all right. There was shock at Leland's death. There was residual terror from the ordeal she'd survived. And there was a tiny sense of exaltation. Brodie had banished her craziness.

He couldn't quite follow the thought, but it seemed that in the midst of the crisis she had ordered her mind to straighten up, and it had. She'd taken control, and now she believed it was possible to keep it. Though Seamus wasn't sure, he guessed Mildred's interference had resulted in a good effect, giving Brodie the feeling she wasn't as damaged as she had imagined.

In a few minutes Bud approached them. "They say I'll live." Scarlet gave Bud her seat beside Brodie in the patrol car and a smile of encouragement before leaving the two of them to talk.

"Hey."

Brodie looked up at him, her eyes wide and shiny with tears. "Bud, are you really okay?"

"I'm fine. What about you?"

Seamus felt her fighting for control. "I thought he was going to kill you."

Bud looked to where several boats searched for Leland's body. "He certainly tried."

"He killed Gramps."

"I know. Did you see—"

Brodie decided a small fib was okay if it made Bud feel better. "I didn't see him fall. Scarlet and the bridge guy got me into the elevator while you two were fighting."

"I'm glad."

"I didn't think he'd follow me up there. If I hadn't—"

Bud took her hands in his. "None of it is your fault, do you hear me? Leland killed Gramps. He kidnapped you. He tried to kill me, and he fell because he wanted so badly to knock me off the bridge."

"Yeah. He was kinda nice at first, but then he went apeshit." At Bud's shocked expression, she rephrased. "Ape. I mean, he went ape." *Sorry, Gramps.*

"I guess so." Bud tried earnestly to make a point. "People do stuff that isn't right, Brodie, and sometimes we can't stop them. But we don't have to let them drag us down too."

Brodie thought about that. "Like my mom."

"Mine too." He chuckled dryly. "Guess we were kids only a Gramps could love."

She smiled briefly at his attempted humor. "Leland said he was my dad, but I knew he wasn't."

Bud nodded. "Your father lives in Muskegon. If you want to, someday we can go and meet him."

Brodie didn't answer, not sure if meeting her father was a good idea or not.

A bridge officer came over and leaned into the car. "We're done here, Mr. Dunbar. Your friend berthed your boat at the marina, so you can return for it when you're ready. We've arranged for the sheriff's department to take you home."

"Home sounds good to us, right, Brodie?" Bud turned to look around. "Where's Scarlet?"

"I'm here." Seeing the look that passed between Bud and Scarlet, Brodie felt a tiny glow of satisfaction. Whatever else happened, those two had gotten past whatever had kept them apart.

The last thoughts Seamus got from Brodie came through clearly, and he realized it was because Brodie was speaking to herself, clarifying what she'd learned in the last few days. *I don't have a DNA-type family, so I can't make an informed decision about what that's like. But some people are family, no matter what. Gramps was right. As usual.*

CHAPTER TWENTY-TWO

Seamus found Millie at the same spot at the ship's rail where they'd first met. She turned slightly as he approached, her silver-blond hair catching the light. He was unsure how to begin because for the first time in a very long while, he found himself reluctant to tell the truth.

He started instead with an update. "I talked to William Dunbar. He was shocked at Leland's betrayal, but he's glad Bud is safe from prosecution."

"Do you think he knew Bud was innocent?"

"I think he hoped that was the case. But it helps them to know for sure."

After a pause, Millie said, "I wasn't very good, was I?"

Seamus chose his words carefully. "Some things you did really well." He turned so she could see the honesty in his eyes. "You care about people a lot, and you really want to help them."

"But I get too close."

"It's kind of a balancing act. You have to care about the case, but you can't let yourself care too much about the people."

"Because they're soon gone." She shook her head. "Or, rather, we are." She blew out a long breath. "I don't think I could do it again."

Seamus turned to the view outside the ship. "You don't have to."

"I know. I've made my decision. I just wanted to—" For the first time since he met her, Seamus sensed embarrassment in Mildred. "I wanted to say that I think you're very good at your job. It was a pleasure to work with you."

Now it was his turn to be embarrassed. "Uh, thanks, Millie—I mean, Mildred. I appreciate it."

There was a twinkle in her eye as she answered. "I think I kind of like Millie when you say it." Her expression changed. "Not that I'll remember my name much longer."

"You're going on?"

"Yes." She put out a hand. "So this is good-bye, I guess."

Seamus took her hand, and in a gesture even he didn't expect, kissed it. "You're quite a woman, Millie."

Mildred backed away, extending her arm until she finally had to let go of Seamus' hand. "For a little while more," she said softly. "After that, who knows what I'll be?"

ABOUT THE AUTHOR

Peg Herring is the author of the critically acclaimed Simon & Elizabeth Mysteries, the award-winning Dead Detective Mysteries, the intriguing Loser Mysteries, and several stand-alone novels. When they're not exploring the world, Peg and her husband of many years live in northern Lower Michigan, where they garden for the benefit of local rabbits, deer, and elk.

As Maggie Pill, Peg writes the Sleuth Sisters Mysteries about two "mature" women who open a detective agency in northeast Michigan in hopes of helping people. They intend to keep their bossy, manipulative sister from poking her nose into their business. Like that's going to happen!

Peg's website: http://pegherring.com
Maggie's website: http://maggiepill.com

About the Dead Detective Mysteries

Dead Detective Mystery #1: *The Dead Detective Agency*

Tori Van Camp wakes one morning on a luxurious ocean liner where she's offered whatever a person might desire: food, clothes, recreation, and the companionship of congenial people. But Tori has no memory of booking a cruise. What she does have is a vivid recollection of being shot point blank in the chest. Determined to find out what happened to her, Tori enlists the help of Seamus, an eccentric but shrewd detective. Together they embark on an investigation unlike anything Tori ever thought possible. Death is all around, the future is uncertain, and if Tori doesn't act quickly, two people she cares about are prime candidates for murder.

Awarded Best Mystery Novel of 2012 by EPIC

Dead Detective Mystery #3: *Dead for the Show*

When Cassie Parker refuses to believe she's dead, Seamus is sent to discover what happened to her. In a small Toronto theatre, Christy Parker takes over her sister's place as wardrobe mistress. Soon it's clear that someone wants her dead too. Seamus does what he can to protect one sister while investigating the other's murder, but moving from host to host, he senses something he's never felt before. Can a dead guy be haunted, and if so, is it a good thing or really bad?

Dead Detective Mystery #4 *Dead to Get Ready-and Go*

No longer satisfied with staying on the ship, Seamus realizes it's time to re-visit his own death and learn why he was murdered. He knows who drowned him in Lake Michigan—his beloved wife and his best friend—but questions have bothered him since that night in 1953. With Ronnie's support, Seamus is determined to finally face the truth—no matter how painful that truth might be. (2016 release)